MY FAIR LADY

BY

J.P. REEDMAN

MW01126734

A Story of Eleanor of Provence, Henry III's Lost Queen

London Bridge is falling down,
Falling down, falling down.
London Bridge is falling down,
My fair lady

--traditional children's nursery rhyme thought by some to refer to Eleanor of Provence, who held the bridge revenues and whose barge was attacked at London Bridge by an angry mob

Prologue:
Amesbury Abbey 1600's: Age of Progress

The two men stood amidst the ruins. Architects, eyes keenly scanning the broken stone, the shattered walls, the little niches. Seeing modernity amidst such ancient decay, these bones of bygone buildings, gravestones to a cast out religion.

Out with the old, in with the new—they were surveying for a potential mansion, a grand house for a grand family, classical design with portico and pillars. That's what the wealthy wanted in the modern age. Greeks. Romans. Not pointed arches and rounded Norman doors, fragments of broken icons and other Papist trappings.

The men, Inigo Jones and his assistant, John Webb, were approaching the site of the high altar, tapping on the walls as if to seek treasure in hidden cornices. Tiny flakes of stone fell away, drifted on the breeze. "Careful, lad," said Inigo, the elder of the two, steadying Webb as he leapt back in fright, narrowly avoiding a piece of masonry that tumbled from the edge of a lancet window. "You must be careful around old places like these. When the time comes to build, you can get stout lads from the village to bring rams, knock it all to ground level."

They continued to walk onwards, though John cast a rueful glance over his shoulder at the lump of stone that nigh-on brained him. Fragments of eroded walling thrust out of the earth all around them, like the decayed stumps of an old woman's teeth. Grasses grew over them, and small wildflowers waved in the wind, dainty harebells, wild daisies, the ever-spreading buttercups. Below, nuns slept eternal sleep. Royal bones lay beside the nuns, silent in the dark.

Inigo Jones lifted his broad-brimmed hat and pushed his long, wavy brown hair back from his sun-bronzed forehead. Nodding, he pointed to a series of low walls that stretched across the flower-strewn field to a tall, jagged fragment of stonework that bore the vague outline of a delicate, glassless, quatrefoil window. A piscina was clearly visible in the wall, speckled with bird dung, a bath for neighbouring starlings. A little further up the wall, attached to another slab of masonry, was a well-preserved row of sedilia, swathed in moss and tangled ivy.

"The church?" asked John Webb, following Jones's nod.

"I deem so, John; look, there's a tomb there. Can you not see it? Attached to the wall, but partly covered by turf. I would wager it is near the site of the high altar. Someone of importance is buried there."

The younger man walked over to where the architect indicated, after looking around carefully to make sure no more precariously balanced stonework threatened his precious pate. "You are correct, Master Inigo...a tomb it is," he said, kneeling down beside the worn stone chest, uncaring that the knees of his breeches became muddied and stained. He scrubbed at the firmly affixed lid with his hands, dislodging a shower of earth and grass, a few frail dandelions that had gone to seed. Their white spores spun away, shimmering in the sunlight like faerie dust. "A fine piece of marble for a lid, but no effigy, no brass...and if there were markings I cannot see them now."

Inigo Jones approached the half-concealed tomb; his shadow fell over John, the bushy hair, the broad brimmed hat perched once again on his head. He had lit his pipe; smoke curled blue around him. "Open it."

His companion blinked up at him, a little perturbed." Excuse me, Master...but sh...should we? It is a grave. Untouched. We have not been asked to. It's not ours to touch."

"We are working at Wilton now but this land is for sale. Soon it will be sold; the Dukes of Somerset are already interested. It may not be my job to build a new house here, my apprentice, but I think it could be yours. Then all this old rubble will be knocked down or buried...under a floor or a fine garden," said Jones. "So does it truly matter if this tomb is explored?"

"It could be the grave of a holy woman," said Webb uneasily. He could not explain why he felt so squeamish. He ran his hands over his jacket, seeking to fasten the neat brass buttons. A high wind had blown down off the plain beyond with its gaunt ring of stones; across the ruin-speckled grassland, across twists and curves of the river Avon, the hill known as Wall after the old Britons who once dwelt on its summit turned dark as night as incoming clouds obscured the sun.

"It could even be a Queen," said Inigo Jones, matter of factly. "And what matter if it be one? This is the age of learning, of science. This very morning you and I visited the Hanging Stones up on the Plain. Foolish legend says it was built by Merlin..." He harrumphed with mocking laughter, his pipe rattling between his yellow teeth. "Men of science like you and me know better. It was Romans, I tell you, Romans. Only ones smart enough to make it."

"But if this tomb *does* belong to a Queen," Webb protested, still uneasy, "wouldn't it be respectful to leave it alone? It's not some stone raised in a time of savagery. It is the grave of a monarch. A Christian grave."

"Papist," shrugged Jones, "and long dead. Old bones will not rise to haunt you if you rattle 'em, lad; does not Queen Catherine, wife to Henry V, lie open to men's eyes in Westminster? They say she is black and mummified."

Webb grimaced."Not a sight I long to see, for all it may be of interest…to…to science. Such dissolution I dread to think of. It comes to all of us, but I don't particularly want it thrust in my face."

Jones' bearded lips parted in a little smirk and he nodded toward the half-exposed coffin. "Come; let us not be coy and fearful like the men of the past with their foolish superstitions! Open it. For the knowledge. Otherwise, we will always wonder."

Webb placed his hand on the coffin lid; the age-pocked marble felt cold, a slab of snow—the sun did not reach here, never did, never would, even with the priory roof ripped away. A little gap between the rim and the interior of the sarcophagus showed a line of utter darkness. Infinity. He began to sweat despite the sharp breeze off the Plain.

"I will need help, Inigo…master," he gulped. "I am not strong enough."

Jones grunted and joined his fellow. His fingers gnarled in the edge of the coffin lid. "Hmm, we'll need to lever it off." He beckoned for their attendants who were lounging lazily about the site. Having enjoyed their morning at the great stones on the plain with Master Jones as instructor, they were not looking forward to getting back to the ongoing building works at Wilton House. Or any unexpected work here, which wasn't even their remit.

A bit churlishly, they joined Webb in the ruins of the priory church, gazed down at the revealed coffin near the high altar. "You, Peter…" Inigo Jones beckoned to a sandy-haired fellow built like a bull, great round head, mighty arms lined with muscles, legs that strained his trousers. "You have plenty of muscle on you. We need help removing a coffin lid. Extra pay for you if the job is well done and without damage."

Peter nodded, anticipating that well-earned pay. Bunching his muscles, he strove to wrest the stone away from the chest. "Won't work on its own," said Jones. "Levers! Come on, man, use this…" He tapped his skull with a bony finger.

The other men were in on the act now, interest piqued. A wooden pole was brought in and then another. One pole was jammed into the split in the lid; something crackled in the dark and Jones frowned at Peter. "Don't break anything if you can avoid it," he said tersely.

The workers all gathered round, the burliest manhandling the coffin lid, while the others used wooden struts to lever the heavy stone away. Peter, strongest of all, neck bunched up and face crimson, was groaning and snorting like a pig giving birth as he swung about, throwing his full weight on the pole and trying to heave the lid of Purbeck marble aside. "I think the pole might break, master!" he panted. "It ain't strong enough!"

Just at that moment, there was a groan like a soul in torment, and the lid screeched aside an inch or two, the dust of uncounted years flowing out from its stygian interior like the long white hands of ghosts.

Face impassive as the façade of Stonehenge on Salisbury Plain, Inigo Jones swiftly walked over to see what was revealed. Webb peered over his shoulder, his hair whitened by the flying dust, looking a ghost himself.

Inside the coffin, *she* lay on her back, gazing eyelessly to the sky, head to the east as in all Christian burials, her arms respectfully folded across her body. A woman's skeleton, wrapped not in nunly garb but the decayed remains of brocade, blue and gold. A dusty ring clanked on her finger, its stone dimmed by age; its band was silver, tarnished. Threads of hair spread out about her head, bleached by death, its original colour robbed out, more like spider webs than human hair.

"No humble nun is this," Inigo Jones removed his pipe, tapped the bowl. Ash fell. "Not even an abbess would be wearing such garb. I believe that is cloth of gold. Here, Webb, you most surely gaze into the face of a queen of England."

Welles stared down. The wind, blowing down from the higher ground, grew stronger; he could hear it whistling in the fangs of broken stone. Hissing like a snake, then murmuring like forgotten voices torn from fleshless throats. A sense of unease washed over him and he glanced away from the heap of presumed royal bones. He did not like to look upon them, science or no. It seemed…intrusive.

Suddenly he jumped back, muttering an oath, crossing his arms defensively.

"What is it?" Jones stared at his assistant in bemused perplexity. "You are white as curds! Did you see a spirit?" He laughed, his tone vaguely mocking.

"Out of the corner of my eye, I saw someone watching us! Not in the ruined church. Across the field, over by the river! A woman!" Webb gestured with a shaking hand toward the swaying trees at the foot of Wall hill, a dark hump beyond the curve of the river. "Watching us. As if to see whether we touched...the bones."

"What a wild imagination, John—most likely some curious lass from Amesbury wondering what we are doing," laughed Jones, but nonetheless he gestured to the rest of the workers with a sudden impatience. "We have seen enough. Cover her back up. Nothing here is ours to take. We are only here to observe and I shall record this day for posterity. Maybe one day others will come here and study these royal remains, if such they are, but it is not for me to do. Besides, I am more interested in stones than nuns...even nuns who were once queens. I prefer them. Roman, you know. One can see clearly by the architecture."

John Webb helped move the coffin lid back into place. The scent of a space long sealed off yet damp vanished...mercifully, the apprentice thought.

He was glad that they were to leave her undisturbed.

Sleeping.

I am old and when the wind shrills down off Salisbury Plain, my bones ache; my knees, my knuckles especially. Much have I seen of sorrow and care but not for much longer—the doctors say there is a canker in my aged body, burning me away from inside. It will kill me in the end, and that ending I fear will be soon.

The nuns I live with in this fair house at Amesbury are kind and treat me well with whatever remedies they can make from herbs found in the garden; pain killing ones mostly, these days. The willow is good for that; I drink tea brewed from the bark every night.

I am an oblate, not a nun, not professed, although I have lived with the order many years in these latter days of my widowhood.

My husband was Henry III of Blessed Memory, Henry of England, France and Ireland. My son is King—he is Edward, that men name Longshanks, set to be a lion amongst Kings.

I am Eleanor, Dowager Queen, and once, with my husband, I ruled all England.

But before that, I was merely a pretty child born to a noble but destitute family in Provence…

When I was a little girl, life was a waking dream, or so I thought in the silly way of little girls. My father, Lord Raymond Berengar IV, and my mother Beatrice of Savoy were like King and Queen within their lands, although they were not so titled…and were really quite poor.

"You are our gems," said my mother, to my three sisters, bright Marguerite, who was eldest, shy Sanchia, baby Beatrice and me…the outspoken one. Mother was clever and very beautiful; her marriage to my father, though contracted as a political alliance, had swiftly become a true love match just like in the romances that we all liked to read. "My four lovely daughters will one day bring us great fame and wealth. God has been good to your father and me, even though He has not given us living sons, but it is a great solace that you are all endowed with comely looks and sharp intellect, even as little children. I do not need a pack of boisterous boys, I do not weep for my lack—you four I shall ever call 'my boys'. My *special* boys."

My sisters and I giggled at being girls who were called 'boys'; we cared nothing for our futures then. Marriage? We dreamed of fantasy knights, like Lancelot and Gawain, handsome and chivalrous. We played at being great ladies of prominence in the gardens of our parents' castle, wandering about with our noses held haughtily in the air beneath a burning sky, while our tired nurses held canopies above our bobbing heads so that our milky-fair skin would not grow red or dusky. Marguerite and I were the worst for affecting airs, and we would parade around the gardens, while the little ones giggled at us and my mother smiled indulgently behind her hand at our youthful pretensions.

Sometimes, when the mood took our parents, we would all ride forth in a chariot to visit their various manors across Provence. My lord father's land was beautiful beyond compare, with the Alps rising like white needles to the east, their peaks darning the azure skies, and the lush valley of the Rhone sweeping down to the banks of the wide, sparkling river, one of the arteries of Europe. The people of the towns and villages would cheer us, for despite their lack of great wealth, my parents always did the best for their vassals and never forgot them. Hence, townsfolk would give gifts of money or of bread and wine to father and sing praises mother's beauty and intellect; some men even wrote in manuscripts that she was as beauteous and astute as the legendary Queen Niobe...a great compliment for an ordinary lady!

My father was acclaimed too, naturally; he was courageous as a bear and a stout warrior who had survived into manhood by the skin of his teeth—when little more than a boy, he had been held in an Aragonese castle while his greedy, disloyal kinsmen battled over possession of his inherited lands. Luckily, he escaped in a daring rescue, shimmying down the high donjon on a flimsy rope, and became the Count of Provence, as was his right.

While on these progresses around the country, we would also attend lavish banquets. My two littlest sisters were confined to the nursery but Beatrice liked to show her eldest daughters to the crowd. I loved to be seen and admired, twirling in the pavane in my green gown, my raven's wing hair tumbling blue-black down to my waist, setting off my wide-set eyes, which were a lucky shade—the colour of the ocean. Secretly I believed myself to be even fairer that Marguerite, who was taller than I, but more angular in face and figure, and whose eyes were warm amber rather than blue.

How glorious the feasts were! We had soup of ground-up capons and almond milk, flavoured with red pomegranate seeds, followed by tender lamb and ducklings on platters of polished silver. Hares and peacocks followed, the latter still wearing their bright feathers. Marguerite and I would beg to keep the feathers after we dined, for we loved their colours so much; later, in our chambers, we would braid them into our hair. Cheese tartlets were also downed, and blancmange, and of course the *entremets*—bream in foil and crayfish quaking in rich jelly.

Our favourite dishes, however, were the subtleties made of sweet marchpane—sometimes they were shaped like animals or castles or shields. Mother did not allow us to over-indulge, however—she warned us about such vice in no uncertain terms. "Remember, my daughters, that beauty and virtue is your wealth, since we have relatively little in the way of dowries for you. You do not wish to end up like your aunt, Gersende, the Infanta of Aragon!"

Such admonishments always made us titter as froth-headed little girls always did. Gersende was father's sister and she was, rude as it might be to say so, enormously fat, with a great moon face and a heaving bosom which she would clasp when excited or distressed. In her wide, elaborate headdresses and sweeping brocade gowns, she outstripped most of the knights in size, let alone the rest of the women! Marguerite and I were determined we should never grow as huge as Aunt Gersende, the victim of many a bawdy jest, and hence limited ourselves to just one helping of the sumptuous desserts.

In 1233, tales of our beauty, manners, and bearing had spread far and wide, exactly as our parents had hoped. Ambassadors arrived from neighbouring France, sent on behalf of King Louis's mother, the fearsome Blanche, known as the White Queen. She was seeking a fitting bride for her beloved son, Louis—she sought a devout, pious girl whose virtuousness outshone even her beauty, and she had heard that a daughter of Raymond and Beatrice might fit her ideals.

Almost immediately, I was deemed too young to be a marriage candidate, which left me in a foul mood; I stomped out into the castle gardens, quite unladylike in my manner, pouting as I sulked under the clusters of heavy purple globes dripping from the grapevines. As much as I loved Marguerite, I did not wish my sister to become a queen if I did not become one too. That just would not be…*fair*.

But Blanche's ambassadors liked what they saw in my elder sister, and soon the deal was struck. Marguerite would fare to France and marry the young King Louis. My parents were thrilled, for the marriage would bring protection for Provence, and a rise in their status before the greats of Europe.

"I am worried though," I heard mother whisper to my father. I was skulking in the hall outside their chamber, eavesdropping, occasionally peering through a crack in the door. "Blanche is over-protective of her boy, king though he may be. I heard she is the true ruler of France, and he does her bidding. She may resent our Marguerite, even though she knows her son must have a wife."

"Marguerite must learn how to win Louis from the hold of Blanche," retorted father. "A man must leave his mother; it is the natural order of things. But fear not, Beatrice, we will journey with Marguerite to Lyon and see that the marriage treaty is properly signed and that she is treated with the respect due her."

Mother bit her under lip, clasped her hands in her lap. I had never seen her look so worried. "Can I ask a boon of you, lord husband?"

"Yes, what is it?"

"For the rest of her journey, and for the wedding, can my two brothers, William and Thomas, accompany her? If anything goes wrong, they are doughty lords who can support her and they are well-versed in politics and diplomacy."

"Nothing will go wrong." Father smiled gently at her. "But you are a most admirable mother, Beatrice, guarding your children like a lioness guards her cubs! Yes...yes, of course you may send William and Thomas to France with Marguerite."

"Thank you, my lord." She took his ring-adorned hand, kissed it.

I slid away into the dark corridors that riddled our castle, lit by only the pale torches flickering in brackets high above my head. My jealousy of Marguerite's new position was abating as the awful truth hit me...Marguerite, who was my best friend, my playmate, would be going many leagues away, and leaving me alone....

I began to cry, childish tears that I wiped from my blue eyes with my knuckles. And then Marguerite herself was there, comforting me. She did not seem the least upset herself, her cheeks rosy, flushed with excitement. "Why do you cry, sister? You have not been your usual merry self even since Queen Blanche's men came to see father."

"Oh, Marguerite..." Words tumbled out. "At first I was wicked, I was jealous of you! Louis is a powerful king and handsome too, and I, as yet, have no suitor for my hand. But that unworthiness has faded from my heart...Now I weep that you will leave and we will never play as sisters in our parents' castles again."

"It is time for us to wed; we are no longer little children." She clasped my cold hand, squeezed. "I am sure a goodly lord will come for you soon, Eleanor—you are even fairer than I. And I swear, even if we must live apart, as good wives must with our esteemed husbands, we will always remain best of friends as well as sisters. Do you agree? Best of friends."

I sniffled; the torches were blurry in my vision. "I do, Marguerite, of course I do. Always friends."

Then her nurses came and guided her away to her chambers, and there was a new respect amongst them, a reverence because she would soon be Queen of France.

Watching, a pang of unworthy jealousy needled me again. My sister was my friend…but I desperately wanted the honour Marguerite had.

After Marguerite had gone from Aix-en-Provence, I moped for many months. My smaller sisters Sanchia and Beatrice were too youthful for the kind of play I desired. Instead, I threw myself into my studies in both crafts suitable for highborn ladies and into the study of Holy Scripture. I was a voracious reader and, hidden in the shady side of the castle garden, would read one or more of mother's romances, stolen from the vast castle library. The Arthurian myths intrigued me most—the tragedy of Guinevere and Arthur, Lancelot the greatest Knight, Galahad who attained the Grail…then died. I scribbled my own stories and poems about these great personages and invented heroes of my own—a great warrior from Cornwall, named Sir Blandin, who slew giants by the score and killed all his foes single-handedly, yet was courteous and devoted to his ladylove, the Princess Briende.

I was intrigued by England, that misty and fabled land lying just a short skip across the fierce waves of the Channel, and found especial interest in Cornwall, where King Arthur was rumoured to have been born on a rocky promontory called Tintagel. I began to fantasise about visiting England one day…but the only way I could do that would be to marry the English King!

Due to my youth, I dared not even voice such a desire, not even to my dear, indulgent parents, but being a girl who listened to the talk of men at table, I was aware that King Henry of England was still unwed, despite being long past the usual age of marriage. He would need a wife and soon….

How could I attract his attention? I was mad with frustration, thinking of Marguerite in her glorious court, feted and admired, while I cooled my heels at home, a captive child with no present prospects.

It was Helewise, one of my nursemaids, who gave me an idea. She was reading my poetic efforts about my invented Cornish hero, scrawled on a scrap of pilfered parchment in my own childish hand. "Could this not be sent to England?" she said.

"Don't be silly, Helewise. A King would not read a Provencal maiden's scribbling!" I said contemptuously.

"Maybe not...but perhaps others might. Your poem—and marvellous it is, my lady—is about a Cornish hero....and the King's brother Richard is a man very like this, a hero and a crusader. He just happens to live on the very rock where King Arthur was born. At Tintagel in Cornwall."

Lightness of being flooded me; my heart soared. Yes, yes, I knew this would be the way! Snatching the parchment from Helewise's hands, I flew to seek my tutor, to beg him to intercede with my parents on my behalf. Please, please let them humour my girlish fancies, and send my humble poem to the great Lord Richard of Cornwall, the English King's brother!

The decision came swiftly, and it was the one I wanted.

My poem about Cornwall went over the stormy sea.

One day, some months later, I was called before my parents in the great hall. I could tell by their expressions that they were both excited and uneasy at the same time. A hard little bud of excitement began to bloom in my belly. I deduced immediately that they had summoned me for news about my future.

"Eleanor," said mother, "God has smiled on us yet again. An ambassador is coming to look for a suitable bride for his lord..."

"Who is his lord, lady mother?" I asked. I prayed it would not be some dull old lord of little worth or power.

"A King...Henry, King of England!" she replied.

I could have danced on the spot, save that it would be unseemly. This was a high match indeed, even if not quite matching the glory of Marguerite's. My poem must have been read, perhaps even finding its way into the hands of the King himself!

"I should be most obliging towards this match, Madame!" I cried.

"You are a good girl, Eleanor," my mother said, reaching out to put a hand upon my head. "But you must contain yourself. Before anything is decided the English Ambassador must meet you, and decide if you are suitable as a bride for his King."

"Why would I not be suitable?" I cried with all the arrogance of a cosseted child. My cheeks were burning.

My father Raymond stifled a laugh with his big, sword-calloused hand. "No reason at all, my beautiful one, but it is part of the formalities of the marriage game. Go now, and prepare yourself to meet the English King's brother."

"His brother!" I gasped. The man to whom I had sent my fantastical poem! I had not expected that!

"Aye, the very same. The Lord Richard was so charmed by your words he said he wanted to come and meet you himself."

Hastily, I was washed, scented and dressed by my tiring women. My chosen dress was a pale sky-blue gown with long, dagged sleeves shot through with green silk, while my hair was brushed down to my waist, where it curled like tendrils of moving shadow. A silver circlet studded with tiny sapphires to match my eyes was placed reverently upon my brow.

"You are so beautiful, lady!" Helewise said, breathlessly…and I knew I was. But would it be enough?

There was no more time to worry. My tutor beckoned to me, guiding me to the great hall, where my parents had feasted Lord Richard of Cornwall, the English King's brother.

The great man was seated on a high chair of estate alongside father's. My eyes raked over him, trying to get the measure of him. He was of middling height with broad shoulders and curling brown hair. Unlike many men of the court, he shaved his chin clean, which made him look quite young. I thought that if Henry looked like his brother I would not be unhappy.

"Our daughter, Eleanor," smiled my mother, as I dropped the lowest curtsey I could muster.

Richard of Cornwall stared, silent; I tried not to sweat, not even to breathe, fearing his disapproval. Then, suddenly, he smiled and I knew I had won.

"Later," he said, "I would like to speak with her ladyship, if it may be permitted."

In the cool of the early evening, we met in the castle gardens, with my chaperones gliding nonchalantly behind us, and the leaves rustling on the vines that climbed the walls and trellises. "I received your poem, Lady," Richard said, walking slowly beside me, a golden goblet in his hand. I studied that hand; strong, manly, a ring winking on every finger. "An intriguing honour...but why?"

"I long to see England, my lord Richard," I said immediately. "I have read about it in the tales of King Arthur. It seems a land of kings and heroes."

He turned and gazed at me, his eyes appraising. His eyes were blue but not like mine; they were paler, with a grey hint, stormy. His brown hair, curling, was damp on his neck; he was obviously not used to the heat of Provence. His hand reached up, pushed the wet hair aside.

I felt a rush of heat of my own that was not altogether seemly for a virtuous maiden, but in my tender years, I did not understand it. I knew I was blushing and hated that I was out of control in this manner.

"They say you are named for the Lionheart," I said, still seeking to flatter. "I would wager you are much like him."

Richard laughed; his pale eyes flashed in the dappled shadows. "He was my uncle...but I fear we are not much alike, at least in looks. The rest...I cannot say. Coeur de Lion was big and bluff, with tawny red-gold hair like a lion's mane. I take my darker colouring from my mother, and my father, John..." He suddenly became solemn, seemed to be thinking of past memories, perhaps not altogether pleasant ones. Then he glanced at me and smiled again. "But luckily I am not as short or fat round the middle as my father was!"

I laughed, my earlier embarrassment fading. "My aunt Gersende is fat. I pray I will not grow like her...I *swear* I will not, as such rondure might not please my future husband!"

"And has anyone yet spoken for your hand, Lady Eleanor?" Richard gazed away from me, out into the garden. The hills were distant, in a blue heat haze paling to purple as twilight encroached; he seemed to be watching the little birds darting over the high walls to seek their nests in the castle rock.

"No, my lord Richard," I said. "Not yet. I..." I knew I was forward here, almost shamefully so, but the chaperones were just out of earshot.

"I must have a hero, Lord Richard. Like those great lords who reside in England."

"Aye, little Lady Eleanor, I would agree with you there." Richard of Cornwall said softly, a little smile playing on his mouth. "I think England is a place where you should come. I will see what I can do for you."

He rode away. From the topmost turret of the castle, I watched Richard of Cornwall's party depart until they were no more than specks in the distance, lost in a cloud of dust. Fervently I prayed Richard would arrive safely in England and speak well of me to King Henry.

I grew restless and fitful upon his departure. With keen ears, I listened in on snatches of conversation between my parents while in their chamber…It was audacious of me, but I was clever and curious. And naughty.

"The Lord Richard seemed most taken with our daughter." That was my father, Raymond.

"Yes. I do hope it was the right thing to do." Mother's sigh was audible.

"Henry is a King, a great King!"

"Yes…but England is far from Provence, and I do not know the English king's character. Remember his father, John? An evil man. He brought Interdict to his country; he hung boys from the walls of his castles and starved prisoners of war instead of ransoming them. He murdered his nephew, Arthur of Brittany. He was full of lust, stealing a twelve-year-old girl from her rightful betrothed and casting off his first wife to marry her…"

"The girl—Isabella of Angouleme—did not seem to mind overmuch," said Raymond dryly. "She seemed to match King John in every way. 'Tis said they would romp neath the sheets till nigh on noon when the King should have been up attending to business! She also diddled her own daughter out of a husband; while as a dowager she sought a match for her child, but decided she fancied the prospective bridegroom and married him herself! As if that was not bad enough…he was the son of her original betrothed! It was virtually incest!"

"Raymond!" My mother's voice was shocked.

"Don't look at me like that, Beatrice! I speak nothing but truth!"

"Then I do not want my Eleanor marrying their son, king or no. I have heard Henry is not so fair of face anyway; he has a squint, his eyelid droops."

Father laughed. "A man is not his parents, my love, and as far as I have heard, he seems untainted by his parents' malice. As for the squint...well, he is not some court fop, some troubadour. He is a king. It does not matter."

"If you are happy with such a match, then I, too, will be happy." Mother's voice was resigned. "By your leave, lord husband, I will have my brothers William and Amadeus go to England and speak on Eleanor's behalf. They are shrewd negotiators and William has done much for Marguerite. The seneschal Romeo can go, too; he is also skilled in negotiation, especially where dowries are concerned."

I pressed my ear closer against the door, hoped my nursemaids would not catch me. I was not impressed by the sound of Henry's rumoured squint but Richard, his brother, had been more than comely enough. As for the infamous John and his wife...ha, they were people from a time past. King John was long dead, having gorged on unfit peaches, and Queen Isabella had departed England for the lands of Hugh de Lusignan, the young man she had pinched from under her daughter's nose.

Henry would be different from his troublesome parents. If he turned out to be boorish, I would surely be able to influence him and *make* him different...

That is, if he wanted me.

Time marched on. I began to fret and then to despair.

Maybe I had been wrong about the way the king's brother viewed me.

Maybe Richard had really thought me forward, unseemly for a girl my age.

Maybe the English had different standards of beauty and he found me ugly but was, of course, too polite to say so.

Maybe...maybe...maybe....

Then, one morning, a party of ambassadors arrived from Henry of England, riding up across the drawbridge through the morning mists, their banners slapping against the azure heaven...though, sadly, Earl Richard had not come in person this time. Richard le Gras and John of Gatesden had come instead.

But it seemed the Earl had spoken kindly of me to his elder brother...Henry wanted me. *He wanted me!*

Unfortunately, he had also wanted a certain girl called Joan of Ponthieu and pledged himself to her by the *verba de presenti*. This pledge, made by a man and women of free consent and legal age, was binding and must end in marriage unless some impediment was discovered that would make such a union void. In Henry and Joan's case, they were in fact related within the prohibited degrees...but the Pope had been asked to grant a dispensation.

My heart sank at this news. What game was the English King playing?

Henry's envoy, John of Gatesden, smiled and tried to comfort me; my expression must have been doleful indeed. "Do not fear, Lady Eleanor," he whispered conspiratorially. "King Henry no longer wishes to wed Joan. He has ordered his servants in Rome *not* to proceed with acquiring the dispensations from the Holy Father."

I clapped my hands, then blushed; I was lacking decorum. I curtseyed to the envoys and fled to my chambers. Oh, how I wished to know that John of Gatesden's words were indeed true and King Henry no longer wanted to wed my rival Joan!

It turned out it *was* true, although some doctors of religion still grumbled about the possibility that any other marriage for the English king would be of dubious legality. I was less worried than they. Without the dispensations from the Pope, the actual marriage was unlikely to go ahead, and since Henry had ordered his servants to stop seeking them, he obviously no longer desired the match. Even if some claimed Joan was Henry's true wife because of the verbal agreement to wed, the marriage could be easily annulled due to non-consummation.

I suspected it would never get as far as that.

I was just thrilled that Henry was more interested in me than Lady Joan, who was a rich heiress and had much more money.

But I still had to wait for an outcome...and I was bad at waiting.

An offer came in October of that year, when the nights were cooling and the leaves withering on the bough and the sky of Provence filled with cold white stars like the glittering snow on the heads of the distant Alps.

Two more men arrived from the court of Henry Plantagenet; their names were Robert de Mucegros and John Fitz Phillip. Henry would wed me, they said…but there was the matter of my marriage portion to be decided.

Seated on his chair of estate, my father Raymond looked a little green in the face at the mention of the portion; my mother Beatrice's visage was impassive as a stone. As ever, we had no real money, we had barely enough to pay our scrvants and keep the borders of Provence safe. If the King was insistent on a huge sum, our plans were doomed.

Six letters were produced by John Fitz Phillip and handed over to father with much aplomb. In each was written a different sum of money, the highest far beyond our means, the lowest much more modest and reasonable, though it still would mean scraping and scrimping and less food on thc banqueting table at Christmas.

Raymond jumped at the lower sum immediately. "*This*…this is good…this is more than acceptable. It shall be done."

Fitz Phillip smirked as the necessary parchments were signed and sealed with wax. "Our Lord the dread King Henry is so entranced by the rumours of his beautiful bride, he told us this before we rode hence… *'If the Count Raymond Berengar is destitute, it matters not. Even should there be no marriage portion at all, Eleanor of Provence must come to England.'* King Henry will have his wife, even if she comes with naught but the clothes on her back."

Within a few weeks, I had been sent to Tarascon and made my vows to Henry using the *verba de presenti*. Henry's ambassador, Robert de Mucegros, stood in for my future husband. De Mucegros was obese and red-faced, and had his hair cut into a bowl-shape; I strove not to giggle as he solemnly spoke the King's pledge of marriage to me. He looked so silly, with a button on his bright crimson tunic about ready to pop open. My real husband would not be so gauche, I was sure.

Then my goods were neatly packed up, and my dresses, my jewels, my beloved books (my mother had granted me several of her tomes to begin my own library in England) set upon carts. I took to my caparisoned palfrey, with a grand retinue around me, filled with servants and soldiers.

Solemnly, my parents, who had come as far as Tarascon, came to bid me adieu. "Be a wise girl, Eleanor!" said Beatrice. "You can make him love you, value you. Do not forget that. Make us proud of you."

"I will. I will be a perfect helpmeet and give King Henry healthy sons who will be the glory of England," I retorted, and then the trumpets were blown and the banner of Provence unfurled, and I rode away from all I had ever known, out into a grey November day with the winds skirling cold from the distant mountains.

I journeyed to Vienne, standing by the sluggish deep waters of the mighty Rhone, and there I met with my Uncle William, my mother's brother, who was dean of Vienne's cathedral of St Maurice.

He kissed me warmly, welcomed me to his home alongside the church. "It is so good to see you, niece. Your mother sent a message to tell me of your forthcoming nuptials. She has also asked me to accompany you on your long journey to England's shores, and I am most honoured to do so. But for now, rest here, in Vienne, while the final preparations for the marriage are made ready."

On December 15, not so long before the blessed nativity of our Lord, the marriage contract between Henry and me was ratified in Vienne cathedral, before the high altar. There was no going back now. Beyond the shadow of a doubt, I would be England's new Queen, bringing hope to a country who's King had been a bachelor much too long already.

Once this formality was over, my retinue set out on the road once more—now containing Uncle William's men, the numbers had swelled to over three hundred riders. William rode proudly next to me in his long churchman's robes and we began the long trek through Champagne and then through France, where Louis and my sister Marguerite sent greeting by swift courier and assured us of safe-passage in their territories.

Finally, the entourage reached Calais. The wind was up and clouds scudding across the grey dome of the sky. The sea was rippled and the gulls screaming and diving about fishing boats in the harbour and about the masts of the tall ships we would take. Squinting, I could just about make out the distant bulk of England far out across the frothing waves—or at least I thought I did.

I had never ridden in a boat before and was beginning to feel a little nervous although I tried to hide it when I saw ships rock and riggings vibrate as the wind and waves buffeted them. "Uncle…" I tugged on William's sleeve, "you know far more of the world than I. It is December and great gales can come up all of a sudden and founder ships. The wind is strong now…Are we safe to travel?"

He smiled down at me, calm, reassuring. "The Channel is always a rough crossing, my dear. Do not be afraid. This is calmer than usual, can you believe! In fact, it is so calm, I would say God has smiled down and decided to make smooth passage for Eleanor to join her husband, King Henry."

I knew he was merely trying to soothe me, but his intentions were good. Head held high, to the accompaniment of the cheers of the locals, I boarded the ship with my ladies gathered around me.

In the early evening, we set sail for England. Surrounded by my women, I stood on deck, watching the shores of France drop away into the gloom. Above, the clouds parted; a star shone out. My favourite lady in waiting, Willelma d'Attalens, chosen by my mother from amongst all the noblewomen of Savoy, pointed to it. "An omen, your Grace," she said. "A good omen. Your star is ascendant, Eleanor!"

In the red dawn, we sailed into the harbour at Dover. Wrapped in a thick cloak lined with miniver, I gazed out at the white cliffs, now tinted a shade of pale red. Before them the waters had gone still, the winds dying away, although I noted the air was much colder than I was used to. Above on the cliff, the adamant walls of Dover castle rose to touch the faded sky. I could see archers marching back and forth upon them and torches burning on poles, their greasy smoke trailing off into the lightening sky.

A welcoming party was waiting on the dock, great lords surrounded by servants bearing more torches.

Waiting for me, their new mistress, and their Queen.

Disembarking, I walked along the bird-haunted quay, wearing my voluminous golden wedding gown, my ladies holding my train out of rain-puddles and a tangle of salt-rimed nets. Then I was placed into a chariot painted with heraldic designs and draped with cloth of gold; the arms of England gleamed on the side. Surrounded by my entourage, and by dozens of my husband's men in full armour, we rode on toward Canterbury where the King was waiting for me.

The city, one of England's greatest, was large and sprawling, surrounded by walls with 'bars'—gateways—set at strategic locations. A grey, squat castle stood forlornly on a low motte, but it looked rather old-fashioned and neglected; Uncle William informed me that it had fallen out of favour when the old King Henry, my Henry's grandfather, built the stern keep at Dover. Beyond its sullen walls, the airy spires of the famous cathedral speared the air, glowing gold against a clear winter sky.

Excitement gripped me. I would soon meet my groom.

The cobbled streets all around were filled with onlookers and well-wishers, waving flags and holding up their children to see. Horns blared, music played, and there was dancing and celebration.

Proudly I gazed from the chariot, waving to the gathered throng every now and then when I remembered. Stone and timbered houses rose up and rolled by, followed by an ancient hospital, where the poor clustered, and the houses of the Franciscans and Dominicans thronging with curious monks.

Entering the cathedral close, the entourage halted abruptly. Gazing out of the window of the chariot, I found myself viewing a large stone building adjacent to the cathedral precinct.

"The Bishop's Palace." Uncle William trotted up on his horse to inform me of our location. "The King will be awaiting you there, little Eleanor."

I was handed down from the chariot, and with some trepidation approached the palace doors. Men were bowing, the doors were opening. Winter sunlight glinted on pikes and armour. My heart was thudding now, despite all my attempts at decorum.

What if he found me somehow unacceptable? Rejected me?

Or, just as important, what if I found him utterly odious? Repudiation by the King would bring me eternal shame, but revulsion on my part would ensure that the rest of my life was an endless, lonely misery…

I was ushered by a welcome party of English lords into the Palace's Great Hall, one of the largest I had ever seen, its roof hung with heraldic shields and its mighty windows filled with expensive stained glass. I blinked against the blue smoke of the central fires and tried to focus at the man seated at the far end, in an ornate chair upon a dais.

It was he! It was my husband, surrounded by all his magnates and by men of the cloth.

As I approached, trying to look eager but not *too* eager, gracious but not pretentious, Henry leapt up and rushed towards me in a way that filled me with alarm, for it was most unexpected and not altogether mannerly.

Without any niceties or introductions, he flung his arms around me and embraced me, hugging me to him while I flopped weakly like a fish, trying to gain my equilibrium.

"Ah!" he cried. "My little bride. At last! Greatly pleased am I to see such a paragon of virtue, an angel possessed of unparalleled beauty. Now I have seen her, I do most gladly accept her. Yes, happily I accept Eleanor of Provence as my wife!"

I should have been glad but my cheeks flamed, and I scarcely dared to breathe. I did not know how to respond to such unexpected ardour—and men claimed the English were cold!

Henry must have realised that his fervour embarrassed me in that high company, for suddenly he dropped his arms and stepped back a pace.

Now I had time—and space—to view my new husband. He was quite old, in his late twenties, but I had known that all along. He was of middling height and neither large nor small in build, with a neatly cut beard that held a reddish hue. His eyes were pale blue, different from his brother's, and to me, they seemed kindly enough. His face was not of great beauty, nor was it unpleasant...save for one eyelid. It drooped a little, giving him a weary look on that side. He was not as attractive as I'd found his brother Richard...but he was King. And my husband.

"Did you have a gentle journey, my dearest?" he asked in a breathless rush. "I am so glad you have arrived unharmed, Eleanor! Ah, I am the happiest man in England on the well-starred day!"

I curtseyed, hopefully with grace and poise. "Your Grace, I am just as happy to meet my esteemed husband."

"Then let us be properly married at once!" Henry clapped his hands, delighted as a child. "We shall be wed before the church doors and nuptial mass said!"

I was a wife. After Mass, we returned to the Bishop's Palace with the Archbishop Edmund to spend the night in a great chamber with a huge bed topped by a silk canopy designed to keep bugs from dropping onto the clean linen sheets. The Archbishop wandered in, swinging a censer, and sprinkled Holy Water upon the bed, speaking words to bless our union and make it fruitful.

Then we were alone. My mother had spoken to me of what was expected. She was an educated and intelligent woman and did not fill me with fearful tales such as I heard amongst the maids in my parents' castle. Whatever came, it was my duty to endure.

And I liked Henry and wanted to please him.

It was funny to see his face when at last his raucous companions were driven from the room and we were left alone together, the fire burning redly on the hearth, casting a sensuous glow over the tapestries, the cold stone ceiling. Outside the wintry winds were beating the stout shutters, but I felt quite warm and safe.

"Eleanor, I do not want to frighten you...you are very young yet," he said uneasily as his two remaining squires unfastened his fine robes and then discreetly left the chamber. Their footsteps clattered away, down the corridor, into the distance.

"Why should I be afraid of my husband, my lord King?" I said bravely, lying naked under the fine quilt, my skin sweetened by fresh rose water. There were doves broidered upon the quilt, pecked out in silver thread; I tried to concentrate on them rather than look at Henry. I heeded my mother's wise words and knew my duty, but I was a little afraid nonetheless. Just a little. I had of course never seen a man unclothed before.

"I promise you, my precious little one, you have nothing to fear," he said, and then he blew out the thick taper beside the bedside and pulled the coverlet away.

We were in London, great bustling London, where great wealth rubbed shoulders with great poverty. A huge wide river ran through the city, coiling like a spitted eel; upon the muddy banks loomed beer houses, docks, while many ships sailed back and forth on the endless swell. Bells were tolling from the religious houses and local churches, sending birds flying up from the river in fright, their wings white and flashing against the slate-hued January sky.

We stayed for a few nights in the stronghold of the Tower of London, as was customary; never before had I beheld such a stern fortress, its keep rising to touch the clouds, the gates frowning and its moats impassable...but I was treated like the Queen I was by the household, and then moved on to Westminster for my Coronation.

It was January 20th. The grey skies parted and the sun shone with weak but welcome yellow light. Together Henry and I walked from the palace toward the great Abbey, its pale towers made radiant by the burgeoning sunshine.

A blue ream of cloth was laid down, stretching out beneath our feet like an azure road towards the Abbey doors. Henry walked before me, accompanied by the chancellor, the treasurer carrying the paten, and three earls who bore aloft the mighty swords of state. A purple silk canopy borne aloft on silver lances shaded Henry, and he wore his full Coronation robes.

Behind him, I walked in slow cadence, holding my head high with pride. A silver canopy trimmed with tinkling silver bells also stretched over me, and bishops and other churchmen processed at my side. My hair flowed free to my waist from beneath a glimmering golden circlet, a dark river lifted by the breeze. I could hear the onlookers whispering, declaring that England had never had such a beautiful young queen.

The open doors of the abbey, gaping like an entrance into heaven itself, parted as we approached. On the front of the church, I could see carvings of angels and saints soaring to heaven. The smell of incense wafted out of the shadowy interior, its cloying perfume rising around me as the coronation procession wound its way into the abbey.

We halted almost at once amid the coiled candle smoke and sweet, rising fragrance. Edmund of Abingdon, Archbishop of Canterbury moved forward, his robes floating about his thin frame, his mitre tall as a tower, and his high, clear voice rolling out the words of the first prayer. Once the prayer was done, the entourage moved forward again, through the endless cavern of the nave, up to the holy of holies at the high altar.

The members of my party, including the King, drew aside. The huge hall of God was hushed, expectant. Now I was truly on my own, a young girl and yet a Queen. On that day, I must acquit myself well in my husband's eyes and in the eyes of his people.

As gracefully and reverently as I could, I walked up to the altar, my shoes making tiny clicking noises upon the tiles. I then lay down upon the ground, humble in the sight of God. The archbishop of Canterbury towered over me, arms outstretched, silk vestments falling in a pale waterfall, while he chanted another prayer over my inert form.

Once the final words of the prayer had faded away, I assumed a kneeling position, still bowing my head in reverence. The golden band was carefully removed from my hair, and the Archbishop anointed me with the sacred oil. I could feel its warm smoothness on my skin, could feel its holy powers seeping into me, imbuing me with my rightful Queenship, a kind of holiness in itself. I was no longer just a girl, just Eleanor of Provence. I was an anointed Queen, made sacred in God's eyes.

The Archbishop was now blessing the ring I would wear, symbolic of my marriage to the King and to my people and to God. He slipped it onto my finger; as small as I was, it fit perfectly, as if I had always been destined to wear it. Then a shadow darkened my head, cut off the light from the painted glass windows high above. Flicking my gaze slightly upwards, I saw the crown, the Queen's crown, heavy with jewels, decorated with lilies.

Down it came as if descending from heaven, settling upon my brow, fitting snugly, though with a certain weightiness that made me sway on my knees a moment, for I was only slight and small. A crown heavy with responsibility. Fervently I prayed I would live up to that high responsibility.

I got up and turned toward the gathered congregation, and bursting forth came the singing of the monks, rising through the roof-arches, reaching to heaven—*Christus Vincit, Christus Regnat, Christus imperat*!

With my sceptre now placed in my hand, I returned to the door of Westminster Abbey, a Queen.

I remembered only a little of the banquet that followed at Westminster Hall. I was too filled by joy and wonder to take in much more than a swirl or colour, a blare of noise, a hubbub of happy voices. There were musicians and entertainers, dancers and stilt walkers. There was a rude jester in a parti-coloured hat. The food was sumptuous, eels in cream and bream in foil, a swan and a peacock still bearing their feathers, and a huge bloated porpoise lying on an engraved silver dish. Jellies wobbled before me, coloured vividly with sandalwood and saffron. A subtlety crafted into a castle portcullis glittered on the table before the high seat, near a saltcellar fashioned into a sailing ship.

That all became a blur as the night progressed and the torches were lit along the walls and the courtly dances began.

What I remembered most, though, were the actions of one man, Simon de Montfort, a Frenchman who had long dwelt in England. His father, another Simon, was infamous for his persecution of the Cathars; he had burned villagers alive and gouged out heretics' eyes. In the end, he had died when hit by shot fired from a mangonel, fired, as it happened, by vengeful girls and women on the walls of the town he was besieging. Although heretics were certainly not to be encouraged, Simon had taken his crusade against the Cathars to cruel extremes, and I thought God had spoken in his embarrassing demise.

But the son! Hopefully not as cruel as his sire, but just as forceful in getting his own way, it seemed. He had been most strenuous in asserting his right to be Henry's steward on the occasion of my Coronation. Earl Roger Bigod, who deemed it was *his* right, had protested with vehemence, his face blood-red and angry, his voice raised in a harsh shout, almost ruining the occasion with his inappropriate rage.

Simon, who had pretensions to the earldom of Leicester, quickly out-talked his rival, his forthright coolness making Bigod look a loud-mouthed lout, and he was duly granted the position he sought. He would be King Henry's steward, Bigod be damned.

I gazed at de Montfort from the raised throne beside my husband, as the Earl held out a golden bowl that the King might lave his hands; a tall, well-made man with sharp cut features and a mass of wild dark hair. There was a dangerous look about him, an unpredictability. A strange, cold sensation chilled me to the heart; at the same time, intrigue took hold. I did not know how I truly felt about this man. Apprehensive, certainly, and suddenly I wished that Roger Bigod, for all his unseemly yelling, had been granted the position instead of Simon de Montfort.

But I dared not saying anything to Henry, at least not here. My position was too new and women did not interfere in politics, not openly and not when they were young, foreign girls, queens or no.

When I retired, alone, to my apartments, leaving the King still celebrating with his companions, in my mind's eye I could see De Montfort standing slightly apart from the others, hands on hips, thumbs hooked in his ornamented belt, looking as imperious as a king himself. Pleased with himself, that he had won the honour of stewardship over Earl Bigod.

Chapter Two

Months passed as months do, and I became accustomed to England…though not to its winter climes! That first year it rained incessantly, turning all the fields to mud and making roads impassable; old men, superstitious, spoke of God's anger. I prayed and lit candles for better weather; I did not want anyone to connect an angry Almighty with the arrival of their new Queen.

Henry doted on me and made sure I had anything I desired: silks, brocade, miniver, samite, necklaces, rings. My Uncle William was still in England, and I begged the King that other members of my retinue should stay as well.

Henry had sighed, knotting his lean hands with their sprinkling of rings. "I do not know, Eleanor. The people would probably be happier if your court was not full of foreigners. They might think you spurned them, did not love them."

"It is not true though, husband!" I insisted. "It is only that I wish to have some family and old time companions near me. They are good, hard-working people who will bring no shame! And most of all, they are dear to me!"

Henry sighed again and took my hand. He raised it to his lips, kissed every finger, then worked his mouth down to the pulse in my wrist—above the silver and gold bracelets he had just presented me. "When have I ever denied you, my Eleanor? They may stay."

We moved from London to the mighty royal castle at Windsor, with its grey drum tower soaring to the sky. I was quite glad to move from London, for at Windsor we could hunt and ride in the spacious park beyond the adamant walls. The air was sweeter than in London, and the river far quieter, with the only boats that passed by there on the King's business.

Henry seemed quite excited when we reached the castle. "I have something to show you," he said.

Leading me to the Queen's apartments, he brought me into the bedchamber. On the wall above the canopied bed, was a wide window that allowed in copious daylight. The window itself was wrought of painted glass that had been crafted by great artisans—it showed the

Tree of Jesse, with a white-bearded, patriarchal Jesse lying sprawled upon the twisted roots and forty-three generations sprouting from him, including those of the wise Kings David and Solomon. At the very top, the Blessed Virgin holding the infant Christ gazed down benignly amidst a spray of golden rays.

I blushed. It was clear that the reference of the Jesse Window was to the continuation of the royal family tree. I had not fallen pregnant yet and I knew Henry was eager for an heir. My personal doctor, Nicholas Farnham, had been summoned, and with great reassurance he said that there was no need to worry, that my lack of fertility was due to my youth, and it was probably better if a few years passed before I conceived. There was no need to call for relics to bring a child just yet.

Henry gave me other gifts instead of a babe, a garland dotted with pearls in silver, an enamelled goblet, gowns trimmed with gold wire, chemises, veils and a horde of shoes—both dainty slippers and stouter goatskin boots to battle the English weather. He told me he wanted to make sure I felt desired and had all the accoutrements of queenship so that men would marvel at my appearance. We travelled together frequently, and side by side gave offerings at the shrine of Edward the Confessor, which had a special meaning for my husband. The Confessor was by far his favourite King of yore. Henry had proposed that the Confessor be made a saint, for miracles had occurred near his tomb, and at the same time, the great abbey of Westminster be remodelled and beautified, with space made for Henry's future tomb and the tombs of all his heirs (and mine) down the long ages.

Dr Farnham, who was a theologian as well as a doctor, taught me all about Edward the Confessor and I came to share Henry's devotion. I was sure the shrine my husband intended to build to his eternal glory would gather pilgrims from near and far.

At Westminster Palace, once we were back in residence after our sojourn at Windsor, Henry ordered many of the walls decorated with scenes from the life of the Confessor. My own rooms, however, were much more secular, complete with a ghostly white figure that represented wintertime painted above the carved fireplace. As with so many of my husband's decorative arts, there was symbolism here: cold winter would never be allowed to flourish in our warm, happy home. It was also a nod to his realisation that I found the English winter harsh after the milder climes of Provence.

A little chill did strike my heart, however, when Uncle William suddenly decided to leave England. A wise man, he had been a high-ranking counsellor to the King and seemed to be making his fortune. "Why must you go, Uncle?" I asked plaintively, calling him to me. "Are you not happy here? Surely Henry has treated you well?"

"Very well, your Grace…my little Eleanor," he said with a sad smile, "but guilt grows within me. I have left my own lands and house unattended for too long. And the Pope has spoken of new offices for me—offices too great to turn down. Do not be afraid, your other Uncle Thomas of Savoy is eager to see England, and make sure you want for naught."

"Yes, that may be so," I sighed, "but you, Uncle William, are my favourite."

He kissed me then, as if I was just a little girl and not a great Queen, and then he took horse to Dover. Sadly, I was never to see him again; he died not so long after his departure from England, without ever receiving those precious offices from the Pope.

I tried to immerse myself in court life in the months that followed. I found it a hotbed of rumour and sometimes full of sinfulness that shocked me; men entangled with women not their wives, and sometimes men entangled with other men. My father's household had been so quiet, so *moral* in comparison.

One day, Henry flew into my Westminster chamber stuttering in rage, his face crimson and his eyes wild, almost starting from his head. Grabbing a crystal vial from the table, he hurled it across the room. It shattered on the wall, sending glittering shards flying across the newly-swept flagstones. My ladies, settled at their embroidery, stifled little shrieks with their hands and dropped their needles.

Henry glared at them, his visage now nigh on purple, and made an angry gesture with his hand, waving them out of the room. Throwing down their work, they clutched up their long skirts and fled, tripping in their haste. The door slammed behind them.

I stood alone, pale-cheeked, not sure how to comfort my husband, for I was not certain what ailed him. I had heard tales of how his sire had rolled on the floors and bitten the rushes when in a fit of rage, and I had no guarantee Henry would not do the same—although he had been of mild temper throughout most of our marriage so far.

"I cannot believe it, Eleanor!" he cried at last, regaining some semblance of composure. "The court is wild and full of defiance and contempt for their King. They insult me …Insult me, I tell you!"

"What has happened, your Grace, my dearest Henry?" I guided him to a stool, hoped he would be comfortable. "Who has upset you so?"

"Lots of people. Simon de Montfort, for one."

I nodded, shivering for reasons unknown as I recalled that tall, stern-face warrior and his hard bargaining to be steward at my Coronation feast.

"And my sister. My sister, who bears your sweet name, Eleanor, but who I wish had even half your goodness!"

"Eleanor! Did you not give permission for her to marry Earl Simon?"

"I did, but what a fool I was! Eleanor had sworn an oath of chastity after the death of her first husband, William Marshal…and she swore it before Archbishop Edmund Rich himself. I tried to appease my sister, get her out of a foolish vow she took in the throes of grief, and now I am being harried."

"Harried? By whom?"

"By Richard, my damn brother Richard!" He thumped his fist on the table, making the glass fruit bowl up-end. Apples rolled over the oak wood, fell bouncing to the flagstones. "And the other lords are fully behind him, bemoaning the fact that de Montfort is lowly in status compared to Eleanor and bewailing that I allowed them to wed in secrecy within my own private chapel."

"Maybe that was not wise, Henry," I said softly.

"You dare to criticise me too?" Henry yelled and he swung towards me, his usually mild, almost sleepy eyes black with rage. I stepped back, a little afraid, for the first time ever…

Heart racing, I thought, *this is how his ill-named father John must have looked.*

Almost immediately, he quietened, gaining control of his own wild emotions. "Richard is in rebellion!" he said. "I cannot believe it…my own brother. And men flock to him."

I thought of Richard of Cornwall, who had come to Provence to meet me. For whom I had written a poem about the English. Aye, I could see why men might follow him. He was a prince of the blood and had been a crusader; he also had a healthy baby son. Henry had never fought a battle, and as yet we had no children…

"What are we to do? What do you counsel?"

"The Tower is safest. Strongest. We will fare there as swift as we may and barricade ourselves inside. With enough food supplies, we can hold out for years!"

Nausea gripped me; my head felt like it might burst The idea of being shut up for untold months within the Tower of London, even with my beauteous rose-painted chambers, did not appeal in the least. It would feel like a prison….

"Surely, surely, some arrangement can be made and Richard and his allies pacified," I murmured weakly.

"I do not know! Start packing your things, Eleanor, without delay…We go to the Tower of London!"

Feeling ill to my stomach, I lay in my bed in my rose-painted chamber in the Tower. Would Richard try to usurp Henry's crown? Such things were well known amongst kings and their jealous brothers. What did he really want, if not that? Just to tear Simon de Montfort and Eleanor Marshal's unseemly marriage apart? As angered as Richard might be by the actions of his sister, and by Henry abetting her wishes, surely rebellion was not the answer?

I stared out the small window above me, a chink in the adamant wall; the sky brooded beyond. It was going to rain again; maybe there was even a storm coming. Sorrow and fear gripped me, and suddenly I felt very young and alone.

Everything was so cramped, with all of Henry's faithful piled inside Gundulf's Tower, and I had heard ugly, ugly whispers that had not been meant for my ears but reached them nonetheless. Nasty, malicious whispers on the stairs, in dark corners. They were calling Henry a bad King, weak-willed and weak-minded; they seemed to favour Richard as their new ruler. And me…they were whispering that I was haughty and that I was barren. Barren! As if I were an old, dried up woman.

My tears began to fall; my ladies glanced in my direction but only faithful old Willelma dared to move, handing me a pretty kerchief broidered with daisies…marguerites. They reminded me of my sister, Marguerite, and I began to cry harder. Oh, if only I could see her…if only I would get with child. But the doctor just reaffirmed I must be patient, that it would take time, and I must eat more (and not worry about becoming as fat as Aunt Gersende with her triple chins and mighty bosom.)

Suddenly there was a flutter of activity in the corridor outside my bedchamber, the sound of footfall on bare stone. The door banged open and the King flew in, and by his wide grin, I knew that the news was good, for once.

Sitting up on my bed, I hastily wiped my tears and tried to affect a regal expression.

"Excellent tidings, my dearest Eleanor!" Henry clasped my hands. "We have no more to fear."

"What has happened to Richard?" I said warily, surprised that this revolt had ended so swiftly. There had been no attack on London or the Tower...just rumours and more rumours, and the oppressive, endless waiting. "Is he captured? Imprisoned?" As much as I had enjoyed Richard of Cornwall's company once, he must not be allowed to assert himself in a way he was not entitled to.

"Of course not!" Henry spoke to me as if I had just uttered the most foolish words ever. "He is content now, and will not bother us."

"Content? How...after he stirred up all the magnates of this land? How can he be content?"

Henry glanced away from me but his voice remained cheerful. "He was happy enough when I paid him. He didn't care much about our sister's honour when coin was placed in his hand!"

"You *paid* him!" Words broke from my lips unbidden; suddenly I flushed red. I knew I had overstepped the mark. Overstepped it by rather a lot.

Henry's lips narrowed to thin white lines. "Yes, I did, my Lady, paid him to leave us be and go abroad on some crusade or other. I presume you will not argue with me—you, who are scarcely more than a child? You are my wife and must remember your place, Eleanor. I don't want a nagging shrew of a woman. Remember that all you have is through me."

He whirled on his heel and stormed out of the Queen's apartments, slamming the door behind him with a resounding crash that echoed through all the corridors in the Tower. I returned to my weeping again, feeling more wretched than ever. The problems with Richard of Cornwall were over for the moment, but his disloyalty had now caused a rift between Henry and me. The King would not be coming to my bed tonight, that much I guessed.

I would never get with child at this rate. Never. And without a babe, my position would be very precarious. Once again, I recalled Henry's father, King John, who had cast aside his first wife, his cousin Hadwisa of Gloucester, to marry Isabella de Angouleme, citing both consanguinity and her barrenness to be rid of her.

Henry was not an angry man in the manner of his father; he was forgiving, hated strife, and soon he sent me gifts as a form of peace-making. We spoke no more of our quarrel and with Richard out of England on some kind of exploit, life seemed much more peaceful and serene.

As late summer engulfed London, drying up the great Thames, and casting heat shimmers over the towers and rooftops, Henry decided we could leave the Tower and move to Woodstock in Oxfordshire. "The heat here in London is too overwhelming!" he stated. "I fear there might be plague, and the humours from the river cannot be good for your health. The palace at Woodstock will be much more comfortable, and I can enjoy myself hunting while we are in residence."

I was glad to get out of London. Although the daily heat did not bother me, the stench of the Thames and the ordure-filled streets offended my nostrils and burned my eyes. I desired to see some green countryside, maybe even to do some riding. It would take my mind off the hard fact that my belly was still flat and that people talked. It did not help that my sister Marguerite was known to have no children either; cruel tongues wagged, saying that we *both* were barren (although others whispered that Queen Blanche kept Louis from Marguerite's bed deliberately since she hated any other woman near her son.)

As our entourage approached Woodstock, I felt my heart lift and soar. Trees swayed in the wind and the forest of Wychwood was a green, inviting blur beyond the palace precincts. A stout wall built by Henry I surrounded Woodstock, separating house and park, and above its broad top thrust pointed turrets and spires with banners flapping.

Passing through the main gate, where locals had gathered to cheer us, we were suddenly accosted by a sinister figure in a ragged robe. The robe was a priest's cassock but the man looked most unholy, with a begrimed face and wild, staring eyes. I could smell the foul sweaty stink of him even from the back of my palfrey, which rolled its eyes in fear and fought against the bit.

The strange man flung himself on the path before Henry, waving his arms in wild abandon. "You are not fit to be King!" he roared, pointing. "You, the weak son of Lackland and his pilfered bride! Give up your throne to one more fitting! I would be a better king than you. Cede your pretty gilt throne to me!" He clutched his middle, laughing in a maniacal fashion, as spittle flew from his lips.

Henry's soldiers rushed forward, pikes at the ready. "My lord!" cried one of the entourage, his face flushed with fury at this unexpected intrusion. "Shall we give this miscreant a good beating?"

Henry was surprisingly unaffected by the disrespectful tirade. "The man is clearly mad, that is apparent to all. He spouts the foolish words of the insane, words that are foul but also nonsensical. Move him on; have him set upon the road leading from Woodstock. I do not wish any more hardship on one who is already afflicted in mind. God has already given this madman a burden; I will not add to it as long as he leaves in peace."

The man was bundled away, not exactly in peace; he was cursing and bellowing as the pikemen jabbed him with the tips of their sharpened weapons. Henry turned his horse's head, smiled reassuringly at me, and we headed on towards the palace. Its shadows fell long over me, bringing a sudden cooling to the heat of the day, and I strove to keep myself from shuddering. The madman at the gate had unnerved me; he had been too close—close enough to strike had he borne a weapon. Uneasily, I also recalled the legends about this palace—of how Henry II, Henry's grandfather, kept a beautiful mistress there, one Rosamund Clifford, a young girl of exceptional beauty. His wife, Eleanor of Aquitaine, had grown insanely jealous, causing him to build a hidden maze with a bower to keep Rosamund safe from her wrath. Legends said Eleanor had murdered her rival anyway, creeping into the maze using a strand of wool as a guide, and then offering her victim the choice between dagger and poison.

The story was scurrilous nonsense, of course; Rosamund had contracted a fatal sickness and gone to the nuns at Godstow, where she eventually died. Nevertheless, my young head was full of foolish tales of poisonings and stabbings, of a young girl lying in a bath being suckled by poisonous toads (yes, that was one of the ridiculous and lurid stories men told!)

Henry and I dined alone that evening, but I found myself lacking appetite even when presented by such delicacies as blancmange, mortrews, and a suckling pig in spiced orange sauce. The wretched madman and his ravings had disturbed me deeply.

Henry did not notice my untouched plate. "I have some business to attend to early this evening," he said, imbibing some claret and finishing off the piglet. "Then I will come to you in your chambers, my dearest, and we will spend the rest of the evening together. Maybe, in the fresh, clean environment of Woodstock, our greatest wish may come true."

I coloured, nodding. I knew he referred to an heir. I doubted somehow if the air would aid in any conception…but on that night, I did not want to be apart from Henry.

As I waited for my husband to finish his business and come to my chambers, I sat sewing with one of my favourite ladies, Margaret Biset. Margaret was a quiet-spoken, homely woman with a long, pale face and soulful grey eyes that were perhaps her most handsome feature. She was very pious, frequently found on her knees in the chapel, and very caring of those less fortunate. Long had her family served the King, and she was held in such esteem she was even allowed to visit Eleanor of Brittany, sister to Arthur whom John had murdered because of his closeness to the crown. Eleanor had been imprisoned for the same reason, passing from castle to castle for safekeeping as her youth fled. At present, she was confined in Gloucester. Eventually, when her childbearing days were long past, she might be allowed to seek a nunnery…Or not…

"I am restless, Margaret," I said. "I cannot eat or drink. I feel quite ill. I was most distressed by the lunatic today."

"He distressed me too, your Grace," said Margaret. "But he is gone and I am sure walking down the road to Oxford, still crying his evil words."

"The King should have imprisoned him," I said grumpily.

"Kings must be merciful," Margaret chided me. "Sometimes."

I thought of poor Eleanor of Brittany then, shunted around a ring of stern fortresses, an inconvenience to all. No one was merciful to her, although she was better off than her murdered brother, stabbed in the heart and his body thrown into a river. He had no known grave. But Eleanor was only a woman and not likely to harm anyone, though in my heart I knew she was dangerous in another way. Through her Plantagenet bloodline.

"What is Eleanor of Brittany like?" I asked, suddenly curious about the imprisoned princess.

Margaret looked surprised, and perhaps a bit embarrassed that I was asking such questions about one deemed as an 'enemy' (despite the fact the King called her 'cousin' in an almost affectionate way). "Getting old…but beautiful still," she said shortly. "Red gold hair, like the early

Plantagenets, and green-eyed. She is an intelligent woman, as are you, your Grace."

"Poor Eleanor," I said. "Kept in all those castles but never knowing a true home."

"So it must be."

"But you said kings must be merciful!"

Margaret sighed. "Not if it is at risk to themselves and their Houses, your Grace. In the end, Eleanor of Brittany's incarceration benefits you and any children you will bear."

I looked thoughtful; the madman was still on my mind, even more than the unfortunate Eleanor of Brittany. " Hmm. And you think the strange, raving man was not a threat? When he said he would be a better king than my husband?"

"The miscreant is long gone, your Grace. With a mind so troubled, he may not even remember the foolish words he spoke. Now, let me come and brush out your hair before his Grace comes to stay the night."

Henry and I were deeply asleep. I lay in the crook of his arm, against his warm shoulder. His breath was a faint rasp; the moonlight, shining through the open window, turned his plain brown hair into an aura of gold. He looked much younger and more vulnerable then, washed free of his cares.

I touched his cheek, moved a strand of hair from his forehead. I could not sleep, still felt an odd unease that churned in my belly. Rising quietly, I donned a thin kirtle and sat in the window embrasure, letting the refreshing night breeze stroke my hot skin.

And then I heard the frenzied shouting from below.

And screaming. A woman's repeated screaming.

"Henry!" I cried. "Wake up! That's Margaret's voice. Margaret Biset. Something has happened!"

Henry was on his feet in a flash, hurling on a tunic and robe and reaching for a weapon as he shouted for his squires to attend him. Outside in the hallway, there was a clashing of arms and more shouting. Feet thundered on the stairs and glancing out the window, I spotted a hundred torches bobbing in the gloom. The entire household was awake and mobilised!

Blade in hand, Henry rushed out of our apartments, and I stumbled a few steps behind him, terrified, wanting to find out what had happened but knowing I should stay out of harm's way.

I was soon to find out what had transpired, however. A flush-faced page rushed into the hallway, skidding on the tiles. He seemed shocked to see me standing there, dishevelled, hair uncovered, and holding a cloak about me. (Maybe he thought I was naked below the mantle—I know not!)

"Your Grace!" He bowed so low he nearly fell over and lost his cap. "The King is asking that you attend him in the hall below; a miscreant has been caught prowling around within the walls of Woodstock. His Grace wants your Grace to attend him when he confronts the criminal."

"I will come at once." I pulled the hood of the cloak over my bare head to keep the boy from staring. "Well, come on, page…lead me to the King!"

The page stopped gawking, bowed again, and then guided me to the great hall. Entering the hall, my eyes were dazzled by a blaze of torchlight. Men at arms were milling everywhere, weapons still in their hands.

Henry was seated upon his chair looking both angry and satisfied. Margaret stood next to him, face white as milk, but seemingly unharmed. It shocked me that she was dressed in a most unseemly fashion, just her kirtle and nothing more…then I remembered I was no different, having risen with such swiftness. And I was Queen.

"Look what we have here, my Lady." Henry pointed to the reed-strewn flagstones at his feet. On the floor, writhing in chains that bound his arms and legs, was the madman who had accosted us earlier in the day.

"This miscreant…" Henry rose and addressed the others in the hall, pointing at the scowling, spitting creature at his feet, "returned to Woodstock to attempt to murder me and my Queen. He broke into my private quarters seeking me, then when he could not find me, came looking for us both…with *this*…" He held up a wicked looking blade, glinting dully in the torchlight. "He planned to cut both our throats. Luckily Lady Margaret…" he nodded toward my lady in waiting, "was still awake, reciting her Psalter. She heard the noise of his passage and seeing the fiend with weapon in hand, raised the alarm. The would-be assassin tried to barricade himself into a room, but the guards pried him out."

"Margaret, Margaret, are you unharmed?" I ran to my lady, clasped her in my arms, despite the impropriety.

"Hush, your Grace, I am fine, if shaken. As we all surely are."

Henry beckoned me to draw nearer. I stood at my husband's side, gazing down at the man who had wanted to kill us. Despite his predicament, he looked unrepentant, snarling at me like some cur, his lips drawn back over his ragged teeth. He looked less man now than a beast.

"At whose behest did he attack?" I asked slowly.

"I do not know but I will soon find out, my Queen!" said Henry, his tone heavy with meaning. Still the attacker did not blanch; he uttered a weird, gurgling laugh then spat at the king's feet, a great, green gobbet that oozed on the flagstones.

"What would you say this man's punishment should be?" Henry glanced over at me.

Showing neither fear nor pity, I stood like a statue. The attacker glared at me with hot, burning eyes, hateful eyes that stripped away my garments and encompassed my very death. Evil eyes. I averted my own gaze from his florid, sweating face. "Death," I said, my voice as clear as a bell in a suddenly silent room.

The man gave a roar like an embattled bear and threw himself forward against the links of his chains. Roughly, he was dragged back by the men at arms.

"So will it be," said Henry, hard as stone, and suddenly that dear, kindly familiar face became like granite, and I could imagine that, with darker hair, here stood the very image of his father, the dreaded John. "Once the man is racked for information, he shall meet a fitting death for the infamy of attempting to assassinate his lawful King and rightful Queen. In the morning, he will be tied to four horses and torn apart before the eyes of all men. Guards, take him away."

As the sentence was pronounced, the attacker suddenly paled and the defiant expression left his eyes. Why he changed his demeanour so suddenly, I did not know. When captured, he must have known he faced death. Perhaps he thought that if he struggled and flung terrible insults Henry would order him killed swiftly on the spot. Now he realised what he had reaped, what his ultimate fate would be.

No quick end for a would-be assassin.

He began to scream, a thin, terrible sound that assailed my ears and made my stomach churn.

"Shut him up!" Henry ordered, his brow like thunder.

An iron fist hit the failed assassin's jaw and he dropped like a stone to the ground, his bloodied face buried in the rushes. With little care, he was dragged away.

Four horses waited.

I was sick for days after the murder attempt, barely able to rise from my bed. My beloved doctor, Nicholas Farnham, tended me with great diligence, and I bade our saviour, Margaret Biset, remain at my side, where I held her hand in gratitude for what she had done for us, at risk to herself. Christ Jesu, what if the intruder has stabbed her to stop her screaming?

"Margaret, how can the King and I repay you?" I said. "What gift do you want? Name it, and it shall be yours!"

At it turned out, she wanted nothing for herself, that good woman, only a little money to give to the women lepers in the lazar house at remote Maiden Bradley. It was a cause near to her heart, and I saw her eyes grow sorrowful when she spoke of those tragic women, but even I dared not ask for the story as it was no business of mine.

Henry sent to my chambers imported fruit, gifts, gemstones the size of pigeon eggs. I grew no better.

I began to be sick, voiding my gut and turning up my nose at even the most delightful delicacies.

And suddenly Margaret's pale face became full of wonderment and her big grey eyes lit like lamps. "Your Grace, could it be that you are *not* ill?"

"Not ill?" I said peevishly, reaching for a brass basin in order to vomit. "I am deathly ill, Margaret—look at me."

"Your Grace, it has occurred to me, these symptoms that you have could be the signs of..."

Holding the bowl for my spew, I suddenly gaped at her. Due to my youth, I knew but little of such matters, but yes, yes, I supposed it could be...

"Oh, Margaret!" I cried, tears springing to my eyes. "I think...I think it is. I am not stricken with some dreaded malady. I...I think I am pregnant! I am carrying my lord husband's much-wanted prince!"

Midsummer was nearly upon England; the heat ran high and the nights were long, with hot sunsets bleeding on the horizons. I did not see the sunrises, sweltering noon, the red dusk, though I felt the heat, rising even to warm the stones of cold castles. I sweltered in confinement, locked away for over a month with my women, awaiting the birth of my child.

The pains of my travail began late at night while I was sleeping. A cramp, a sudden dampness. I called for my women, who summoned the midwives.

I was afraid, as all women are the first time they give birth. No amount of reassurance or tales from my ladies of their own travails could prepare me for what was to come. I had written my will, as all sensible women did before enduring childbed, and I could think of nothing else. Nothing but death and the tomb.

Gentle Mary, protect me!

Gasping as the pains took me, I writhed on the bed, possessed by agonies such as I had never imagined. My women clustered around, laving my brow as the midwives examined me. Margaret Biset was there and the indomitable Sybil Giffard, an intelligent and industrious woman who had looked after me as her own daughter during my confinement. The women had loosed their hair as well as their girdles and their jewellery; to unbind such items was rumoured to help free the unborn child from the ties of the womb. Special sacred stones were pushed into my hand for luck; I clutched them with a death-grip as pain washed over me in waves.

"Is it stuck?" I cried at one point. "Is the baby going to die? Am I going to die? Ah Mary, Mary, have mercy."

"No, your Grace." The midwife was a fat woman whose cumbrous body bore the signs of having borne many children. "Everything is as it should be. You are young and strong. Your pains are not exceptional, just the burden we must bear because of mother Eve..."

The torture went on. Sweat rolled down my skin in gleaming rivulets. I ceased to talk but grunted embarrassingly, like some animal spawning its brood.

Sybil sang to me, trying to soothe; sometimes her mannerisms changed and she spoke sternly, telling me to stop weeping and to bear down.

Then...it was over.

I lay there for a moment, surprised, chest heaving, my burden removed.

Did the infant live? Was it male?

"Your Grace, you have a healthy son!" A baby's strident scream pierced my ears.

I began to weep, any pretence at queenliness lost in that moment, as the midwife held up the King's son and heir, who let out a piercing scream and thrashed his tiny red limbs as if already fighting this new world into which he had been thrust. A warrior already.

"It is a prince!" I cried. "A prince. Let King Henry be told! Let him be told at once!"

Sybil Giffard hastened to the door, summoning a page who waited outside. Shortly thereafter, the sound of cheering sounded in the courtyard below, and then the bells of all the nearby churches began to ring, and ring, and ring…

The King was elated at the birth of his son; he sent me a collar of rubies as a gift and then he got drunk with his favourite lords. "A boy!" he kept slurring. "It is a boy! I knew it would be, what else could it be? My heir, my wonderful, long-awaited heir!"

The child was taken to Westminster Abbey with great pomp and baptised at once; he was called Edward, after the Confessor, whom my husband revered so much. Sybil was given a pension for assisting me during my travail, and all other babes baptised the same day as my son were given monetary gifts in honour of Edward's birth. Surprisingly, Henry asked Simon de Montfort to act as our child's godfather; I supposed he did it to show his sister Eleanor that he had forgiven her for her former transgressions, but I still had my doubts about Simon having any part in my baby's life. And I knew his marriage still rankled with Henry, due to the difficulties it had brought.

In the weeks that followed, Edward thrived, just as we hoped and prayed he would, suckling from his plump wet-nurse without difficult and swiftly putting on weight. Henry and I still treated him like fine glass, however, for we knew babes could be suddenly snatched away— a blast of stagnant air, soured milk, bad humours. To protect from this as best we could, we donated money to the poor, hoping Christ and his blessed Mother would intercede, and had a little silk tunic, tailored to be child-sized, sent as a gift to St Mary's at Southwark, where it would lie as an offering on the high altar.

Once the required month had passed, I was ready for my official churching, my purification after which I would return to public life and re-enter my marital bed. Now that Edward was born, it was my duty to swiftly become pregnant again, and have a second son in case anything untoward happened to the first.

Surrounded by my women, clad in a pure-white robe and veil, I entered the incense-bound shadows of Westminster Abbey. Thousands of candles flickered before the Shrine of the Confessor and the monks were singing, their voices deep and melodious, echoing down the vast cavern of the nave.

Great lords and ladies gathered round to witness the purification. The ceremony went smoothly enough and with great magnificence, but when we returned to Westminster Hall, the King was presented with a letter delivered by the Treasurer. The man looked grim, Henry even grimmer. I chewed my lip, dared not asked what had gone wrong.

The King started looking wildly around him, ignoring a perplexed Archbishop of Canterbury, who had been trying to engage him in conversation. Henry suddenly released an animalistic yell and stormed away from the Archbishop towards a tall figure lounging in the corner of the chamber. Simon de Montfort.

My heart hammered against my ribs, then sank; I had rarely seen Henry so enraged and de Montfort always filled me with unease.

"You!" Henry shouted at the nobleman. "You dare to show your face here…you, and my whorish sister!"

Eleanor de Montfort, Simon's wife and Henry's sister, made a low curtsey and then tried to assuage her brother. "Your Grace, why are you so wroth? We come in love for you and the Queen. I believed any misdoings on our part had long been forgiven by my beloved brother, our dread King."

He glared at her, looking as if he might explode, his fists curling dangerously. "You presume, Madame. I do not know if I can ever truly forgive your unseemly and shameful behaviour in marrying this odious man!"

De Montfort's face was stunned, colour burning on his cheekbones. He could say nothing to defend himself, dared not. "You…your Grace!" he managed to stammer. "I do not understand. You allowed us to use your chapel, you made me steward, you made me the Prince's godfather …"

"You are a miscreant!" Henry roared at him. "Not content with seducing my sister, you are a debtor too. Yes, I know about your debt, de Montfort! A huge debt that you owe. But what care have I about your finances, you might ask?" He was almost screaming in Simon's face now, spittle flying from his lips. "Well, I will tell everyone in

Westminster Palace, shall I?" You used my name as surety against that debt, you wily knave. My name! How dare you, you presumptuous bastard!"

De Montfort began to stammer out an excuse, while his wife Eleanor gasped in horror, staring wildly between her brother the King and her red-faced husband. Henry raised a hand as if to strike Simon; horrified, the Archbishop reached up and grabbed the King's sleeve, a dangerous motion even for a man of such high standing. "Your Grace, you must not do this violent act! Not on the day of the Queen's purification!"

"I will do as I must!" yelled Henry. "Get you gone from my sight, de Montfort, and you my sister too—you fickle wanton carved in the image of our inconstant mother! Stay here at your peril."

De Montfort began to look as angry as the King, his eyes crackling fire and his nostrils flaring like those of a maddened bull; his wife Eleanor clung desperately to his tunic, dragging him out of Henry's presence and toward the hall door. "We will go, brother!" she cried over her shoulder. "I swear we will trouble you no more. We will go from England's shores, go far, far away!"

Together the disgraced couple left the hall and the iron-bound doors clanged behind them. In silence courtiers, barons and servants stared after their departing forms.

Henry's anger began to abate as soon as the couple were out of his sight. He clapped his hands and gestured to the musicians clustered in the gallery. "Play!" he shouted. "Come on, minstrels—play! Play a sweet song for my beautiful Queen, Eleanor! Let us forget this ugliness as best we can!"

The feast in honour of my churching proceeded, but I could not relax, thinking of my husband's suffused face and de Montfort's own red-eyed glare before he stormed out of the room. The day got even worse when a Fool waddled in wearing cap and bells and wittering about cuckolds. Henry, losing his temper once more, accused him of an inappropriate jest, then tore up his cap and threw him bodily into the gutter outside the palace. My churching, my special day, had been marred; there were no two ways about it.

Two days later, a messenger arrived with the news that Simon de Montfort and Eleanor had indeed sailed for France. Relief flooded me. With luck, they would settle and never come back.

If they did, the Tower would surely await them. I saw Henry's father, King John, in the depths of his son's angry eyes.

Henry worried for months over Simon de Montfort's departure. He was fearful he might brew up troubles with the French. I tried to reassure him. "With my sister as Queen, you need not fear overmuch. Marguerite will have Louis's ear, she will not allow de Montfort to ease himself in like some gnawing worm."

"I pray you are right, wife," murmured Henry, staring down at the floor. He was stalking around our apartments like a captive beast, thoroughly miserable. "He could bring me so much trouble. Already I have lost so many lands in France, and have no aid from my she-devil of a mother, Isabella. She is so entranced by the brood of brats she spawned with young Lusignan, that she has forgotten her children of England."

I was glad I had not met his infamous mother. I imagined her with horns and a tail; a lustful succubus like the she-demon Lilith.

I tried to lighten my husband's mood. "Did you hear? My uncle Thomas of Savoy is coming to court!" I said brightly. "I will be so glad to see some of my kinsmen once again."

"Yes, yes," mumbled my husband, obviously not the least bit interested. "It will be a joyous occasion for you, Eleanor."

Indeed it was. In private, I fell upon Uncle Thomas with a squeal of joy. We retreated to my garden and he told me all about my parents and how they fared. "They are so proud of you and of Marguerite," he reassured me. "Your marriages have brought them great status."

"And what of my two younger sisters, Beatrice and Sanchia?" I asked. "I wager I'd not recognise them now!"

"Probably not. Both are very fair to behold, just like their elder sisters. Hopefully, they too will make worthy marriages one day."

"And you, how are you, Uncle Thomas?"

"Struggling, as ever." He held out his hands. "Even though I am a count. You know how it is, money is ever short. So short."

"You will not have to worry. I will make certain of it," I said reassuringly, kissing his cheek.

He beamed at me. "You were always a dear girl, Eleanor...."

I went to Henry. He was still so elated with me because I had borne him a prince that he was ready to grant me anything I asked for. Five hundred marks soon found their way into Uncle Thomas's purse. He was also granted a tax on English wool entering his territories in Flanders.

Uncle Thomas was elated and so was I. The English barons, however, were furious. They even refused to accept my husband's seal upon the documents pertaining to the tax.

Henry would not be swayed by such discontent. The money was his to give; after all, he was the King! With a curt hand wave, he dismissed the grumbling protestors from their offices and had them driven from the hall.

"How dare they rail against me?" he said to me later, when we were alone in his private closet. "Who do they think they are? The money is mine to give to loyal kinsmen. Don't you agree, Eleanor?"

"Of course, my lord husband," I said. I had no qualms about giving the wool taxes to Uncle Thomas, but the way Henry gained the 500 marks brought a vague disquiet. The treasury was rather bare, as ever, so Henry had gone to the Jews of London—not for a loan, but to levy a punishing tax on them.

"Will the Jews accept this tax in silence?" I asked. "It is heavy."

"Yes," said Henry arrogantly. "They have no choice; I have threatened them with expulsion from England if they do not pay up."

"Is that wise?"

He gave me a stern look. "They are only Jews. They are here on sufferance. What I have done is for the benefit of *your* family, Eleanor. Remember that."

I did, and seeing Thomas's joy and my husband's satisfied face made me soon forget the plight of the Jews.

Richard of Cornwall's wife was dead. The news reached us by fastest courier. Henry and I glanced at each other. Richard had made an unusual, not altogether fitting marriage many years ago, despite much protest from his family. He had married Isabella, the widow of Gilbert de Clare, a woman much older than he, though still beautiful to gaze upon. She had borne six living children to Gilbert but unfortunately produced only stillborn babes with Richard, save for one boy, his heir Henry, aged five.

In bearing one more, final, child Isabella lost her life, and the infant died with her.

Richard sent her heart to Tewkesbury since she had written in her will that she wanted to lie in the abbey there, next to her long-dead husband Gilbert—rather a reproach to Richard, who had, truth be told, neglected her, leaving her on her own in the shabby castle of

Berkhamsted. He had loved her deeply once, men whispered, but had swiftly grown tired of her, and so he dallied with other women and harlots, and even tried in vain to get an annulment.

Now he needed no such decree, for she was dead, but Richard had another problem. He was about to go off on crusade, and his son had no mother to care for him. He asked if he might send young Henry to join his uncle's court.

I was delighted at the thought. If I did not quicken again soon and produce another son, this young boy might be a good childhood companion for my Edward. It would be better to forge ties with cousins and have them stoutly at ones' back than have them distant and possibly troublesome.

"Let us have Henry here at court," I said to the King. "It could work out well for all of us."

Richard sent the child a few weeks after that, rolling up to Windsor in a painted chariot with Richard's dark eagles blazoned on the side. Young Henry was a handsome boy who resembled his father, with curling brown hair and bright eyes. He was dressed in deep blue silk and a short damson cloak and bowed before me like a little courtier, despite his youthful age. Whatever flaws his mother Isabella may have had, she had trained him well in manners.

"Welcome to our Court, Henry." I beckoned him closer so that I could get a good look at him and him at me. "I am your Aunt Eleanor."

"You are the Queen!" he said, awestruck.

"I am that as well, little Henry!" I laughed.

"You are very beautiful, Madame," he said in a hushed, reverent voice.

Sitting next to me, Henry burst into laughter. "You have an admirer, that is clear, my Lady wife. A little flatterer. He has scarcely noticed me—his uncle the King."

Young Henry immediately went down on his knees before his Uncle's seat. "I hope I have not been rude, Uncle…King Henry."

"No, you are not rude, my young namesake. You are correct. The Queen is indeed beautiful."

"Would you like to meet your cousin, the Lord Edward?" I asked. "I hope you and he will become good friends when he is a little older."

Henry nodded solemnly. I made a gesture and the child's nurses took Henry's hands, and we left the King's presence and retired to the royal nursery. Inside, amidst a cavalcade of hangings, silks, rich carpets and imported toys, Edward lay in his tall, carved cradle, wrapped, as was custom, in swaddling.

My healthy son once again entranced me, his burgeoning curls forming a silvery-white halo, his small round face breaking out into a toothless smile as his nurses lifted him up for inspection. His only flaw was a drooping eyelid…but at least none could ever deny he was his father's son with such a distinguishing mark.

"He is much smaller than me," said young Henry dubiously.

"Yes, for now, but not for long. In a few years, hopefully you can play together, train together to be warriors. "

Henry walked briskly to the nurses carrying Edward, and to my surprise bowed courteously before his cousin, before grasping the baby's hand and kissing it. Edward gurgled with delight.

I laughed. My son the prince was already building up his army of loyal followers.

I was pregnant again, just as I had wished. In the warm month of September, when the tips of the trees' leaves were frosted with first gold, I gave birth, easily and swiftly to a daughter. Henry and I named her Margaret—the English form of Marguerite—as a tribute to my sister, the Queen of France.

My churching passed without incident this time, and as a gift, Henry gave me an expensive candle to carry at the ceremony—a token of his gratitude for producing another healthy child, albeit a girl. Later in the year, shortly before the Christmas celebration, he presented gold purses to little Margaret and me as a further sign of his esteem.

My Christmas was made complete by the arrival of Peter, another of my Savoyard Uncles. Like my mother Beatrice, Peter was affable and intelligent, with a handsome face that drew maids and goodwives alike. He was clever too—as a younger son, he had been destined for the religious life, for which he had no taste. On his own, he had managed to wrangle a propitious marriage for himself instead and hence escape the monastic confines.

Henry took to Uncle Peter immediately and knighted him along with many other goodly young men that winter season. He then proceeded to shower him with honours and with lands. I was thrilled that Peter got on so well with Henry, but men began to mutter that the king should not be so free with his wealth, especially to foreigners.

They also whispered about how angry Earl Richard would be when he returned from his crusading.

Peter was intelligent; he had his ear to the ground where the rumours were concerned. He knew he had been rewarded more than was perhaps wise. When news reached England that Richard was soon to return, Peter began handing some of his newly acquired castles back to Henry.

But when Richard returned, to everyone's surprise, the expected confrontation never happened. The Earl of Cornwall seemed quite preoccupied with other matters. With his wife Isabella dead and only one living son, he had turned his mind to remarriage.

And that remarriage was very personal to me.

On his way to the holy land, he had acquired safe passage through the lands of my father, Raymond Berenger, and as kin by marriage, had been invited to a feast at one of my parents' castles. There, he had seen my younger sister, Sanchia, and become smitten by her. She was betrothed to Raymond VII, an alliance no one much liked, as Raymond was a violent and unappealing man, but which had been deemed necessary to ensure stability in the region. However, there was still time to call the union off.

Richard pushed for it, promised many things to my parents. It did not take long for them to decide against Raymond VII, an old enemy, and plump for Richard instead.

Sanchia would marry the Earl of Cornwall, and so two royal brothers would wed two Provencal sisters, and my father's blood would be forever mingled with that of the royal house of Plantagenet.

I was most pleased by the news about my sister and the Earl. To have one of my close kinswomen residing in the same country would please me very much. So much shared history to talk about, so much good companionship to be gained. I would endeavour to bring many of my kin as possible to England, and strengthen its ties with Provence and Savoy and vice versa. The barons and their ilk might grumble, but it would be for the good in the end. My family were clever, determined people, not afraid of hard work. Yes, they would need lands and manors befitting their stations, but they would work hard for them.

I knew I was doing the right thing.

A few months later, I found I was with child yet again. I did not feel so well this time around and spent much time in the privy with my head hanging over the edge and my concerned ladies fluttering around me, laving my brow and dabbing at my mouth as I retched. When not being ill, the rest of the time was spent abed, which irked me, as I knew matters of great importance were afoot and I hated to be left out, woman though I was.

There was going to be a campaign to Poitou. Henry would be fighting against the French…and hence my own sister Marguerite. This filled my heart with great grief, but there was no helping it; my allegiance had to be firmly with my husband's cause.

Everything had gone wrong in Poitou. Once an English territory, King John lost it due to his ineptitude; it then became a fiefdom, which both England and France claimed. In the past summer, King Louis's mother, the fearsome termagant Blanche, had insisted Louis knight his own younger brother, Alphonse, and make him count of Poitou.

It was unacceptable. There was a count already—Richard of Cornwall. The move to raise Alphonse to the position of count had been shrewd and deliberate; Blanche and Louis knew Richard was far away on crusade and could not defend his territory.

Henry and Richard's mother, Isabella, who so seldom took interest in her English children, threw herself into the fray at the insult to her son…and the perceived injury to herself.

That was not all she had thrown… After the feast held when the new count and his wife arrived in Poitou, she had taken every pot, pan, plate, chair—everything touched by the French—and hurled it out the window of her chamber into the castle moat!

"The French are vile miscreants!" she had reportedly screamed as she watched the luxuries sink into the foetid water. "They looked upon me with scorn! I am a Queen! They made me stand before them like some sorry kitchen wench! They did not let me sit beside King Louis, as is my right! Shame on them, they who have stolen my son's lands!"

Her young husband, Hugh de la Marche, had been mortified by her behaviour. First, he tried to comfort her, without success, and then, when that failed, to restrain her from throwing more valuables about in a frenzy.

Her response was not altogether unexpected, knowing Isabella's character. "Leave me be, you wet sop of a man!" she had screamed at Hugh and flung a heavy gem-encrusted goblet straight at his head.

While he nursed a bleeding cut and howled in agonised rage, Isabella stormed from the castle, leapt astride a horse and rode like the devil to her own castle in Angouleme, where she barricaded the door against her husband. Head bound with bandages, he followed her and ended up waiting outside the gatehouse for nigh on a week before she decided to 'forgive him' and let him in. She seemed to have forgotten *she* had struck him, not the reverse, and, strangely enough, so had Hugh.

Once all was forgiven, the pair descended to plotting against their *true* enemies, the French, and when Alphonse held his first court, Isabella burst through the doors with her armed guard and flew into his presence like some Greek harpy, shrieking, "Usurper! Usurper! Get out of Poitou!"

Hugh had chimed in, angrily denouncing Alphonse as having unlawfully stolen his stepson Richard's title and lands while he was selflessly fighting for God's cause. A man could not be eviller than that! As Alphonse stared, struck dumb by their effrontery, Hugh had stormed from the hall and set the building aflame in one huge final act of defiance.

Returning from the Holy Land, Richard had been informed of the dramatic turn of events. He was furious, but seemed to have suddenly lost his taste for fighting—he was more eager to marry Sanchia than to recover his pilfered lands.

Ignoring the situation in Poitou, he immediately began negotiations to find a new bride for the jilted Raymond so that there would be no hard feelings and he could wed Sanchia unhindered; Hugh kindly stepped in and offered up one of his own daughters, who Raymond accepted in his usual brusque manner.

I liked to fancy that Richard, who had entranced me so as a green young girl, had had the same effect upon Sanchia, and that he was equally smitten with her. However, unlike Henry, Richard was not content to receive no dowry with his bride…and it was well known my parents were not wealthy people, for all that they were respected as the parents of two Queens.

"Henry," I wheedled to the King, plying him with sweetmeats, wine…and my kisses. "Can you not aid my sister Sanchia and your own dear brother in the matter of their marriage? It would be so disappointing for all if they should not wed. And after the fiasco in Poitou, Richard surely needs some cheering up."

Henry had frowned for a bit (the treasurer was always chiding him about his lack of finances!) then relented—he would bestow a handful of manors and three thousand marks to Richard on Sanchia's behalf. That would suffice as a dowry.

I breathed a sigh of relief. My sister would not be shamed and the marriage would go ahead.

"I am coming!" I was angry; Henry looked helpless and dismayed. He had planned to sail to Gascony with his forces…but he seemed to have forgotten one thing. Me.

"But Eleanor, this is madness, you cannot possibly go. You are with child!" He pointed to the slight swell of my belly beneath my heavy samite robes.

"I know that, Henry, but there are still months yet before the birth, and my place is at your side, not waiting here like some feeble invalid."

"But it…it would be dangerous!"

"Dangerous? What do you think I will do, go running toward the enemy swinging a sword above my head?"

Henry paused, obviously imagining such an unlikely scene, then he burst into laughter.

"I probably indulge you too much, wife, but so be it. You may come, but you must be kept well away from any conflict."

I threw my arms around him. "You know I am as stalwart as any soldier, even though I am a mere woman. I want to be with you, win or lose."

Henry sent me to Bordeaux to deliver my child. On the journey, illness overtook me, and I became feverish and afraid I would die. I halted at La Reole, where my ladies bathed me with cool water and begged for the best doctors in town. The local lords were suspicious and surly, making excuses. They did not wish to help; they were playing both sides, unsure of how the forthcoming battle would go.

Margaret Biset was in a panic, fussing about me. "Your Grace, I heard them whispering….I am fearful they might betray us to the French. Can we not press on?"

I was too weak to do more than motion with my hand. "Yes… at first light…on to Bordeaux. We must pray to God that nothing untoward will happen before then."

I was a little better come sunrise but still weak and shaking. I was placed in a litter and we hastened away before anyone in La Reole might summon our enemies or think on the reward they might get for capturing England's Queen.

After many hours' hard travel, in which rain lashed down, soaking through the canopy of my litter, we reached Bordeaux, only to find it nearly as unwelcoming as La Reole. The castle was strong, but the castellan sullen, and the servants spoke gruffly and without grace, as if they resented our presence.

Sybil had travelled with me, along with Margaret. "Oh Lady, we should have remained in England!" she wept. "I am afraid to go out the door. The castle residents glare at me, and I am afraid of the food they give us. What if it is…tainted?"

"You think it might be poisoned?" I was propped up on some cushions in a bed; I had many of my own linens and quilts, hauled with me in the baggage train, but the chamber was unclean, the tiles damp and growing mould and the fireplace black with ash.

"I do not know what to think, your Grace, only that I fear we may never see England again." She hid her face in her hands and began to weep bitterly.

"Hush, Sybil!" I chided. "That will not help." I shifted uncomfortably in the bed; little cramps were rippling across my belly. Soon we would have more to worry about than Sybil's fears.

Beatrice of England was born the next day as dusk descended into night and the stars came out, cold eyes watching over unfriendly Bordeaux. A pair of pouch-faced, sullen midwives attended, carefully watched by my worried ladies. A wet-nurse was dragged in from the local village, as miserable and suspicious as her fellows, and not too clean, but she was plump and hearty and seemed to have plenty of milk to feed the new baby.

I was exhausted and in much more pain than I was after birthing my last two children. My fever returned and I lay abed for days, in a frightening dream-like state. Once I thought I had died and gone to hell and demons chased me with forks…and I knew not why I should be so punished, for I was a dutiful wife. I called out for my mother and prayed to the Virgin to save me, but even Our Lady seemed to shun me; I envisioned her statue from the chapel come alive and rocking menacingly towards me, and she was scowling. "You have been wicked, Eleanor…proud and pushy. Your punishment, Eleanor…"

And then the fever broke. The nightmares faded. Suddenly I felt cool and my mind returned to its normal state. "Margaret," I called, "bring me a drink. Where is the baby? How fares Princess Beatrice?"

"She is fine, your Grace." Loyal Margaret rushed to my side, cup and pitcher in hand. "But we feared for you. So long you were ill…"

"How long?"

She told me. My eyes widened. "Jesu, *that* long! What news from my husband the King?"

Margaret chewed her lip uneasily and stared at the grimy floor. "Not good news, I fear. Poitou is lost. Lost utterly."

"Lost!" I sighed and fell back against my pillows. I stared at my hands, so thin, so white. But I was feeling hungrier now.

"His Grace the King and his brother Earl Richard are making their way here to Bordeaux even as we speak."

"I must rise then, Margaret…must be strong for Henry, even in defeat."

"Madame, do you think it's wise to get up?"

"I must! Bring me some food to give me strength and then bring me my raiment."

I was churched without the splendour I was used to, a paltry affair with a few half-hearted nobles in attendance, my women and those who were my guards. I cared not; as long as it was done adequately in the sight of God, that was enough.

Henry was returning and I was eager to find out what had befallen. As it was, I only heard rumour and evil mutterings, and I could feel the growing hostility of those around us at Bordeaux. They had never been friendly, and now what little warmth they had evaporated like morning mist.

Great relief flooded me as I saw my husband's banners fluttering on the horizon. Dusty and weary of aspect, he entered the castle hall in Bordeaux with a grim-faced Richard of Cornwall and the even grimmer-faced Simon de Montfort, who had made a reconciliation of sorts with the King.

After the initial niceties were over and the great lords and magnates had refreshed themselves, Henry and I sought our own quarters.

"I worried so for you," he said to me. "News was sent of your illness."

"I worried for you, too. The dangers of your battles were ever in my mind, not my own woes." I embraced him.

"Our child…I heard it was a girl. She is well?"

"As well as can be, though I was in great fear during her birth. I have named her Beatrice, after my mother, if that is acceptable to my lord. Henry, Henry, let us not talk about my doings…Tell me what happened in Poitou!"

"Taillebourg…" Henry spat the name as if it were venom. "When we reached Taillebourg to meet my mother's husband, Hugh de la Marche, we found blasted Louis already there with his forces. We had been betrayed; the townsfolk had let his army in."

"Christ, no, that is terrible! Who could have played us false?"

Henry's face reddened. "I was furious, as you might imagine, my dearest. Right or wrong, I put the blame on Hugh. I told him that he had allowed us to come too poorly armed; in his letters to me, he had told me he needed my money more than my armies."

"And what did he say when you confronted him?"

Henry's teeth gritted. "He said it was my damned mother who sent the letters, not him!"

The King swirled away from me, began to pace the grubby flagstones of the keep. "I would have been lost if not for Richard. He saved me. Amongst the French hordes, he spied some knight who he had freed from imprisonment among the infidels. Summoning him, he asked him if he would do a favour in return for Richard saving his life. He went to the French commanders, laid down his sword in peace, and asked that I be allowed to go free. Thankfully, they were not out for my blood and agreed as long as I departed at once. What shame! We even had to leave our train behind, so great was our speed of departure."

I tried to comfort Henry, laying my hand on his shoulder. He gently shrugged me off. "There is more to tell, Eleanor. Hugh tried to rally the men, with de Montfort to aid him…but they were defeated in their efforts; they had no chance against the French. And my mother…that…that she-wolf…"

"What did she do?" I dreaded to hear, knowing Isabella of Angouleme's fiery reputation.

Henry took a deep breath; I could see him shaking with rage as he tried to control his anger. "She tried to poison them."

"Who?" My voice came out a shrill, high whisper.

"King Louis, his mother Blanche…and your sister Marguerite."

I pressed my hand to my mouth then let it drop. My sister…but what could I say? My best friend in childhood but now, separated by the politics of war, my enemy.

"Do not fear, they are all unharmed," said Henry. "My mother's 'plot' was not terribly well thought out, as usual, born out of rage with no proper planning. She sent her own cooks to the French camp to prepare the evening meal for Louis and his family. As you might imagine, everyone wondered who these strange cooks were, and they were swiftly apprehended and executed. Realising she had failed and made herself look foolish at the same time, mother then tried to down the poison and kill herself, but her ladies managed to wrest the elixir away after she had only swallowed a mouthful. Along with Hugh, she was forced to kneel before Louis and Blanche and suffer taunts and humiliations…although they left her alive. Hugh wept like a woman, as all his castles and lands were stripped away. Mother has now left him and gone to Fontevrault—to become a nun."

"A nun? Queen Isabella?"

"Yes, extraordinary, isn't it?" sneered Henry, shaking his head, his face bitter as he recalled his unpleasant childhood with the vain and cruel Isabella.

"What will we do now, Henry? Now that Poitou is lost."

"What can we do? We will go home. But, by Christ, I am afraid to do even that. The Barons will be angered because of the loss and wasted expenditure."

I was silent. Henry was afraid? What had we come to, where this unfriendly, hostile town felt safer to my husband than our own realm?

Sadness gripped me as night settled over Bordeaux. Marguerite's star had risen; France was supreme in Europe, the mightiest country of all. Henry had been made to look an incompetent fool, freed almost through…pity.

Things were not as I had foreseen. Unwillingly I was brought to the realisation that my husband was great at neither statecraft nor war. Many of his policies had no forethought and were damaging to the country…and to his reputation.

Recently, Henry had spoken of giving Gascony to Richard, for his assistance in saving him at Taillebourg. Although I naturally appreciated the Earl's intervention, I thought this a foolish move; Gascony should go to the Crown, to our young son Edward. Otherwise, all the traditional holdings in France would be lost. Richard could have…*something else* as a gift.

"Henry…" I slipped my arms around my husband, ran my fingers down his chest beneath the loose robe patterned with lions in gold thread that he wore for bed. "You know how you have spoken of giving Gascony to Richard…"

"Mmmm." Henry sipped from a gem-encrusted goblet, more interested in what my hands were doing than in what I was saying.

"I do not think it is a good idea."

"Don't you?" He shut his eyes as my hands slipped even lower. "Why…woman, why?"

"He…he will be too powerful," I said bluntly, suddenly halting my ministrations. "Gascony should be reserved for our Edward and Edward alone."

"Richard would be furious. After the loss of Poitou, he has his heart set on Gascony."

"Let him be furious. He is not the heir presumptive to England any longer. You have a healthy son"

"You do not know his temper, Eleanor. Richard may have charm, but beneath it, he is a hard man. He would not take a change of plan lightly."

"If you speak to him, I will come with you to back you up. Surely, you can find other gifts with which to reward him. But not Gascony."

I leaned over, pressed myself against him in my thin shift. My body was still plump, soft, pliant, after the birth of Beatrice. Henry growled, clutched me to him. "So be it…I will speak with him, Eleanor. You are right…you are always right. A lucky man am I to have a wife so clever…and so beautiful…"

Smiling, I peeled my shift away, let it fall to the flagstones. Shadows from the candle flames dappled my bare flesh. Henry's eyes were like globes, his breathing ragged.

I would have my way.

We met Richard in the dismal, sun-browned gardens of Bordeaux castle the next day. He exuded suspicion from the moment he arrived; his blue eyes narrowed and his lips compressed into thin lines. "You wished to see me, your Grace?" He bowed to Henry, but there was a curt stiffness in his movements.

Henry fumbled around, playing with the stem of his wine goblet. He could not meet Richard's probing gaze. Standing behind my husband's chair, shielded by a cloth-of-gold canopy, I shifted in frustration—I wished my husband would be more forceful, more decisive. Just say, 'I am the King' and let no one gainsay him.

"Richard…" Eventually, he spoke, faltering slightly, almost stammering. "I have come to a decision. One you won't like overmuch. You will be handsomely compensated, of course…"

"What?" Richard's voice tore from his throat, a snarl. I jumped, hid my alarm. It was a dangerous noise, like the growl made by a cornered wolf.

"Gascony." Henry was staring into his lap.

"What of it?" A flush began to grow on Richard's cheeks.

"It must go to my heir, Edward. It is only right. I have given it long thought."

"It was promised to me!" A muscle jumped in Richard's jaw and his hands clenched. I was glad he had no weapon; I knew the Plantagenet temper could strike swift as lightning, blotting out all rational thoughts.

"I know how much you desired it…As I said, I will compensate you."

"I do not want compensation, I want what was promised to me! Brother, how could you betray me so? I saved you in Taillebourg! What are you thinking? Why do you insult your own kin? You…you fawn over your wife's family, more than you care for your own."

I was shocked by his harsh words; I had no idea Richard felt so about my uncles and other relatives who Henry had aided in the past. It was right that he built up relationships with them, surely!

"My family will soon be yours also," I chided him, keeping my voice calm, "when you marry my sister Sanchia."

"Aye, but I swear they will not bleed my coffers dry!" he spat. "My wife will know her place."

Henry's eyes flared now. "You forget yourself, Richard. You speak to your King and Queen. This is not acceptable talk. I demand an apology."

"You're not getting it!" Richard flared.

"I command you…"

"No, you will not. I am leaving this vile country and returning to England. I can bear it here no longer. It is full of snakes…" He suddenly whirled, slammed his boot heel on an innocuous little serpent that rustled through the grasses. The creature writhed, spitting, then coiled up, dead. "I don't like snakes. Treacherous things."

Henry's face was glowing red; we both knew what Richard was implying. "If you leave the army, it will be without my consent!" he roared, slamming his fist on the arm of his chair. "I'll have you arrested!"

"Do what you must," said Richard coldly. "Or should I say, *try* to do it. Henry, my brother, at the moment you are in no position to threaten anyone. You are a laughing stock; the French think you are a buffoon. Remember what Simon de Montfort called you, to your very face, when you were nearly taken in battle?"

Henry scowled, suddenly looking as embarrassed as he was angry.

"Did he not tell you, Eleanor?" Richard turned to me, mouth quirking in an unpleasant, mocking smile. "No, I suppose he would not. He told Henry to stand back out of the way, that he needed to be 'shut up like Charles the Simple.' Do you know who Charles was, Eleanor? An old king who abandoned his men, who gave favours to the undeserving at the expense of better men. A King known not only as simple but stupid and inferior, who spent half his life imprisoned by his nobles!"

I was mortified, both by the fact de Montfort had spoken such harsh words and that Richard was repeating them. I always felt a certain unease around de Montfort, but to speak such treasonous words and then go unpunished was unheard of! What had Henry been thinking of? True, he had been in grave danger at the time, but he should have quelled de Montfort's tongue, perhaps permanently. The reconciliation between them had been brief indeed.

Richard was striding away, leaving the King and me in the garden. Our attendants stood still as statues, shocked by the shouting and dishonourable behaviour.

"I want my brother punished!" Henry stamped his foot on the ground, more like an angry child than an angry king. "He cannot walk away from me like that and get away with it."

But Richard did.

Henry was not going to let it lie, however. He remained furious at his younger brother. Summoning a couple of unsavoury rogues he found lurking in the castle stables, he paid them from his own purse to go capture Richard and throw him into the deepest dungeon in Bordeaux. On borrowed horses, they galloped off in a cloud of dust, laughing like loons and swigging from a wineskin.

Worry gripped me; Richard had behaved disgracefully, if somewhat understandably in the circumstances, but I wanted no harm to come to him…not least of all, for the sake of my sister Sanchia. She was rather old to still be unmarried—seventeen! I did not want her to fret for years while her betrothed rotted in some foetid dungeon.

As it turned out, Richard had soon realised he was being pursued by Henry's hired thugs and took refuge in a church, barring the doors against his assailants. The priests helped him hold out against the mercenaries; while Henry stewed on hearing that his plans were thwarted.

My husband's wrath did not last long, however. As days dragged out, he started to reconsider his actions. "Richard was rash in speech and manners," he said, "but he's always been like that ever since boyhood. I understand his disappointment. I want to be reconciled with him. This siege at a church…it's unwholesome, unholy. I'm going to call my men off…and seek to repair our friendship."

"But he won't get Gascony?" I said sharply. "That is for our son alone?"

"He won't get Gascony."

A reconciliation of sorts took place. With assurances that he would meet with no ill, Richard emerged from the church where he had taken sanctuary. Coming back to face Henry, he went down on his knees and begged forgiveness for his behaviour in a voice that I thought didn't sound very regretful at all. But no mind. The words of apology were said. Henry seemed happy enough, and apologised for sending his hired thugs; he then fawned on his brother, handing him jewels and embracing and kissing him. Richard, begging leave, was granted it, this time, and he headed in all haste for the nearest port.

We lingered, despite not being entirely comfortable in Bordeaux. Henry did not want to return to England just yet. The barons were still muttering, and he remembered what had become of his father at their hands.

"We will wait for Sanchia," I said, trying to make him feel we had a purpose in Bordeaux. "It would be most gracious of the King to meet her and my mother before proceeding to England."

Sanchia and my mother Beatrice arrived in May, having journeyed with much personal danger through war-torn lands. I had not seen them for nigh on seven years, and my heart swelled with excitement.

As their entourage arrived at Bordeaux castle, I waited anxiously, clad in my most stylish gown, fashioned of rich blue sindon, with its borders stitched in silver thread, and designs of lilies and butterflies upon the skirts. My hair was confined in a pearl hair *tressure* imported from Paris and a necklace of tear-shape rubies lay upon my breast. I prayed I would look queenly enough, and that my kinswomen would not look askance at Henry and me because of our recent misfortunes in war.

A trumpet blared, then another—a cacophony of brazen noise. I almost jumped in fright as a herald announced '*Beatrice Countess of Savoy and the Lady Sanchia*'. As my mother swept into the hall, she shocked me at first—she looked much older than I remembered, her face a little thinner, a few lines beneath her beautiful eyes. However, she was dressed in the most stylish russet *bliaut* with a flared skirt and dangling sleeves, and she held herself upright and dignified... *She* had not grown fat like the dreaded Aunt Gersende.

Sanchia, my little sister...she was a wonder. Rumours had spread across Europe of her burgeoning beauty, and they were true. The little girl I remembered was gone, replaced by a slender young woman with flowing black hair and greenish eyes beneath a fringe of long, curling lashes. In some ways, she resembled me, as one might expect in two sisters sharing similar blood, but only in appearance, not in her mannerisms. She was much shyer than I, hesitant to speak. She blushed and looked down at the floor frequently, not with coyness but with real shyness. This inborn timidity gave her a slightly softer appearance to mine, as did her frequent blushes. Some men might find that appealing; others, I suspected, might find it irritating after a time. A lack of sophistication.

I frowned a little; such meekness might not be to her advantage when wed to a strong figure like Richard of Cornwall. I would try and advise her if I could.

Rising from my seat, I approached my kinswomen, and they folded in deep, respectful curtseys. Reaching out to them, I raised them with my hands, my mother with my right, and my sister with the left.

"I am so pleased to see you; it has been so long," I said, as my throat suddenly closed and tears sprang unbidden to my eyes. I had not foreseen such a rush of emotion! Eleanor, proud queen, trying to affect a regal air, yet reduced to tears by the sight of much-loved family and memories of a youthful life in Provence. "Come...come to the solar with me. We will speak in private there—so much to talk about! I cannot wait for you to travel to England with me...Mother, you shall be most proud of your grandson, the Lord Edward, and the other children too. I named my youngest for you. I wish father were here also…How is father?"

"Afflicted by the little ailments that plague us all as we get older but well enough," said my mother, with a thin smile, but I noticed a little flicker of uneasiness within her eyes.

"I will pray for him every night…I will have a *hundred* priests pray for him," I said fervently. "Now let us seek some privacy, and you can tell me about the everyday happenings in Provence! Tell me everything! I miss home so much sometimes…the warmth, the grape vines, the colours of the distant mountains at twilight!"

"Is Richard here?" asked Sanchia timorously, glancing around the chamber.

"No." I shook my head. I would not tell her of the recent violent argument over Gascony if she had not already heard of it. It would only worry her, and besides, Henry was no longer at loggerheads with his brother—at least for the moment. "I beg you, Sanchia, do not look so crestfallen! He has returned to England to prepare for your arrival. He is most enamoured of you, my sister, and no wonder…you have grown so beautiful. I'll wager you are indeed the most beautiful woman in Europe!"

"Beside you, I am but a little mouse," said Sanchia, with a brittle, scared-sounding laugh. "Grey and uninteresting!"

In truth, she might have been a little fairer of face than I, especially as I had been ill—her skin blooming, rose-petal soft; her face sculpted, not knowing the strains of childbirth; her eyes big and docile and expressive, but in one way Sanchia's statement was indeed true…in her manner, she was mouse-like.

"If you are but a mouse, sister, then you must learn to squeak loudly," I told her with firmness. "You would not want to be so small and quiet you got crushed under foot!"

Henry departed for Portsmouth, taking the rag-tag remains of his army and leaving me to catch up with my mother and sister for a month or two. In November, we finally sailed to Dover, watching the white cliffs loom up as we stood in the prow, just as I had done when I travelled over from Calais to marry Henry.

As we stepped ashore, we saw that the port was decorated with banners and garlands of wintertime greenery and that all the onlookers wore their best festive dress. Lit tapers glimmered in the November gloom, and the church bells pealed and pealed, their clangs echoing from townhouse to church to the bastions of the great castle on the cliff. Atop the castle's ancient lighthouse, a beacon was burning brightly like a second sun.

A horn blared out, and the castle gates gaped, and Richard of Cornwall rode forth on his destrier to greet his bride. I saw his eyes rake over her with delight; she had only been thirteen when he first met her, and in the interim, a pretty and winsome young maiden had grown into a stunning woman. I hoped he would remain faithful to my sister, as Henry seemed to be with me…but I knew Richard had a weakness for women and had kept many mistresses throughout his first marriage. Never mind, whatever the case, Sanchia had to adapt, for such was the way of many men. Sinful, but natural.

Richard bowed his head and kissed her hand; she blushed beneath the sweep of her raven hair, worn loose beneath a circlet to proclaim her maidenly status, and in the streets of Dover men whispered that she was 'beautiful beyond compare.'

With great fanfare and even greater joy, the wedding party then moved on from Dover to London, where I was reunited with my husband and children, who had been brought in garlanded carriages from Windsor castle. Little Edward, already so tall, flung himself at me, grasping my gown with his strong little fists, till his nurses pried him away and settled him.

Within the week, I was once again reunited with my Uncle Thomas, who had come from Flanders for the wedding, and watched with happiness as he met with mother and they gave each other fond kisses, and she lovingly teased him and called him by his Savoyard name, Tommaso. "I feel like a little girl again!" she said.

In the spacious vault of Westminster Abbey, with gladdened hearts we watched as my sister wed the King's brother in a lavish ceremony where no expenses had been spared. I wore a rich, ruby-red gown made of fabric embellished with gold, which had been a gift from Uncle Thomas upon his arrival; he had presented my mother and Sanchia with similar. Sanchia, however, was dressed in a blue gown of imported Araby silks, with a silver-hued train that was so long she had to have six women carry it.

After the ceremony was completed, we processed in splendour to Westminster Hall, where three thousand souls were served at the wedding feast. Porpoises, eels, bream in foil were carried in on gilded dishes; silvered pies with decorations of crowns on top graced every trestle table. Roe deer and wild boar festooned with sprinkled ginger, and spiced chicken covered with egg yolk were amongst the first courses, while pomegranates, almond tarts and plums stewed in rosewater followed. Finally, there were the ever-popular subtleties that included jellies made into family crests and a giant castle with sugared turrets.

My mother was busy about her usual statecraft, speaking earnestly to Simon de Montfort's wife, Henry's sister Eleanor. She had managed to soften Henry a little regarding the Earl and was allowed to return to England, despite de Montfort's disrespectful words to the King during his fruitless campaign. Simon himself, however, had not been permitted to attend Richard's wedding feast.

Mother, finishing her conversation with Eleanor de Montfort, then sidled over to Henry himself. "My dearest son in law, dread King of England..." She cast him a radiant smile, curtseyed most delicately. I knew she wanted something then...and looking at Henry's beatific, drink-flushed face, I thought there was a good chance she would get it. "I have had the most delightful conversation with your sister, the Lady Eleanor. I doubt not her husband the Earl of Leicester would be a most stalwart aid to you, if all ill events of the past were forgiven, and Eleanor could truly be welcomed back within the family fold, despite her misdeeds. A happy family is one that is not fractured; it is also a safe family for those of high estate. A wall of relatives can be as unbreakable as that of the stoutest castle."

"But de Montfort insulted me, madam, " Henry slurred, rather deep in his cups. "Likened me to Charles the Simple! Can you imagine that? The impudence!"

Mother held up a graceful hand sparkling with rings. "Your Grace...it was a wicked thing to say...but perhaps he spoke foolishly when under pressure. Which of us has not, at one time or another? He regrets his rash talk but is too prideful to say so. Lady Eleanor told me this herself."

"Truly?" Looking interested, Henry tried to prop himself upright in his high seat. "He needs to lose that pride then."

"True," mother inclined her head, "but perhaps he would be more sweetened if he felt truly part of your family, your Grace. As it stands, he does not. I am sure he would change in his outlook if he did. Since coming to England with my daughter Sanchia, I feel as if you are indeed all my kin, and I will weep when I must leave again, though leave I must. If Earl Simon were made as welcome as I have been, being the husband of your own blood sister…"

Henry looked thoughtful. "Perhaps you are right, Countess Beatrice. Perhaps I should be less harsh on De Montfort. His conduct with my sister was disgraceful, but I played a part in it, I must admit, when I was persuaded to let them use my own chapel for their forbidden marriage. Anyway, what's done is done. No use in mulling over the past. Maybe I *should* build a bridge with de Montfort rather than attempting to destroy all ties. The Bible says to forgive; maybe I should. One more time."

"I implore you to try the way of forgiveness, your Grace," said mother, nodding emphatically "Loyal friends and family are more valuable than gold and gems."

Later on, mother wandered up near my high seat and I beckoned her over to my side. "Why that speech to my husband the King?" I whispered in her ear. "Did the Lady Eleanor really so enchant you? I must tell you, I do not much like Simon de Montfort. His is hard-minded…and men follow him."

"I do not like him much either, from what I know, though he seems to have a certain…attraction," said mother. "However, I think it would not do well to alienate him further. I would rather see him serving his King than opposing him."

"You are wise, mama," I laughed, completely informal. "I see I still have much to learn."

"Another thing…" She leaned in even closer, her lips brushing the shell of my ear. "Think on it…Richard is a powerful man, and from what I have heard is often at odds with Henry. He has royal blood; history tells us that bad things can happen amongst feuding brothers. You might need Simon on one side as a shield."

"Richard and Henry may fight but surely you do not believe…" I said, aghast.

She gave a small shrug. "I will be blunt. Your husband the King is a generous and decent man, it seems. But he is not a warrior. Nor does he seem inclined to statecraft. His main loves are building and grand ceremony…and you, my dear. He has few real friends, the Savoyards at court are tied to you, and his Lusignan half-brothers…Ugh, that lot use him for their own ends. His barons are never satisfied… Now Richard…" she nodded toward her new son-in-law, seated above the salt with Sanchia glowing like a dark ruby at his side, "he is clearly more gifted in these arts of war and politics, though not *much* more, truth be told. The Barons might well turn to him, with no other choice before them. Kings have been replaced before now. Think on this, Eleanor. Think hard."

I did.

The very next day I invited Henry's sister Eleanor to walk out into the gardens with me. I found out she was actually quite pleasant, and that her nickname was Nell. For all that I felt uneasy around Simon, she clearly adored him; spoke of him as if he were some kind of god. I would have to look at him again, with new eyes, I swore to myself; find *something* to like, even if I found it difficult.

I told Henry of our new friendship and saw his face fill with pleasure. After listening to mother's advice, he wanted the rifts in his family sewn up. Several weeks later, he cleared some of Nell and Simon's debts and gave them 500 marks to live upon. In a sudden burst of magnanimity, he even presented the mighty fortress of Kenilworth to Simon as a gift. It seemed my husband had decided after all to forget being likened to Charles the Simple and let bygones be bygones!

My mother's visit to England ended in sorrow, alas. An urgent message arrived from Provence; my father was gravely ill, Beatrice must come at once. Mother took ship from Dover as fast as she could, taking with her considerable monies gifted by Henry for the military protection of Provence. Sanchia and I prayed for our father Raymond Berengar's wellbeing, lit candles, put offerings on the altar.

Side by side, unified by our love for our family, we two sisters stood staring into the grey mists of morning where mother had departed.

My father's condition worsened. Many Provencal and Savoyard lords began to fare to England, fearful of the developing situation abroad, with the French threat looming alongside the decline of the Berenger's strength. I welcomed them and so did Henry, caring not that the Barons grumbled about expenses paid and favouritism. They were just jealous, those sullen old lords; the court was much brighter and more urbane with my kin to bring cheer and fashion and knowledge.

My Uncle Boniface was one such arrival; Henry had promoted him to the See of Canterbury. I thought him a splendid choice for archbishop…but almost immediately, he had fallen out with the King over the election of the Bishop of Chichester. Henry had favoured a man named Passelewe, a harsh judge despised by most of the local populace, while Boniface put forward the saintly scholar, Richard Wych. Henry's man was discarded, and the King grew very wroth that his wishes had been ignored.

I preferred Wych myself; I had met the man on many occasions and was impressed by his intellect and piety, but knew not if my uncle had the authority to appoint him and discard Henry's man. Boniface was greatly disturbed by the King's anger, so, at his prompting, I sought to bring up the subject with Henry.

Gingerly, I approached the King in his closet, where he was busily sealing documents. "Yes?" he barked, not glancing up; his mood was clearly foul.

"Your Grace," I said. "I must speak to you. "About Uncle Boniface."

Henry's jaw stiffened. "Let him not be a turbulent priest…" he growled. "That could end up very ugly. As it did in my grandfather's day."

"I doubt any ugliness will be necessary." I tried to hide my nervousness behind a veneer of confidence. "He knows he has done wrong, you know. He wrote to me and I have chastised him for his presumption in choosing Wych and rejecting Passelewe."

"Has he? Good! I hope he comes to me to humble himself and beg forgiveness."

"But…" I walked to Henry's side, placed my hand on his shoulder, "I must say I agree with Uncle Boniface. I think Passelewe too…harsh for the role of Bishop. He is better at collecting money than praying, while Richard Wych is a holy and learned man…"

Henry knocked over the sealing wax; squires leapt to keep it from spattering the desk and his ermine-lined robes. "So, you are really saying you agree with your uncle? That you think I am wrong in my choices?"

"I am just saying, your Grace, that Richard Wych seems to me an appropriate candidate for the bishopric. Not so much Passelewe. Ultimately, it is down to you, and no other."

"I will think on it," said Henry petulantly. "I do trust your judgment Eleanor, woman though you are."

"Thank you, your Grace," I said. "Perhaps we could discuss this again later on tonight…within my apartments? We could dine alone…"

He glanced up at me sharply. "Are you trying to seduce me, woman? To get your own way using your wiles?"

"My Lord King. You wrong me. I merely want to spend time with my dearest husband, who has been working so hard of late in administering his kingdom. How will we ever have another healthy son if we seldom see each other?"

At the mention of a son, his face became grave. I knew he wished for another boy, just in case, Christ forefend, anything happened to Edward.

He peered up at me then sighed. "Forgive me for my neglect, Eleanor. Now…where is that scribe of mine? I suppose I should send a missive to Boniface."

I raised my brows.

"You win. He wins. Passelewe goes back to collecting money; this Richard Wych shall have his bishopric. Are you happier now?"

"I will be happier tonight," I said, and casting a seductive glance over my shoulder, exited the room.

I was pregnant. The King was ecstatic. He was also very frightened for my health and for that of the child. He ordered thousands of candles to be lit before the shrine of Thomas Becket in Canterbury and at nearby St Augustine's Abbey. Prayers were spoken for the safe delivery of a son. Humbly, he told the Abbot of Bury St Edmunds that he would name a boy-child after the great martyr Edmund if only the child should be born safely.

I had been very ill throughout this latest pregnancy, unable to eat and as weak as a lamb, and this was why Henry feared for my wellbeing. Nevertheless, when the time came, I was delivered of a male child, screaming and strong, while the antiphon of St Edmund was chanted.

Immediately there was celebration, and chasubles sent to Westminster in thanksgiving.

They say sometimes a birth is followed by a death; it is the way life runs, the way the Wheel of Fortune turns. Several months after Edmund's birth my father Raymond Berengar died. It was not unexpected, as he had long been ill, but the sorrow still tore my very heartstrings. Henry knew well how it would affect me; he held back from delivering the sad news until he had returned from a campaign in Wales.

But not long after Raymond Berenger was buried in the Eglise Saint-Jean-de-Malte, my husband's solicitude suddenly turned to anger—not at me but at my widowed mother. "Eleanor, I cannot believe what Countess Beatrice has done!" he roared. "How could she treat us with such ingratitude, after the money I gave her?"

I flinched. "What is it? Why are you shouting? What has she done?"

"Your father left all of the inheritance to your youngest sister, Beatrice."

"Not entirely unexpected, Henry. She is the one who is unwed and has the least of us four sisters. And what is that to do with my mother? My father wrote his own will; my mother did not write it for him!"

"It is not the loss of any wealth that bothers me so much; it is that your little sister is now a very powerful heiress. Many men have sought her hand already…and your mother—this is what enrages me—she has gone ahead and procured a match with Louis of France's brother, Charles of Anjou! The enemy French! To cap it off, your uncles Boniface and Philip have been involved with the matchmaking from the start. I feel betrayed, betrayed utterly."

"We can make good of this, Henry." I tried to soothe him, though my own mind was churning, rattled by the news about my sister Beatte marrying Charles. How could I ease his worries?

It was a lengthy process, but eventually we managed to strengthen England's ties with Savoy. Henry made a treaty with Count Amadeus, granting him a thousand marks in order to become Henry's vassal. The passes of the Alps would be shut against invasion, guarded by a barrage of Amadeus's stern castles.

I worked Henry round about my mother. She had made a terrible mistake, I told him. She was suffering too; in fact, far worse than we were. French troops surrounded her castles, and French lords made rules in Provence at the command of Charles of Anjou.

Henry and I travelled around England, eager to show the populace that the disturbing news from abroad did not intimidate us. It was imperative that my husband not be viewed as a weak, ineffective ruler but as a confident king. We held celebrations full of great pomp and splendour, jousts and tournaments and feasts…but our long journeys from castle to castle, and the banqueting and merriment that came at each stop caused us to fall seriously in debt. The treasury verged on empty; the treasurer's face was as grey and frowning as a mountainside as he examined the ledgers. But we could not stop spending—the people would disrespect us, maybe topple us…

Sometimes we took the Lord Edward on our travels, for the commons loved to see the little prince who would be their future king. He would sit high on his well-trained horse, wearing a tabard of Ypres silk and a tunic of camlet, already a tall boy and mature for his age. He would wave while the sun spilt through the darkening gold of his hair and the people threw flowers over him.

However, not all journeys with Edward went well. When we were attending the re-dedication of the monastic foundation at Beaulieu, Edward began to feel unwell. He grizzled at my side, shifted from foot to foot as we were led through the abbey's eleven radiating chapels; I chided him at first, then noticed the sweaty pallor of his face, the drenched curls sticking to his brow. He was swaying like a leaf blowing in the wind.

"Edward, what is it?" I hissed in his direction, suddenly alarmed. I attempted to keep my voice moderate; the abbot was on a podium, speaking to the assembly, which included not only the King and his entourage but Sanchia and Richard—Richard's first wife Isabel was buried at Beaulieu, along with poor little Nicholas, the baby boy that had died at the birth that killed her.

"I am hot…I feel like I am on fire, Lady Mother!" Edward gasped, clawing at his tight collar. "My throat swells, I cannot breathe…"

"Henry!" I cried, as Edward's eyes suddenly rolled back and his knees went from under him. "Edward is ill! Call a physician! Get someone at once! *At once*!"

Panic broke out amongst the lay brothers and certain members of our entourage as they saw the prince lying in a swoon on the cold new tiles of the abbey. Edward's attendants ran to him and lifting him on to a makeshift bier, carried his inert form down the cloisters, with the monks running alongside him, praying and crying out to God for mercy.

He was taken in to the infirmary and two of my physicians who travelled with the royal party at all times, Peter de Alpibus and Raymond de Bariomono, dashed in to attend him. I refused to leave the room, stood by my son's bier with his nurse, Lady Alice, wringing my hands as the doctor's assistants splashed Edward's brow with cool rosewater and the learned men felt his brow and the pulses in neck and wrists. Edward began to come to consciousness, which brought a rush of relief to all of those assembled, but his skin was blotched by some kind of hideous, growing rash that spread and deepened even as we watched.

"How serious is it?" I grasped Bariomono's dangling sleeve, dragged him in my direction with a strength that must have shocked him—he nearly fell over. "Tell me the truth and do not hold back. I must know what ails my son, even if you must tell me the worst."

"My colleague, Dr Alpibus, and I believe it is one of the many childhood maladies," Raymond de Bariomono replied gravely, recovering his equilibrium.

"Not the pox, please tell me it is not the pox!" Fearful sweat broke upon my brow; I had seen those whose faces had been scarred by the devastation of the pox. If they lived.

"I think not," said Dr Bariomono. "It is more likely to be *mezils*. However, it is still a serious illness, without a doubt. The prince must be bled and he must not be moved. He needs to stay in quarantine here for around twenty days, and he must rest another twenty after that while he mends. A monastery will be a fitting place for his lordship to regain his good health."

The abbot of Beaulieu, Azo of Gisors, was standing in the room behind me; I had hardly noticed his intrusion such was my concern for Edward. "Fear not, your Grace," he said. "The brothers at Beaulieu will take great care of the Lord Edward while he is ill. You can go upon your way assured of that."

"Go upon my way!" I flared. "You must be mad, lord abbot! I am not leaving my son! I am staying here while he is unwell. The King can go on. I will stay!"

Abbot Azo looked shocked, his jaw dropping in surprise at my impassioned outburst. "Your Grace, what you desire cannot happen…"

"Why can it not?" Fire flew from my eyes.

I realised my voice had risen; on his pallet, Edward began to moan and groan, the rash on his face flaring. Not wishing to disturb my sick son further, I grabbed the front of the Abbot's habit, which seemed to terrify him, though whether because I was the Queen or because I was a woman, I wasn't certain, and dragged him out into the cloisters, shutting the wooden door of the infirmary firmly behind me.

"Now you will tell me why I cannot stay with my son. I, the Queen of England." Defensive, I stood with my arms folded, under the vaulted ceiling with its gilded bosses of wild men and the Tree of Life and Jonah and the Whale. A wild woodwose, pulling his mouth open to release a tumble of foliage, seemed to be sticking a green ivy-frond tongue out at me…or maybe at the Abbot.

"Your Grace, no disrespect to you…but …but you…you are *female*!" Azo of Gisors squeaked. His visage was the hue of fire.

"What of it? Are you not born of a woman, lord Abbot?" I raged at him.

Azo flinched. "Your Grace, surely you must understand…this House is Cistercian! We are forbidden to have women staying within our walls. Even Queens!"

"You will change the rules then…just this once!" I said imperiously. "Fear not, lord Abbot, I won't attempt to ply the wiles of Eve on you or your monks!"

The Abbot's mouth moved and he gibbered, as if I had reminded him of all those uncomfortable and sinful fleshly lusts he had given up. His hands flapped like an anxious old woman's. "Your Grace, I do not know what to say…I must speak to the King!"

"How dare you try to involve the King when he has so many other matters on his mind? You attempt to override me, your Queen…and obviously have little regard for the prince who will one day be your monarch. Shame on you, and shame upon this narrow-minded, sanctimonious, self-seeking House. God will punish you for your unkindness, I am sure of it! Now get away from me, and let me tend to my sick son!"

Abbot Azo fled down the cloisters as if a devil was chasing him, his cassock billowing behind him in the wind of his speed.

I returned to the infirmerer's chamber, where my son lay, still hot and sweating, half in this world, half in that terrible dream-place I remembered from my own illness in Bordeaux. I caressed his wet brow lovingly. "Don't fear, Edward, no matter what anyone says, I will be staying with you until you are well."

Chapter Three

Edward soon recovered and was as well as if he had never been ill. No marks marred his face and he crawled from his pallet and began running around the abbey cloisters annoying the monks as any young boy would. We left Beaulieu riding upon our palfreys, with my guards around us, and the locals appeared in droves to celebrate the prince's recovery. The monks cheered too—I deemed they were glad to see me gone. I heard later, that some of them were dismissed because they had served secular food to us upon saints' feast days.

In Windsor, and in a string of castles and palaces across the west, my beloved family lived in what seemed a happy time, even if the coffers were bare and Provence and Gascony still under threat.

I enjoyed my Wiltshire manors the most, the castles of Ludgershall and of Marlborough, where men said Merlin of the Arthurian legends once lived. Strange arrowheads and ancient bones came out of the huge, conical mound on which the castle stood, so I could only suppose the tales were indeed true. I told them to my children; hoped they would have the same interest in the nobility and chivalry of King Arthur's court as I did. Certainly, the tales made Edward's eyes shine brightly.

Winchester was a regular stop on my travels, with its enormous great hall and ten-foot-thick walls. Next to the Great Hall was a little garden Henry had planted for my pleasure, where I could relax with my ladies in the wan English sunshine and do needlework or play chess or read one of the romances I had bought from William of Paris. A bronze fountain spewed water into a copper basin, there were turf seats and wall embrasures to sit in, and trellises made of interwoven withies where roses and other flowers climbed. Strawberries grew in the beds in season, along with bay, mint, vervain, rosemary and other herbs.

When the weather would not allow the joys of the garden, I would retire to the hall's interior, where I would study the huge chart known as the Mappa Mundi, which hung on the wall of the Great Hall, and ponder its detail. It was a map of the known world, with Jerusalem at its heart. Paradise was there, unreachable, ringed in fire, a civilisation long gone, like those of Babylon and Crete, where the monstrous man-bull called the Minotaur still menaced in drawn form. The Red Sea bled, and Noah's ark still sailed, and Lot's wife became a pillar of salt near now-vanquished Sodom and Gomorrah. Egypt was there, roped in by the wending blue Nile, and mighty Rome, complete with a phrase, in Latin, that read *Rome, the Head, holds the reigns of the world*. In the northern section of the map, lay England and Scotland, surrounded by scaled dragons and images of the four winds, and beyond them, a mythic figure from Norway called Gansmir, who raced upon skis accompanied by a bear and an ape. I was fascinated by the long-bearded Norwegian, and wondered what it might be like to ride on skis—would it be similar to flying like a bird?

Passing on from Winchester into Wiltshire, another favourite residence was the palace of Clarendon, on the road to Salisbury. There I hunted with my mewed hawks in the nearby forest, surrounded by my brightly dressed damsels, Margaret Biset, dear old Willelma and her daughter Isabel, dark-eyed, fierce-tempered Roberga, delicate little Christiana, and the indispensable and practical Sybil Giffard, who rode up from Oxford where she had quarters in the castle with her scholar son, Walter.

The palace was beautiful, set against stands of forest near the old Roman road. Salisbury's cathedral spire pierced the sky in the distance, rising through stands of fragrant trees. Beautiful arrangements of pale pink and grey tiles graced the palace floors, and the windows of my two floors of private apartments were filled with fine *grisaille* glass, allowing in a muted, hazy light that washed across the floor. I called it 'dream light.' My private hall extended a great ways back into the building's core and was artfully designed so that the eyes of visitors were drawn to the fireplace at the far end, which was flanked by polished marble pillars and crowned by a carving of the twelve months of the year. My chapel had an altar of the same luminescent marble, and a painting of St Katherine on the wall, and a gold crucifix bearing the figures of the Blessed Virgin and St John.

I spent much time in prayer, for rumours were running rampant again and many barons were openly hostile, especially towards any foreign residents of England. It pained me—even after being crowned, even after my success in producing Henry's heir, I was still regarded as an interloper, a troublemaker, not to be trusted. Henry's own half siblings were considered unwelcome, as children of fractious Isabella de Angouleme, and even my Uncle Boniface came under attack, although the dislike the English felt for him was partly of his own making. He had been unwise in his stern criticism of the canons of St Bartholomew's in London, and this caused a row with the tough old prior. It had come to blows, and Uncle had drawn his sword and had to be restrained from killing the venerable churchman. London—and the rest of the country—had not forgotten his sudden eruption of violence.

It wasn't just rumours and unrest that troubled me. I was also worried about Edmund, my younger son, the much longed for second prince. He was far sicklier than his brother and two sisters; a solemn-faced, pallid child with big haunted eyes and a poor appetite. He seldom travelled with me but remained with his nurses in Windsor. I called my own doctors to tend him and brought him gifts to make him feel better...little toys and silk tunics and some sticks of sweet barley sugar, which he loved to chew on.

Then my sister Marguerite's husband, King Louis, went abroad on crusade. Thibaud, King of Navarre, a man of greater girth than sense, started encouraging the Gascon lords to go on the rampage in Louis's absence, sacking other men's castles and setting the land aflame. My uncle Gaston de Bearn, renowned for his fighting skills, fought back with a fury, aided by the might of Castile. However, he fought for his own personal gain, not to help his niece or keep the lands for England.

"I will have to send someone out to Gascony," Henry said to me, frowning. He strode about our chamber, hands knotted behind his back, fretting. "This situation cannot be allowed to continue. As much as Louis and his Frenchmen have caused me grief, at least they kept the peace."

"Who do you think would suitable for the job?" I asked, although I already guessed Henry's answer.

"Richard, of course. He showed great skills in diplomacy on his earlier crusading and he also has plenty of this..." Henry made the motion of rubbing two coins together. He also knows the place well... Did you know, Eleanor, that he fought there when just sixteen? He helped hold the region for England."

"And that may be the problem," I said flatly. "You promised him Gascony back then and reiterated his claim once again after the disaster at Taillebourg. But, as you must remember, my King, we *both* then decided Gascony should be reserved for our Edward. If you send Richard to Gascony, you and I both know what will ensue—he will demand to be given the county for his services."

Henry began to splutter; his face suffused with colour. "What else can I do, Eleanor? He is the obvious choice to go!"

"Choose another, I beg you. Gascony is Edward's. Maybe...What about Simon de Montfort?"

"De Montfort? I thought you had no love of him, wife?"

At the irritation in his voice, I stirred uncomfortably. Over the last few years, as I became friendlier with Henry's sister Nell, I had grown easier with de Montfort, too, which surprised me. When he entered the room, there was something…he both repelled me and fascinated me at the same time. There was a certain primal magnetism about the man, and when he glared at me with his yellowish eyes, I thought of a wolf. Now, you might not say it would be nice to be gazed at by a wolf, as if you were a lamb to the slaughter, but his lips would smile, belying the hard, pitiless scrutiny of those dangerous eyes, and I would have to glance away. That seemed to just make Simon smile the more. It was unnerving and strange. No other man, not even the King, could make me avert my gaze in that manner.

"He has much experience in warfare," I said slowly, "and would not ask such high payment as Richard. Will you not at least consider my choice, Henry?"

"I will think on it," retorted the King, "but what does a woman truly know of war and warriors? Go and attend the children, Eleanor; I am sure Edmund needs the comfort of his mother!"

"As you will it," I said and retired to the nursery, where I gave Edmund some more amber-coloured barley sugar…but next morning I found out that Henry had indeed appointed Simon de Montfort as the vice-regent of Gascony (he refused to be just seneschal—impertinent, but that was proud de Montfort all over).

Richard of Cornwall would be furious; I, however, was rather pleased. Henry was listening to me, and though he was a pompous man, Simon could have no legal hold on Gascony.

"Simon's captured Uncle Gaston? And is sending him here in chains?" I gaped at the King, stunned. Messages had just arrived by swiftest courier from Gascony.

Henry nodded, crumpling the parchment in his hand. "Yes, it is true. Your uncle should be arriving at any moment. My guest…and my prisoner."

At that moment, trumpets blared in the inner courtyard. Iron shod feet crashed on the cobbles.

"Indeed," said the King, "the entourage bringing your Uncle Gaston would appear to be here now."

We hastened to our seats of estate, beneath their elaborated canopies bearing the Arms of England. I felt quite sick to think of my father's own brother, no matter what he had done, being brought before me in chains.

The doors at the end of the hall banged open. Pikes bristled like shining, deadly trees. Two burly knights strode into the hall, dragging my uncle Gaston between them, chains binding both his hands and feet, making him stumble and teeter.

Gaston was a heavily muscled man of low stature but great girth; of all my male relatives, he was the most pugnacious and war-like. He wore his hair cropped, and his skin was bronzed from many expeditions in the sun. He had handsome features, like my own father, but they were marked with white scars from various frays. Today, new bruises and cuts made those scars even more livid; he had not easily been captured.

He looked up at me, chains rattling round his wrists, and managed a grin. There were more gums than teeth—he had lost several teeth in his battles, too.

"Unbind him!" My voice burst unbidden from my lips. "Take off his chains at once."

The guards looked startled, stared uneasily one to the other. The King made a noise beside me as if he were choking. "Eleanor!" his voice hissed in my ear. "He is a rebel, a prisoner. He has fought against us."

"He is also my Uncle," I whispered back fiercely. "He is not a bad man...he is just of a war-like nature that has, this time, got the better of him. Think on it, Henry...What will the commons say if they hear that the Queen's own kinsman is in chains! What will they think of me?"

"Nothing. You are not your uncle."

"We share blood. And we are Provencal! Please, my love...let him be released from his bonds. Let him speak to us about what has happened in Gascony before any decision is reached as to his fate. If his answers do not satisfy you then, let him be thrown in the deepest dungeon you can find."

Silence from Henry.

"Your Grace, I beg you...one chance. For me. Are not my other uncles good men?"

Henry slowly rose from his feet, resplendent in his cloth of gold and ermine. He motioned to the guards. "Remove Gaston le Bearn's chains."

A gasp came from the assembled courtiers. The guards looked even more uneasy.

"You heard me!" Henry barked.

A gaoler ran up, bowed, and unlocked Gaston's chains. They dropped clattering to the flagstones. Unsteadily—no doubt his ankles were raw from the rub of the cuffs—he approached Henry's high seat, while a row of pikes was levelled at his back in the event he should try to attack the King.

I tried to catch his eye; suddenly he glanced at me and winked. I knew things would be well then.

Obediently, Uncle Gaston prostrated himself before the King's feet. "Forgive me, terrible Prince!" he cried in a great voice that rang out to the farthest reaches of the hall. "Spare me, and my sword will be forever at your service."

"Why should I spare you, Gaston de Bearn?" Henry glared down at the man crouched at his feet, humiliating himself by fawning at his toes. "You have caused great distress in Gascony, and helped make the area unstable. Gascony is England's. You not only betray me but bring sorrow to your own niece, who is England's most fair Queen."

Gaston lifted his head, gave me another surreptitious wink. "I am a warrior, not a thinker, your Grace. I have been a fool. When fat Thibaud started to encourage lords to fight against each other, I deemed myself no man if I did not join in. I should have thought more deeply." He rapped his cropped head with his knuckles. "Sometimes I know not if anyone is home anymore!"

A ripple of laughter rang throughout the chamber, and I suppressed my own smile. Uncle Gaston might have been a battle-scarred ruffian but he still had the cleverness of his family on both paternal and maternal sides.

"Will you swear to me, Gaston de Bearn, that you will cease to fight against us in Gascony?" Henry glowered down at the bristling, scarred head.

"I do, my liege." Another reverent kiss to Henry's painted leather shoe.

"And that you will return in peace and stay in your castles and molest no one?"

"I will tie my sword into my sheath if need be," said Gaston. "But I have no castles to return to. Your man, Simon de Montfort, confiscated them all."

"That is too much, he had no right," I said sharply, causing Henry to glance in my direction with equal sharpness.

Henry bent towards me. "He had the right. He is seneschal. He represents me."

"He was far too harsh," I retorted. "We both know de Montfort can be a hard and unyielding man. Uncle Gaston's castles must be returned."

"Only if he swears to be peaceable!"

"I swear, I swear!" said Gaston eagerly, his keen ears picking up our conversation. "I will be loyal to you forever more, you can rest assured."

"Then…" Henry raised his voice so that everyone in the chamber could hear, "I pardon you, Gaston Bearn. Your lands and castles shall be returned immediately. You will dine with the Queen and me tonight, as a beloved kinsman."

Gaston returned to Gascony a very happy man, his wealth returned and his castles waiting for him to repossess them. I doubted Simon de Montfort was so pleased, however. His anger at the rebellious Gascons knew no bounds; men of all stations were imprisoned, hanged, banished. Simon hung on grimly to the territory, and complaints about the Earl's conduct arrived in England daily. Henry grumbled as they were received, one after the other, borne by grim-faced messengers; he knew not what was the best course of action, and I dared not advise him, for I had been the one foolish enough to insist on de Montfort's appointment instead of Richard's.

Eventually Simon was ordered to return to England to face trial. His behaviour in Gascony was seen as too harsh, too brutal; an echo of his father's treatment of the Cathars many years ago. Too many men had perished in dungeons, too many times had the gallows-tree groaned beneath the weight of its swollen-faced fruit. The loss of life was intolerable.

Richard of Cornwall attended the trial, speaking not for his brother the King, but Simon. "You must not arrest or otherwise harm de Montfort," he told Henry sternly. "He is not a convicted traitor; he must not be detained as a prisoner. If you harm your own man, Henry, the people will rise against you…de Montfort is hated in Gascony, but in England he is decidedly popular amongst both the barons and the commoners. You, brother, are not."

Stung by the criticism, Henry was furious but he backed down with his idea of charging Simon with many crimes. He remembered well his father John's various entanglements with the barons and what they had forced him to do.

Simon de Montfort returned, his behaviour unchecked, his manner haughty, to Gascony, and the troubles there continued.

The threats abroad could not take over our whole lives, however. We had a kingdom to rule at home, and children to look after. Our daughter Margaret was now eleven and we had a good marriage offer for her. The counsellors of the King of Scotland, Alexander, a boy of ten, suggested their young lord should marry a princess of England as part of a peace treaty.

I called Margaret to me. A pretty, slim-boned girl, she stood in her pink silk gown, her long brown hair flowing in waves to her waist. Her eyes were pure leaf-green and her lips very red...but her courses had not started yet and she still was very much a child.

With consternation, I stared at her, uncaring that I had been scarcely older when I wed Henry. Somehow, I'd had a maturity that Margaret did not. The thought of sending her hundreds of miles to cold, forbidding Scotland, the territory of England's enemies, did not much appeal to me as a mother. Yet I knew such an alliance would be beneficial to the country, and a Queen should not grow over-attached to her children, who had royal duties to perform.

"Meggie?" I used the pet name her nurses gave her; I would have called her Margot, the short form of Marguerite, which is how I thought of her, but she responded only to her English name, as common as it sounded.

"Yes, mama?" She glanced at me quizzically.

I took her soft pale hands in mine, bent close to her. "You are not a little girl anymore. You are well educated and taught in all womanly arts, are you not?"

"Yes, mama," she nodded again. "I have had good training from Dame Sybil and others. I know my letters and my prayers, and I can dance and do needlework."

"Then you will not be surprised to know your father and I have been thinking of a marriage for you."

Meggie blinked; a little, surprised gasp escaped her lips. "Marriage? To whom, mama?"

"Alexander of Scotland. He is ten, just one year younger than you."

Her face crumpled and I felt my own belly knot up. What had come over me? It was Margaret's duty to marry whom her parents wished, as it had been my duty. "You will be fine, Margaret. At least your husband is not an old man. You will grow up together."

"I do not want to leave you and father and Edward, Bea and Edmund," she said tearfully. "I like it here in Windsor."

"I am sure you do…but your father promised Scotland a marriage alliance as early as 1244. He will not break his word. And think, Meggie…you will be a great Queen and bring peace to a troubled land. You want that, don't you…to be a great queen like your mother?"

"Yes, I want that." Margaret's voice was a whisper and her chin trembled. But there were no tears, and for that, I was wildly thankful.

The wedding was held in York. December roared in with its cold snows and gales, but it did not dampen the festivities. Riding under Micklegate, we processed to the Guildhall and then on to the great Minster church of St Philip, which Archbishop de Gray was rebuilding in a new fashion. Tall and golden, it stood out against the ice-blue northern sky, while at its feet the people clustered, eager to see their king and his consort, and the royal Plantagenet princes and princesses.

We lodged in the bishop's palace to the side of the Minster, and de Gray's servants raced around like madmen bringing us everything we needed. The streets were so busy with people trying to view the activities that fights broke out, especially amongst those of different nations—many Scots and even French had come to view the wedding—first with quarterstaffs and later with swords. Bailiffs and beadles wandered around attempting to keep the peace, aided by soldiers of the crown.

Henry and I walked through the streets clad in samite decorated with gold braid; we wore our crowns and gleamed like angels. Edward was with us, now a towering lad of thirteen, along with his three youthful companions Nicholas, Bartholomew and Ebulo, all the sons of prominent lords. All four boys wore cloth-of-gold tabards patterned with the leopards of England. All four were handsome and upright, but none could compare to Edward, a head taller than the others, his curling hair like a halo around his princely head, even if its one-time golden gloss was now tending toward brown.

A gaggle of bishops and prelates brought the young King Alexander before us, a thin little lad with soft reddish hair, a pale face, and thoughtful eyes coloured a deep hazel brown. He wore a deep green tunic and a golden circlet on his head. Dutifully, he knelt before his future father-in-law, the King of England, and Henry knighted him before the watching throng, to the delight of all.

Then our daughter Margaret, wearing a gown of imported brocade and a golden belt whitened with clusters of pearls, was guided to the Minster doors. The Scottish King and his ministers greeted her, bowing in respect, and in the presence of the Archbishop de Gray and the bride's royal parents, the new couple were bound together in the eyes of God.

As the bells boomed from the mighty towers of St Philip's, sending birds flying heavenward, the underside of their wings glowing against the low winter sky, my eldest daughter was wedded to her husband and made a Queen.

We stayed in York until the end of January, enjoying all that the city could offer, the goldsmiths and silversmiths, the booksellers in the little shops along the bridges. Then the Scottish wedding party, with a heavily armed guard for protection, travelled swiftly northwards toward the border, with little Margaret accompanied by a newly chosen governess, Matilda de Cantilupe, who would see to her education in the years that followed.

I cried that night, though I hid my tears from Henry. Miserable, I retreated to my chambers in the Bishop's palace, where even the warmth of a roaring fire and a warbling minstrel could not comfort me, so great was my distress at my daughter's departure.

"Do not weep, your Grace!" said that dear lady, Sybil, handing me a kerchief to dry my eyes. "Meggie will be fine, I am sure of it. She will be a most splendid queen, like her mother."

"I am being foolish." Gratefully I took the kerchief, daubed my wet face. "But somehow…somehow I cannot feel happy about this Scottish marriage. Not because of the little King, who seems a fine, intelligent boy…but because of his counsellors, his guardians. Ah. Stone-faced, heartless beasts, one and all! They hardly looked at Margaret; she was just an object to them, a means to an end! I hope my fears are but the foolishness of a too-possessive mother…but how I wish I could be with Meggie now to guide her and ensure she is not mistreated!"

I leaned upon the window casement, staring into the swirling darkness outside. A few flakes of snow were falling; I could see them illumed by the rows of torches in the courtyard below, where Bishop de Grey's men were hauling in kegs of drink and pallets of food. I thought how cold it was here and how much colder it would be in Margaret's new land, in an unfamiliar, unfriendly castle with the stern Scottish lords all about her. Jesu help her, they hardly even spoke the same tongue!

The tears came again. The wind, whistling over the pinnacles of the nearby Minster, gave a sob too.

Sybil gently beckoned me away from the window, while Margaret Biset wrapped a martin-lined cloak about my shoulders and Christiana reached for a comb to attend to my hair. Dear Willelma, looking as sad and solemn as if her own daughter had been sent away to a foreign kingdom, stoked the fire even higher, to try to chase the chill and the fears away.

The chill departed. The fears did not.

We returned to London. Henry was preoccupied with further trouble in Gascony and I brooded over my young daughter far away in Scotland. We saw each other only rarely, and when we did, certain unease hung between us.

I went about my business and let Henry get on with his; hence, I thought nothing was amiss when I awarded a living to my personal chaplain, William. He was a pious and dutiful man, and I believed it was a just reward for his service to me.

The trouble was, at the same time I presented the award to William, Henry decided to present the *same* living to one of his own favourite chaplains. Summoning me to the solar, he went into a screaming rage, the likes of which I had never seen before—and I had seen a few of his rages.

"You make a mockery of me yet again, going behind my back as you did in that business over Passelewe!" he bawled, his face crimson with fury. "You make me look weak, a chinless ninny to be jeered!" Angrily he hurled a bowl of fruit across the room; little round apples bounced over the reed-strewn flagstones. "Women's arrogance runs high if it goes unchecked; I should take my hand to you! I will not have you shame me, Eleanor! Your interference is too much!"

I tried to calm him with pacifying words but I could not—he thrust me aside and stormed from the hall to seek his own apartments. The entire castle had heard his shouting and I was mortified. What must they think of me?

I was also in a predicament. I could not just cast William out; he had been legally appointed in his position.

I would have to go to court.

Against Henry, my husband.

My King.

The court ruled in my favour! I was surprised but my pleasure on William's behalf was tempered by my fear of how Henry would react. He had taken the news with glowering silence but I feared a terrible explosion of rage later. I thanked Bishop Grosseteste of Lincoln for assistance on my behalf and then sought out Henry's sister, Nell. I needed help against my husband's anger and Nell had certainly felt the brunt of that wrath in the past.

Nell was sitting in the solar of her manor house, reading her prayer book. She glanced up as I entered; then gracefully rose from her stool and curtseyed. I noticed how attractive she was, her neck long like a swan's, her eyes pale blue against skin pale as snow. No wonder Simon has desired her so much, despite the oath of chastity she had sworn. And what a waste it would have been had she retired to a convent, although her veiling would have saved much fighting and grief.

"Nell, I need your assistance." I tried to sound serene and confident but my voice wobbled.

Alarmed, Nell looked at me. "Your Grace, what is wrong?"

"Call me Eleanor while we are alone, I beg you. It is Henry I am having problems with. He is sore wroth with me. He glares and we do not speak, let alone…" I swallowed, ashamed to reveal our unhappy situation, where he did not come to my chamber anymore.

"How may I help you?" Nell's brow furrowed. "Tell me, Eleanor, that I may help if I can."

"You have known him far longer than I, grew up with him. You have felt his anger too. Tell me how to win him back. I have given him two sons and two daughters. I have supported him in all his endeavours…yet I have failed and am ostracised just because I wished to give my chaplain a gift!"

"Henry is generous," said Nell slowly," but he hates being made a fool, or thinking that others may deem him so. That is why he reacted so badly to my marriage to Simon…egged on by Richard, of course, who thought it a matter of the family's honour. Henry really did not mind so much; as you know, Eleanor, he even allowed us to use his private chapel to wed. But when the barons objected, he was made to seem weak and his whole manner changed. He became unreasonable, even dangerous."

"So you think I should have allowed Henry's chaplain to have the church living instead of William? Even though he was granted it first, and all was proper and in order? It was truly a matter for the courts to decide once it had reached that point."

Nell sighed. "I would have ceded to my husband, Eleanor, even if you were legally in the right. You could have found another position or some other fitting gift for your chaplain, I am sure."

"Will you speak with Henry? You are his sister, and you have become good friends with him in recent days. I am so fearful, Nell. I do not want to lose my husband's love. Not over a matter as trivial as this."

Nell smiled, patted my arm as if we were both just two matrons, not royalty. "I will do my best, Eleanor. Henry can be a stubborn man. Both our parents were the same…only worse, much worse. When my father and mother fought, I thought they would murder each other! Henry can be stubborn and temperamental…but at least, unlike father, Henry has a heart."

Nell spoke to Henry but still my husband did not come to my chamber. However, when I saw him, he had at least ceased to scowl at me. I judged I was undergoing some kind of a punishment for my presumption over William's living, and that soon the ice that had touched Henry's heart would melt. He would surely return to my bed before long. He would realise how much he missed me, needed me, and how this quarrel was foolish and needed to be put into the past.

And then, unthinking, I made another dreadful mistake, and it was all the fault of Henry's half-brother, Aymer, the bishop of Winchester. Once again, it was over a church living. Aymer had granted the living to one of his own when my Uncle Boniface wished to grant it to one of his servants. I thought Aymer a grasping sort—I disliked all of Henry's Lusignan half-siblings, finding them fractious, pushy and rude—and therefore supported Boniface wholeheartedly against Aymer.

Henry went mad.

I was in my garden, surrounded by my sweet herbs and flowers, when I heard him coming. I say, heard him, because he was shouting and screaming, his voice echoing down the halls. A cold flush rushed over me, turning my blood to ice. I froze, the beauty of the day fading away.

Craning my head around, I could see Henry storming towards me across the manicured lawns, his robes blowing out in a great red cloud, a haze of blood. I swore I could see foam upon his lips, like that around the muzzle of a mad dog.

"Henry! My lord!" I cried, seeking to break his crazed charge.

My ploy did not work. He grasped my arm and shook me as a terrier shakes a rat. My ladies stared in horror; some began to weep. "Get you gone, you bitches!" he spat between gritted teeth and they scattered like roses thrown about by an ill storm-wind.

He shook me again. "Nell nearly had me fooled!" he hissed. "Saying you were sorry for your meddlesome ways. And what have you done? Shamed me again! God's teeth, woman, have you gone mad? Well, you will not get away with it this time!"

"What will you do, husband? Please do not be rash!" I clung to his arm, praying he would come to his senses. He flung me off; I staggered and nearly fell amidst a bed of lavender. "I meant no harm. Aymer was in the wrong…"

"That is not for you to say, Eleanor!" Henry screamed, spittle from his lips blasting into my face.

Grasping my arm, uncaring that his fingers bruised my flesh, he dragged me across the garden. My women were still lurking, running hither and thither, hiding from Henry's wrath behind the shrubbery but not willing to leave me altogether.

"I have had enough!" He waggled a finger in front of my face. Sparks seemed to leap from his eyes. "You will be punished as you deserve for this new interference."

"I beg you, do not imprison me," I begged. I thought of his grandmother of Aquitaine, and her long imprisonment on Sarum's windy cone. "Please do not beat me!"

"I don't want to touch you!" he snapped, seemingly even angrier because I thought he might lay hands on me. "But I am removing all your lands, Eleanor…confiscating them. So, you learn what is like to lose face and be humiliated. I will do exactly to you what you have done to me. Maybe I will give your lands away to those more loyal and truer. Leave you in penury. A queen with nothing."

Tears leaked from the corners of my eyes. "You do me wrong. There is none more loyal than I. Mistakes have been made and I am sorry…"

"You did it twice!" he raged, sticking up two fingers before my face. "Twice within a short time, you silly trull! Anyway, it matters not now. Pack your things."

"Pack my thi…"

"You heard me. Get your robes, jewels, everything. I am banishing you from London."

It was a harsh sentence but at least I was still free…though destitute without my lands.

I did not dare argue.

Heart hammering, tears brimming, I ran for my quarters with my ladies running after me, many of them weeping with fear in the aftermath of Henry's wrath. Helplessly I stood in the middle of the room as the tapestries and linens were stripped, my jewels boxed, my garments flung haphazardly in a chest then carried out of the room on the brawny backs of male servants.

I was bundled into a covered chariot and driven at a great speed out of London and into the countryside.

I ended up in Marlborough, at the stern, thin, castle keep on its tall, strange hill. I had enjoyed my former visits there, near the deep forest of Savernake and the winding River Kennet, but I had never dwelt anywhere for long without my children or my husband. It was lonely, and it seemed to me the household there now gazed on me with suspicion…even mockery.

I had been at Marlborough for a month when I was suddenly summoned to London. I received no personal letter, just a summons from the King brought by a solitary rider in a cloak bearing no device. Rattled and distressed, I was sick in the chariot as it rolled at unnatural pace over the rutted roads towards the capital.

When I reached Westminster, I was perfunctorily handed out of the carriage and without preamble or any ceremony, escorted straight to Henry's private closet. As he saw me nervously approaching, he rose from his bench, dismissed his squires of the body and other attendants with a word, and motioned me to come before him.

Shivering, my arms folded across myself, I gazed at my husband with a mournful expression, not certain why he had called for me in this manner after driving me forth mere weeks ago. Was I to be castigated further? Would he even seek some kind of ending to our marriage? The spectre of imprisonment loomed in my tortured mind yet again.

To my surprise, though, Henry's face bore no signs of anger. In fact, he looked near as distressed as I did. "Eleanor, Eleanor, forgive me," he murmured. "I am so glad you are here."

"Your...your Grace?" Startled, I blinked at him.

"I was rash. Too rash. Sometimes we Plantagenets cannot control our emotions. I should never have sent you away. I need you."

"You...you do, your Grace?"

His cheeks were burning red above his luxuriant coppery beard. "You are beautiful, my Queen, but there is more to you than beauty. In your absence, I have considered many things. I know I need you to help me...to help me rule this country justly and well. You are a brilliant negotiator and of high intellect; you remind me of my grandmother, the other Eleanor of great esteem."

"Henry..." Relief flooded me. I sank to my knees, not so much from respect for the King, but because they suddenly felt weak and wobbly. "I have missed you so, husband. And the children."

"I have missed you too, more than I ever believed possible." He suddenly gathered me up, lifted me as if I was weightless, just like a hero in one of my romances. It was most unlike the Henry I knew. "We must never let anything come between us again. You must promise me, Eleanor, to confer with me when you make grants of livings or give out other appointments. You must not be seen to be contradicting me, the King. Cruel harmful rumours may start. A wife should not undermine her husband...especially a King's wife. Hard times are coming, I fear, and we must stand together. Do you understand, my dearest?"

"I understand!" I murmured weakly. "I hope we never quarrel so again."

He took me to his large bed with its quilts bearing the Royal Arms. "Your lands will be returned as soon as possible," he murmured into my ear.

"Lands be damned," I murmured back. "I care nothing for them, only for the love of my husband."

But in my secret heart, I was glad to have them back.

Chapter Four

Simon de Montfort had left Gascony. Unable to recover his dignity after being dragged back to England for trial, he at last resigned his position and galloped for Paris in a wild temper. My son Edward was now put forward to claim his birthright. He was only thirteen.

As war-like as my tall, fair son was becoming, he was far too young to go and attempt to quell the rebellious Gascons.

Henry knew not who to trust amongst his men…so he decided to fare to Gascony himself and assess the situation. Fuelled by wrath, he would have happily sailed within days, but my husband had a serious problem that prevented such action—money.

As ever, England's coffers were notoriously empty and the barons were grumbling darkly into their beards, unhappy at the thought of foreign conflict. They gazed shiftily at Henry, even when parliament sat, and insisted he swore new oaths upon the Great Charter signed by his sire, John. It was humiliating, and Henry insisted he would do it only if he could make a grand spectacle of the act—and so the Archbishops of Canterbury and other bishops appeared in droves, milling about in their pontifical robes, bearing lighted candles and threatening excommunication on any who transgressed the charter of common liberties. "*Let all who incur the sentence of excommunication stink in Hell!*" they had cried, flinging down their candles, while Henry, with mild and tolerant expression, swore that as man, knight and anointed King, he would never dream of defiling the charter's terms. From the looks the Barons gave him, no one much believed him.

Not only did the nobles grumble about the possibility of foreign war, the commons groaned when fund-raising initiatives took place. The people of Winchester even said he ruined their Christmas celebrations by demanding 200 marks. I could not understand their reticence to assist. Surely, they did not want to see their monarch lose Gascony and be shamed before all the crowned heads of Europe? They had to cease their constant moaning and opposition. And if they did not, to hell with them. We must not lose Gascony, not at any price.

In August, Henry was finally ready to depart. The royal army marched to the harbour of Portsmouth; Edward and I rode with them to say our farewells. Banners fluttered and clarions blared as we entered the thriving town that had been founded by Jean de Gisors in the last century. The local people swarmed the streets, cheering and throwing flowers; despite the increased taxes to pay for these expeditions these folk remained loyal to their monarch; their charter had been granted by Henry's uncle, the Lionheart, on one of his rare visits to England, and that was not forgotten.

We journeyed to Domus Dei, the House of God, an almshouse and hospice that stood on the green overlooking the torrential waters beyond and prayed for safe passage and for victory in the church of St Nicholas. Then it was on to the harbour, where Henry turned to us to say his farewells before taking his ship.

He wept, uncaring that many saw his sorrow, and embraced Edward, who was now fourteen. "I will hold Gascony for you, my son," he promised. "Your birthright will not be lost to evil, grasping men."

Tall and striking in his tabard with the arms of England on it, Edward began to weep too, tears tracking down his smooth young face. "Father, take me with you! I am old enough! I beg you! I can use a sword!"

"You are too young, my son!" Henry put his hand on Edward's shoulder and shook his head. "One day you will be a great warrior, no doubt about it...I have heard that already you excel in horsemanship and in the joust. But that time is not now."

Edward looked crestfallen, wept some more as the company of noble youths who always followed him shuffled their feet and looked embarrassed.

"I need you to stay here, Ned," Henry said kindly, still seeking to pacify. "You must remain to take care of your mother the Queen...and the small brother or sister she carries beneath her girdle."

It was true. I had fallen pregnant again. I put my hand to the small swell of my belly. After a gap of several years, I had wondered if my childbearing days were over. But no....The pregnancy was one of the reasons I would not be accompanying Henry to Gascony. I had not felt well since becoming with child, and the memories of the fraught delivery of Beatrice while Henry was on campaign would not leave my mind.

Edward wiped his steely blue eyes on his sleeve. Now that his lord-father had given him a task, he seemed slightly happier, although I knew that his nature was not one inclined to the tending of the gentler sex. "I will do as you bid," he said bravely to Henry. "I will aid my mother the Queen and see that neither she nor England comes to harm in your absence."

Henry turned to me; our eyes met. "I will be victorious; I promise you before man and God that Edward's inheritance will not be compromised. And while I am on the continent I will also seek allies by offering our son in marriage; the king of Castile I have heard has great armies…and a marriageable daughter."

I nodded in agreement. A princess of Castile would be a fitting match for Edward…though how strange to think of my eldest wed! Somehow, it seemed even more alien than Margaret's wedding to the young Scots king. Meggie was a girl, born for such alliances. Edward…he was *everything* to his parents, and to his country.

Then Henry said his last farewells and boarded his ship with clarions blowing and kettledrums rattling, and his flotilla of three hundred English war-ships sailed out of Portsmouth harbour with a clean wind in their sails.

Edward's mood turned sour as the ships passed the harbour wall and swiftly hastened out to sea. Pulling away from me as if I were an old doddering crone that held him back from glory, he paced like a trammelled beast upon the salty flagstones and strained his gaze into the distance, watching as the last sail, flaring red as the sunlight caught it, drifted over the horizon.

Once the flotilla was gone beyond view, his earlier weeping resumed with extra fury, an angry sorrow that became a harsh grinding sob in his throat. His face was the angry red of a screaming baby.

"Edward, you must not take on so," I chided, "not here in front of the entire entourage. Remember that you are a mighty prince!"

"I do not forget, Madame!" he cried, using a tone of voice far colder than any I had heard from him before. "And that is why I weep! Not because I cannot bear to be parted from my father the king or fear for his safety…but because I want to go to war with him, to raise my sword to claim what is mine! And you don't understand that…you are just a woman, despite that you are my mother and the Queen of England!"

"Your father bade you protect me and help me in his absence," I said sternly. "Is that not enough for a fourteen-year-old boy?" I would curb my son's tongue a bit before he said too much.

"No, it is not enough! I will do my duty, for I am sworn to it, but soon I shall not be held back, nursing babes and weak women!"

He stormed away from me, and I stared after him in shock, my heart hammering, unnerved by his insolence.

A weak woman…

That I was not.

Before he sailed, Henry had broken with English protocol.
He had given into my keeping the Great Seal.
I was the Regent of England.

Chapter Five

"Money, we need more money."

At Westminster, I conferred with Richard of Cornwall, who Henry had appointed to assist me in running the country. Richard was seated at a long table, maps and documents spread before him, while I paced the room, holding my huge belly, uncomfortable and ill at ease, fearing the strain of these uncertain days might bring my unborn child some harm.

"I know, your Grace, I know it well," said Richard peevishly. "But as ever, it is in short supply within this land. I will do my best."

Hard-eyed, I gazed at him. He had not fared abroad with Henry, despite his military experience, and that irked me—he was punishing his royal brother over his own thwarted desire for Gascony. Edward's Gascony.

"How is Sanchia, my sister?" I asked, changing the subject. "Could you not have brought her to court with you?"

"Sanchia..." He looked startled by the change of conversation.

"Yes, I would like to see her as Sanchia seldom comes to court these days. The people hardly know her, for all that she is married into the Plantagenet line. They do not even get her name correct. They call her Cynthia. Her little son Edmund...my nephew and your son, Richard, also calls for his mother, although he is happy living with his royal cousins in the Windsor nursery."

"Sanchia has spells of illness and besides that, she is busy, Eleanor. As we speak, she is consumed with works at Hailes Abbey in Gloucestershire, which we plan as our eventual family vault. As for Edmund, when he reaches the age of his elder brother Henry I shall take him..."

"Ah Henry, your eldest boy from Isabella Marshal...You two are more like brothers than father and son when you are together and away from the niceties of Sanchia's household. I know what you two get up to; it is common knowledge. How is Joan de Valletort, your mistress?"

I folded my arms. Richard was notorious for his affairs with various women; he had bedded others all through his marriage to the older Isabella Marshal, and he did the same with my sister, despite her radiant beauty. It saddened me. I was sure the King was faithful to me, and I knew poor Sanchia was unhappy about her husband's behaviour.

Richard scowled. "I came here to help you, as my brother decreed. Not to be scolded for my sins."

"Just remember that you have a wife and that she is my sister. If you must slake your urges...be discreet, Richard. Find a path for yourself on the continent and put a crown upon Sanchia's head, and maybe she will overlook your indiscretions."

He looked at me with startlement.

"Is that not your desire? A crown? There are many kingdoms where kings are not necessarily upon their thrones by right of blood but through having been chosen. Think on it... and be nice to Sanchia. She doesn't warrant your disdain. Now, about that money."

"The Jews," said Richard. "It will have to be the Jews again."

"They will not be pleased. What will you say to them...this time?"

"That they have caused the King displeasure, and that they must come up with ample monies...on pain of death or imprisonment. What else can I say? They are hardly going to hurl bags of gold at me willingly."

I bowed my head. "If threats are the only way, it will be done. I myself will contact Florentine bankers regarding loans, and even take money from my own allowance if necessary. And...we can, of course, fine the unwilling, with my right of Queen's Gold. Richard, we will win Gascony."

Richard merely shrugged. He would do his duty, of that I was certain, but, having no stake in it himself, he clearly did not care overmuch if we should hold Gascony or not.

News came from Henry, news pleasant to my ears. He had swallowed his pride and asked Simon de Montfort to return to his side and aid him. He apologised for having him dragged to England on charges of inappropriate actions while on campaign. Surprisingly, Simon had agreed to aid him, leaving Paris with a large, armed force to join Henry in the siege of La Reole. Of course, he did demand payment of various monies still owed him by the crown...but he was there with his sword.

The rebels began to weaken. De Montfort was a fierce warrior and much feared in France. Disreputable lords were brought to heel, and soon they began to renew oaths of allegiance to Henry.

During this tumultuous time, I gave birth to my daughter, Katherine. She was the most beautiful of all my children, even more lovely than

Edward—round and rosy, with abundant red-gold curls and eyes the hue of a summer sky. I was glad the birth was over; going into my confinement when the country was at war had placed great strain upon my mind and body. It was difficult to sit for days on end in a shuttered room, with women trying their best not to bicker, the windows closed and the whole place smelling of sweat and close-packed bodies, even though herbs were sprinkled around. Nothing to talk about, no business that could be accomplished, and the lingering thought in my head that I might, as many mothers did, die in childbirth or shortly after.

But now Katherine was here and settled in with her wet-nurse, and I, after a glorious churching that I arranged myself, having none other to do it for me, was back to dealing with matters of state as regent of England.

Over the months that followed, interesting news arrived from Henry. Hearing of English victories, Alfonso of Castile had agreed that the marriage between his half-sister Eleonora and Edward would go forward. There were conditions, naturally—Edward had to be given lands as befitted a prince, and he would have to travel to Burgos in Spain on the day Alfonso specified and none other. I suspected the Spanish king was taking a petty revenge on Henry, who had rejected the girl's mother Joan of Ponthieu in order to marry me.

Henry had been gone a year. Hostilities were ceasing. It was time to join my husband in Gascony. The royal party had to fare forth in style, to appear as conquerors to the defeated. In order to do this, I tasked the shipwrights of Yarmouth with providing my son Edward a mighty warship, while those of Winchelsea would provide a smaller ship for my household and me.

Gathering my retainers, and both of my sons, we departed Windsor for the port of Dover. The entourage trundled on slowly, unmolested. However, as we approached the seacoast, on the horizon I noticed black clouds of smoke rising into the sky, staining the blue dome of heaven with lurid streaks. Leaning from the window of my chariot, I called out anxiously, "Halt! Halt! Something is amiss at the port. Look, there is a great fire. It is as if the whole town is alight!"

The entourage halted, waiting in the muddy fields beyond the town. The captain of the guard ordered outriders to go and assess the situation while keeping the two princes and I ringed by a wall of steel. It was an anxious time…I feared the town had been attacked by sea pirates or even the Gascons themselves in retaliation for their losses.

Before long, the riders returned. Their faces were gloomy and filled with shock but not fear. The captain marched toward me, dour, mouth pursed, his boots squelching in the mud.

Quizzically I glanced at him; a fine haze of rain was blowing in my eyes, making me blink. "What is it? Are we safe to journey on?"

"Aye, your Grace, the road ahead is safe," he answered. "There is no invasion, no uprising. But there has been trouble in town. It might be best to turn back, for now."

"Trouble? What kind of trouble? My ships are waiting; I will not be delayed by fire, flood or fools. We press on."

The man shifted uneasily. "So be it, your Grace. Perhaps her Highness must see for herself."

Mounted on his white destrier, Edward drew up next to my chariot. He was wearing armour with a surcoat bearing the Arms of England and looked less a fifteen-year-old lad than a stern young warrior. "Go on, man, let's get this train moving," he said forcefully. "I will deal with whatever lies over the hill."

Our retinue marched onwards into the town. People buzzed like flies in the streets and there were signs of fighting; over-turned market stalls, patches of spilled blood, shattered doors and windows, smouldering houses, men with broken heads who sat on street corners, moaning.

Beside me in the chariot, Edmund stared out at the scene of devastation with wide, frightened eyes. Passing by this appalling panoply of wreckage, we came to the harbour, where our ships were waiting for our embarkation...or should have been.

One vessel was in utter ruin, half sunk in the bay, the turgid waters slapping at its half-submerged prow. A fire had been kindled on deck and was still burning cheerlessly where the timbers stuck up out of the deeps. The mast had been torn down and seemed to have been clumsily fitted onto the smaller ship moored in the next berth. Far too large and heavy for the ship it was now attached to, the pilfered mast shook and swayed in the rising wind, dangerously close to tumbling into the waves.

"What am I looking at, my lords?" I asked the advisors and nobles who gathered around me, stunned into silence as they view the ransacked harbour, the ruined vessels.

"Your Grace," said Uncle Boniface, who was journeying to Gascony with us, "I fear that the sunken ship was the one intended for the Lord Edward; the other one is yours."

Astounded, I gazed ahead. "And what has happened? By Christ, what has gone on here?" I felt my temper rise, flare. "What is the meaning of this outrage?" I gestured to the wreckage of my son's ship, sinking lower into the bilge even as we viewed it. I could now see dead bodies bobbing in the water—the crew, slaughtered.

A local man was dragged before my chariot, shaking and shivering as he bowed before me. It was the harbourmaster. "Your Grace, the shipwrights of Winchelsea grew jealous when Lord Edward's ship pulled into port, as they deemed it much fairer than the one they crafted for you. In a jealous rage, they attacked the crew before they even came ashore, slaying many in their anger. Not content with killing their rivals, they then destroyed the vessel, carrying the mast away as some kind of trophy."

"This is madness!" I tried to control the wave of despair that washed over me. I had readied myself to leave England, and now there was no transportation.

"They must be punished, all of them!" I heard my son's voice behind me, deepened by anger, strangely mature and commanding. "I want them brought before me so that I may administer punishment myself!"

"Peace, Edward!" I gave him a hard stare; the last thing we needed was a young royal prince flexing his authority. I placed a firm hand on his shoulder, holding him back. For a moment, I thought he would cast my hand off; he was trembling with rage. But after a second or two, he took a deep breath and stepped away from me.

"What is your will, my mother?" he said, his tone sullen.

"That we find a way to reach Gascony—that is more important than teaching these wretches a lesson," I retorted, trying to sound confident.

But in my heart, I felt only dismay.

The next morning, I had gathered my wits after the shock of the sinking of Edward's ship and the ruination of mine. The instigators of trouble were rounded up and arrested and several more ships requisitioned for the use of the Crown. They were not new vessels and not particularly beautiful to gaze upon, battered by many storms and crusted with glittering salt, but they would suffice for my urgent purpose. Appearances would have to be thrust aside.

While we waited for our supplies to be loaded on the ships, a messenger arrived from Henry, sailing in on the morning tide. He went on his knees before me. "Your Grace, news from Gascony. A letter from the King."

I stretched out my hand to receive my husband's missive, uncurling the battered parchment with trepidation. *My dearest wife,* he had written, *I bid you stay in England with Edward. I have had word that Alfonso plays us false and is set to lead an army into Gascony against us. Do not risk yourself and our sons.*

My breath railed between my teeth. What was I to do? My newly acquired ships lay in the harbour, waiting for our departure, manned by doughty seamen with years of skill. If I went to Gascony, I might be in danger and the boys too. But if I did not, there was every chance the territory would be lost forever, and England seen as a weak nation.

I glanced over at Edward, staring with his eyes full of longing at the waves. Such an intense young man, so eager…

I cleared my throat, raised my voice so all could hear me above the rush of the tides and the mewing of the gulls. "Troubles have arisen, but nothing we cannot deal with; we are ready to set sail. The wind is in the west—it is favourable for travel; we shall depart upon the morning tide."

A sigh of relief passed through the assembled throng. Edward's face filled with an almost luminous joy. I saw him finger the hilts of the dagger he wore at his belt.

As trumpets rang out and banners were unfurled, we processed in majesty onto our ships.

We sailed, unafraid, into the sombre morning.

The King was ecstatic when we arrived safely in Gascony. Forgetting his royal dignity in a burst of enthusiasm, he ran to embrace Edward, Edmund, and me. "I am so glad you have arrived. I thought you would not come due to my earlier message. As it turns out, there is nothing to fear," he said excitedly, taking my hands in his own. "The intelligence I received about Alphonso's ambitions was proven wrong, God be praised! King Alphonso was not intending to attack Gascony as was believed, but rather Navarre! The wedding of our son to the Princess Eleonora is still viable, though Edward must journey to Spain as soon as possible to meet his bride."

I was dismayed, having assumed the marriage was off. "It is so soon, we've only just arrived…I need to prepare, need a wardrobe…."

Henry stroked my hand. "I know you won't like this, but I think it best, my dearest wife, that Edward carries on to Burgos in Spain on his own. We should stay in Gascony to keep the area under control. To leave it, would be to tempt fate. Edward's councillors will go with him to make certain all goes well."

"But…but what of his knighting? You were to knight him, or have you forgotten? It will have to be postponed."

Airily Henry waved his hand. "I have taken care of it. I won't knight Edward—King Alphonso will, in my place. In Burgos. I am sure that will be more exciting for Edward and raise him in the esteem of the Spanish people."

I bit my lip, displeased that my eldest son would travel alone into areas so recently hostile, even more displeased that I would not be able to wear my best gowns and jewels before the Spanish nobles. And Edward…knighted by a former enemy! Then I sighed and shrugged my shoulders. The whole idea was to make Alphonse an ally. I could say nothing against my husband's plan. "So be it. I cannot hold on to Edward and protect him forever. He must go on to get his knighthood and his little bride on his own, while I wait here, sighing."

"Let little Princess Eleonora shine, Eleanor." Henry looked at me, and I could see desire in his eyes. We had been long apart. "I want you here with me. If you went to Spain, your beauty would blot out that of the bride…and we cannot have that, can we?"

Edward's cavalcade left the next day, resplendent beneath a riot of banners and pennants. Hiding the fear in my heart, I waved my kerchief madly like a ninny, held back a tear or two…but Edward did not seem at all bothered by departing without his parents; indeed, he seemed excited at the prospect of faring into unknown territories alone. He was, of course, curious about his bride too, as one might expect of a young man in his teen years.

Little Edmund was as worried as I; after Edward had gone and his entourage a mere dusty blot on the distant horizon, he warily slid up beside me and clutched my hand. "He will be all right, mother? The Spanish king isn't wicked, is he? He won't cut off Edward's head if he doesn't like him?"

"Don't be foolish, Edmund," I retorted, laughing, but my laugh sounded forced and brittle. "He is going to be Edward's father by marriage. He wouldn't dare harm him. As for liking him, what's not to like? You couldn't find a better match for his daughter."

Edmund said, "Oh," but sounded dubious. I turned and looked for the nearest spire of a church. Bordeaux was full of them. If I had to, I would have masses said in each and every one for my elder son's safe return.

Within three weeks, Edward returned from Spain, a married man. The Infanta Eleonora, a girl of thirteen summers, travelled with him in a magnificent litter decked in cloth of gold and covered in vast canopies bearing the insignias of her house, gules and a three-towered castle.

Henry and I waited on a high dais in our castle at Bordeaux to greet the wedding party. I was greatly relieved to see my son return, his face darkened by the strong Spanish sun, a new air of maturity wrapped about him.

Clad in damson robes, he swaggered into the castle's great hall. "I am a knight now and a man," he said proudly. "I would present you to my wife, the Infanta Eleanora. I am most pleased with her, father."

Surrounded by her ladies-in-waiting, Eleonora entered the great hall. She was a small, slender girl, with rich red-brown hair, and a pretty, oval face with greyish green eyes and a small curved mouth. She wore a gown of stiff blue brocade, embroidered with the Castilian coat of arms, and a jewelled circlet over a long, diaphanous white veil. Coming before me, she affected a deep curtsey with a great deal of grace for one so young.

"Let me see you, child." I beckoned her forward, smiling as kindly as I could.

Eleonora rose from her curtsey and stepped daintily in my direction. I took her face in my hands, gazed into her eyes. Honest eyes. Intelligent eyes, though mild. Despite her young age, she was not afraid. That pleased me; a timid wife would be a poor choice for Edward.

"Are you well read, Eleonora?" I asked. If Alphonso had been remiss with his sister's education, I would see that such a lack was soon rectified. My son's wife would not be a fool, either.

"Yes, your Grace," Eleonora said to me, unexpectedly speaking in my own Provencal tongue. "I am lettered and well-read and have knowledge of languages other than my own. I hope this acceptable to you…and to my dearest husband, Prince Edward." She glanced over at my son, who was watching his new wife with an adolescent adoration I found surprising but heartening. I had not thought my son, often so stern, with such longing for manhood and war, would gaze on his bride with such open affection.

"It is most acceptable and pleasing to me, and to his Highness the King. From now on, you will be called Eleanor...the same as me. That is how your name is pronounced in English, and it is what the English people will know you as."

Eleonora, Eleanor of Castile, nodded. "His lordship, my husband the Prince, has already begun calling me Eleanor, your Grace. When we first met, he told me it was because in many ways I reminded him of you."

I smiled. I thought we had made an excellent match for our son. Made even more attractive by the following Peace Treaty with King Alfonso, in which he released any claim on the land of Gascony and swore to let it remain in the hands of the Kings of England, both now and for all time.

Henry looked less careworn than he had in years; he laughed more, smiled more. Gascony was ours, the rebels subdued, and a dangerous foe, Alfonso, had been turned into an ally by a profitable marriage. Full of energy in a way I had not seen for years, the King paced our chamber, looking as if he might like to leap upon a steed and ride like a madman to unknown destinations.

"Henry, you are like a caged beast!" I exclaimed. "What is on your mind? I can tell you are planning something."

"I am. I do not think we should return to England just yet, wife," he said, "although I would dearly love to see our newest daughter, Katherine, and I am sure you miss her too..."

I bowed my head. The baby was often on my mind, but I knew my duty was with my husband and sons. The nurses would look after Katherine well.

"First, I would visit the great abbey of Fontevraud, where my mother was recently laid to rest, dying as a nun of the House, her former sins and capriciousness atoned for at the end. Fontevraud is also where the mighty Lionheart, and my grandparents Eleanor and Henry lie."

"If it is your wish to go, we shall," I said. "It would be a noble and respectful journey to make. We must not forget those who made us what we are." I crossed myself.

"I also think there should be something in this journey for you too, Eleanor."

"I am your wife; it is my duty to accompany you, Henry. I ask for nothing."

"No, I insist. After I have prayed at the tombs of my forebears, how would you like to see your sister, Queen Marguerite? I know you were once close!"

My face lit up at the thought of seeing my sister again. "Oh Henry, I would be so pleased! Much has come between Marguerite and me, as is to be expected of two queens in rival countries, but I would build bridges with her again. She is my much- beloved sister. And oh, to see the glories of Paris and King Louis' court! I have heard it is magnificent."

I paused, suddenly shaking my head, my mood darkening. "I scarcely know what to say. Can it truly be possible, Henry? To go there in safety and amity? You and the French King have often been at loggerheads."

"Louis has invited us for Christmas," said Henry. "I know it sounds impossible, but it is true. He wishes to make amends."

"A miracle," I breathed.

"From what I hear, Louis is a much changed man," Henry warned. "As you are aware, he went on Crusade in the Holy Land and failed miserably in his task. Thousands of French soldiers were killed. It has twisted his heart, making him monkish and subdued with grief. He hates sin with a passion—more than most pious men—hence he even burned the lips off a man he found guilty of blasphemy."

"Burned them off? That is a cruel punishment, even for bitter sin. Surely, death would have been kinder than such torture. My poor sister, if Henry has been so turned in his mind. It makes me want to visit her even more, to ensure that she is well."

"We will go, Eleanor. We will go to Paris, to Louis's court. We have made allies with Spain…now let us work upon the good will of the French!"

Shining in the sun, Fontevraud Abbey appeared through the morning haze, layers upon layers of white finials and soaring arches. In the humble nun's graveyard, the Abbess Mabile greeted Henry then guided him to the unadorned tomb of his mother, the infamous Isabella of Angouleme. The grave was a simple structure, marked by just a stone with a cross; exactly the sort of thing Isabella, ever mindful of her station, would have despised...unless she did indeed have a huge change of heart once she was veiled as a nun.

Henry dismounted his horse and to everyone's surprise, not least of all mine, flung himself on the grey stone and began to weep. "This is not good enough, this humble stone!" he cried. "I want my mother moved!"

Abbess Mabile looked startled. "Moved?"

"Yes!" Henry rose, tears still streaming down his face, and pointed at the abbey. "She may have become a nun but she was once a queen...and the mother of a King! Her bones must be lifted and taken inside the choir, to be buried near my dear grandparents, Henry and Eleanor! I will pay for a marvellous coloured effigy to lie above the grave."

The Abbess still looked a little startled, but much less so once Henry had mentioned that he would *pay* for the Queen Mother's new monument. "I am sure, my lord-King, that we can make this possible. A fine tomb...and perhaps a donation to the Abbey, for prayers for the soul of Her Highness, Isabella."

"Whatever you wish, Abbess, whatever you need," said Henry, nodding and wiping his tears. "Take me to the abbey's guest house, where we can talk and make arrangements for the tomb and the reburial."

Henry went off with Abbess Mabile, so obsessed with thoughts of his mother's monument he did not even glance back at me, and I was left to seek my own quarters with my ladies. We sat in the gardens awhile, resting, but then grew fidgety as boredom set in. "Dare we go out?" asked Willelma. "I am curious to see the church, and the effigies of the King's illustrious grandparents."

"Of course we can go out," I scoffed. "I am Queen, and I have a need to pray!"

I took Willelma with me into the church. There, in the nun's choir lay the colourful *gisants* of Henry's kin. Crowned and stately, Henry II lay in repose, a fierce man now at peace; at his feet was the great Lionheart, who had expressed his wish to be buried by his father while on his deathbed at Chalus.

But it was Eleanor of Aquitaine who intrigued me the most, appearing tall and sturdily made, with skin touched by the sun, a benign smile on her lips, a book held in her hands. An effigy of a woman in life, not in death. She seemed to smile at me…but surely, that was only from the movement of the candle flames?

"We will pray for them, Willelma," I said to my old friend… and so we did, up by the altar, ringed by fluttering candlelight, but I said the most prayers for Eleanor…and *to* her.

I prayed *this* Eleanor would be as tough, intelligent, and well-remembered as the former Queen of England.

Once the business of Isabella's new effigy was sorted, the royal party journeyed on to Pontigny, where Henry and I paid our respects at the Shrine of Edmund of Abingdon. Edmund Rich was now considered a saint; he had wed us in Canterbury all those years ago. He had often fought with my husband then, but in his newfound holiness, such secular matters were forgotten.

Then it was on to Chartres, where the French people ran out to greet us. We had not expected adulation from those who had been our enemies, but they came out in the thousands to greet us, wrapped up in warm woollens against the biting northern winds.

It was magic…To the bellow of brazen trumpets, we entered the city gates nearest to the magnificent cathedral, where Louis and Marguerite were waiting. Snow was falling, thin as lace upon the manes of our horses, and all down the streets gleamed rows of torches to light the way. Chapels and monastic churches lifted stone spires into the sky, reverberating with bells, and on the nearby river, blue-green with a thick, immoveable rind of ice, men, women and children skated on skates made of bone.

Henry loved every moment of our procession. He knew he was not popular in England, but strangely, here, in a place of supposed enemies, he was admired. He waved and smiled, and his face shone like a beacon in the winter gloom.

At the Cathedral, we met King Louis and my sister, Marguerite. Louis surprised us both; we had heard the rigours of his failed crusade had changed his manner, but to our eyes, now he did not even appear a king. He had cropped his hair nigh as short as a monk's and wore dull brown robes that looked itchy and worn. A black cross inlaid with chalcedony glittered on his chest, its harsh colour drawing any warmth from his face, which bore the last traces of ravaged beauty, for he had once been a handsome man.

Marguerite had changed too, grown older, stouter. She was still beautiful, but there was a hint of sorrow in her thoughtful eyes and the first lines of worry scoring her brow.

While our husbands talked, treating each other, surprisingly, like old friends rather than one-time enemies, I went with Marguerite to her solar, where fires in pits on the floor kept the room warm and cosy, protected from the snow and ice outside. Huge tapestries hung from the ceilings: blue and gold, the lilies and the fleur de lys, a sea of bright-eyed daisies (also known as 'Marguerites') and kneeling unicorns with horns of silver laid in the laps of fair-tressed maidens.

Dismissing our women, we embraced as if we were young girls. "It has been far too long, sister," I said to Marguerite.

She nodded. "Yes…but so it must be. A wife must follow the will of her husband, even if she must lose the love of her sisters. Especially if she is a queen."

"You have never lost my love, Marguerite," I retorted, shaking my head emphatically in denial. "Not even in the worst fighting between our respective kingdoms."

"I know, Eleanor…but in truth it was not you I was thinking of, but our sister Beatrice! Beatte loves us not, I fear, and often causes mischief. Our father was foolish when he granted all of Provence to her in his will. And she did not even have the decency to give us the money he willed to us! "

I thought of my youngest sister, remembering a winsome child indulged by my mother in a way contrary to the rest of us. Marguerite and I had been strictly schooled to excellence, our learning extending far beyond mere womanly arts, encompassing philosophy, politics, history and religion. Sanchia, being of somewhat lesser intellect than the rest of the 'boys', was adept at all the graceful, womanish things— sewing, singing and dancing, and her piety was notable.

But Beatrice was…*different* from all of us. Our mother had allowed her to have her own way in most things. She had grown up beautiful and spoilt, holding tightly to what might not have rightfully been hers, and yet envious at the same time—little Beatte wanted a crown like her older sisters.

Sometimes such ruinous indulgence came about when a child was last-born in a marriage. I thought of my own new baby, Katherine, that tiny, pretty child left with nurses at Windsor, and felt a sudden gulf open beneath my heart. For all that I wanted to see Marguerite, my mother and even erring Beatrice, I needed to see my infant daughter.

I tore my thoughts away from Katharine, not even two months old. "For all her faults, though, Beatrice is on her way to Paris with mama. She could have refused to meet us and kept up silly grievances. We must not argue with each other this Christmas. It will be almost as old times."

"Yes, it will," Marguerite smiled, "the four sisters, all of high renown, and their wondrous mother. The 'boys' of Provence! Sanchia is coming too, is she not?"

I clapped my hands in delight. "She is indeed, the desire to see you, mama and Beatte conquered even her natural timidity! Oh Marguerite, this shall be such a special time for all of us."

"I wanted the whole family here, for my heart is sore…Louis's Crusade, the disaster of it all has grieved me. It started so well when Damietta fell…but then…" she took a deep breath, "the weather conquered the knights where men did not. The blazing sun…and then the rising of the stagnant Nile. They were weakened already before they fought the battle of Al Mansurah, to disastrous consequence. Louis was taken prisoner …."

"But you have him back!" I said brightly, not wanting her melancholy to mar our reunion, as selfish as that might seem.

"I do…but the cost of his ransom was at great cost to France, in terms of money and reputation! And he is a changed man. Failure changed him." Marguerite sat down; the winter light, streaming through the slit of a window made her face look unexpectedly old. "Life has not been easy for me, Eleanor, although you might not think it. When Louis's mother Blanche died, I believed relations would improve between my husband and me without her interference, but Louis loved her dearly despite her possessive nature and sank into even greater despair over her demise. Eleanor, Eleanor…"

Marguerite leapt up again and began to pace about the chamber, her long skirts swinging over the rush mats. "You can see what has become of Louis. He does not dress like a king, as you've observed with your own eyes. He eschews royal ermine and says he despises scarlet dye. He forbids dicing at court and banished most of the Jews from France. He has harlots flogged if he can catch them. He even had a noblewoman publicly executed for murder; the punishment was just but I had begged for a private death to spare her family the shame. Louis said no, the people would watch a sinner die. I said I did not think that was a very Christian attitude and told him so. He went mad; I thought he might strike me."

Marguerite beckoned for one of her ladies to come in from where she lurked in a doorway embrasure. She brought a goblet of wine; I could see my sister's slender fingers trembling as she took it. "He wears a hair shirt, Eleanor. Wears it all the time, till his skin is red and oozing. Even then, when he can bear the shirt no more, he dons a hair belt in its place! Frequently he scourges himself with rod and chains; many a night he wanders about the palace with his robes soaked in blood."

I winced. "And that is not all, sister," Marguerite added hastily. Her cheeks were flushed. "He even suggested we give up our positions and join holy orders, living at separate monasteries!"

I was now truly shocked. "But he is the *King* and you are his wife! That is what has been ordained for you!" I protested.

"I managed to convince him that God would be more pleased with us if the country was adequately run," said Marguerite. "Eventually, he decided I was right and backed down. But I do not think he will ever be the husband he was, Eleanor. He wants to go back to the Holy Land some day, you know… He hopes to make good of the disaster that was."

"My poor sister," I said in a low voice. "Well, at least you do have a good pack of children to cheer you…a surprise to us all, for in early days did men not whisper that you were barren? Cruel creatures. They did the same to me."

"I have borne nine children so far, and all but two still live." Marguerite laughed bitterly. "Barren? Not I. Do you know what the problem was, Eleanor? It was Blanche, the King's mother. She could not bear that we bedded together and did everything within her power to keep us apart. And Louis loved her so, he would not hear a word against her! In the end, though…" she folded her arms, "I won."

"You certainly did," I said, though privately I thought that with King Louis's recent monkish behaviour, maybe Blanche still was trying to gain the upper hand from somewhere in heaven. But the White Queen had failed ultimately to scupper her son's marriage, for my sister did indeed have a huge brood of children, several born in recent years, despite Louis' over-zealous piety. "Now I would like to meet all these nieces and nephews of mine!"

Marguerite smiled; the lines of care on her face vanished. Turning from the cold window-light, she was now like the Madonna, warmed by the fire's orange glow. "Yes, you must meet them…Come with me."

She guided me to the chambers that had been set up as a temporary nursery for the royal children. The youngest there were two girls, Blanche and Margaret, the latter only a few months old. Both were beauties and I thought once again of little Katharine at home in England with her nurses. She would have changed so much by the time I returned home. The next youngest of Marguerite's brood was Peter, a quiet, shy and rather mousy boy, and then John Tristan, who had the black hair of our family and striking blue-green eyes. A handsome child.

"What an interesting name you've given him," I said to Marguerite.

"Yes. Named for Tristan in the Romances. I loved them nearly as much as you did, Eleanor. And my little son has already had such an exciting life, just like an Arthurian hero. He was born in Egypt, you know, while we were on Crusade. I was in Damietta, and heavily with child when Louis was taken prisoner. As I lay in my confinement, I could hear the arrival of the Saracen army outside the walls. I had an old knight at my side, guarding me…"

"Even as you gave birth?" I cried, horrified. A man in the royal birthing chamber?

"Yes, even then. I told him that if the city fell, he must cut off my head immediately. I would not allow myself to be taken. Death would be preferable to what would befall a female captive."

My breath rushed through my teeth. And I thought I had been through a perilous situation in La Reole! I dared not ask what she had asked the knight to do with the newborn child had the gates fallen….

Marguerite moved her hand dismissively. "But it is all over now. Damietta held, although at great personal cost to the crown, and Louis escaped with his life. Now, come, you must meet my older children, including Louis's heir. Soon they must be introduced to their two cousins, Edward and Edmund…"

Just before Christmas, we moved on to Paris. Beatrice, Sanchia and mother had now joined the royal party. My mother was her usual diplomatic self, pleasing all with her intelligence and grace. Sanchia was tearful, overwhelmed at our reunion, holding her boy Edmund by the hand as if only he, young as he was, could give her support.

Despite the rumours about her allegiances, sister Beatte was pleasant enough, if a little distant from the rest of the group. All of us danced, feasted, and compared garments, and then feasted and danced some more. And chattered like magpies, not of serious things but of frivolities...but it *was* Christmas. A time of celebration and thanksgiving.

Surprisingly, for old time enemies, Henry and Louis treated each other with almost brotherly amity and had not fallen out once on any matter of policy since Chartres. They admired each other's piety and were soon talking as if they were long time friends instead of foes.

I watched them carefully, listening in as best I could as they conversed upon the royal dais. The French King's drawn face brightened and he gestured to my husband with a hand that looked as frail as a stick. "My kinsman of England, you must come on a little journey with me. I have a great wonder to show you. A great building project, which will be pleasing, I pray, to the eyes of God."

"What is this project?" asked Henry, his eyes glistening like a fervent young boy's. Henry loved to build—Clarendon and Westminster were testimonies to his talents. If he had his way, every cathedral and great abbey across England would be beautified for God and man alike. If his father had enjoyed hoarding gems and money, Henry enjoyed spending wealth on his various projects, even when the coffers were dangerously bare. That had brought him the admiration of Louis's nobles; they were impressed that the English king, their former enemy, had paid for banquets over the festive season and given them gifts of plate and gold.

Louis was rising from his gilded throne, looking almost like an ascendant angel as the torches behind him made a halo of his sparse blond hair. His thin limbs were fairly trembling with excitement. "I have dismantled the old chapel in the palace and built another, much finer, much more beautiful...the Sainte Chapelle. I must show you my work, my friend, but first let me tell you about the wonders it holds. The Crown of Thorns is there, and fragments of the Holy Lance and the True Cross. I have the Image of Edessa...all purchased from Baldwin, Emperor of Constantinople."

"A wondrous collection," breathed Henry, intrigued. "I am interested in collecting relics of my own. I bid you show me at once, Louis, that we both might venerate these relics together, bound in our new friendship!"

Our husbands headed for the glorious new chapel, surrounded by their retinues.

Mother looked at me, smiling smugly. "Time for us to enjoy time together without interfering husbands, my 'boys'," she said, openly calling us by our collective childhood nickname that had irked so many who wished to damn her for producing no living sons.

We all began to laugh, even demure Sanchia and the slightly reticent Beatte. Marguerite took hold of my hand. I felt like a young girl again, back in Aix-en-Provence.

Henry and I finally departed Louis's court in January. Marguerite kissed me warmly upon our departure and presented me with a stunning gift—a bowl wrought into the semblance of a peacock, with coloured gems in green and blue to match the hues in the feathers of the actual bird. The eyes were made from pearls, and more sprays of pearls augmented the rim of the bowl.

But my sister's leaving gift paled beside Louis'. The French king, for all his piety, could still on occasion be extravagant.

He sent us neither jewels nor plate.

Louis sent us a live elephant for the Tower menagerie.

The only elephant west of the Alps!

Chapter Six

Edmund needed a crown. His brother was set to be King of England but there was nothing for my younger son. I was not happy with that prospect, if for no other reason than I did not wish for the situation to become as fraught as it was between Henry and his brother Richard, with Henry ever fearing what his brother might do, and the brother chaffing at the bit for power of his own.

I had my mind set on Sicily.

This little kingdom in Italy was in need of a ruler. The throne had been vacant for several years, following the death of King Conrad, who died of a fever. Conrad was infamous, a wicked man who had poisoned his half-brother, Henry, a boy of fifteen, in order to strengthen his claim to the throne. This grieved my husband deeply as the murdered Henry was the son of his own sister, Isabella, but before he could mount any action towards Conrad, the usurper had died of illness, and the Emperor Frederick II's bastard Manfred marched into Sicily and seized power himself, holding grimly onto the region with contingents of imported Saracen troops. The pope's forces had tried to oust Manfred's paynim mercenaries from Sicily, but the infidels had slaughtered them with their curved, lethal blades. And so the Mamluks—and the covetous bastard Manfred—remained.

The pope had offered the Sicilian crown to Richard once, but despite his burning desire for kingship, he had refused it as too great an expense; he had no wish (and no money) to lead an army abroad, especially against Saracens. Slightly miffed, the Pope had swiftly withdrawn his offer and instead made approaches to Louis's brother, Charles of Anjou, who also declined the crown, being 'too busy' with Louis's unfortunate crusade.

I thought Sicily might be fitting for Edmund; with relations between England and France improved, perhaps we could drum up enough support for a massive invasion to unseat Manfred...although Richard might prove a problem, rather than a support in our endeavours. For all that he had rejected the foreign crown himself, he might well resent a ten-year-old boy assuming what could have been his in different circumstances. I had grown to know Richard's mind well throughout the years. He was not quite the brave, selfless Arthurian figure the twelve-year-old Eleanor had imagined.

But, even putting Richard's lack of interest in Sicily aside, Edmund would be the better choice, for all his tender years. It need not be all about bloodshed. A peace treaty with Manfred, who had a young daughter of marriageable age, could stop the fighting altogether.

But could Richard be mollified if he was unhappy about his nephew's accession? We needed to have him at our backs if our plan for Edmund was to succeed. Needed his support, his soldiers, and whatever money he could offer...

"I am to be King of Sicily!" Edmund raced down the halls of Westminster, skidding on the ornate tile floors and veering around servers, courtiers, and heralds who tried desperately to avoid the energetic young prince. "Bow to me, you all should bow to me!"

I gestured to Edmund's frantic, harassed-looking nurses, who were trailing in their charge's wake, their faces red with exertion as they tried to exhort him to behave with promises of more barley sugar sticks. Unfortunately, he had grown a bit beyond bribery with sweet fancies.

"Stop him." I was frowning. "This roughness is not acceptable. See that the prince behaves with more decorum."

The nurses did not reach him, however. His elder brother got there first, towering over Edmund like a threatening giant, his visage stern and his hands placed firmly on his hips. His legs were like tall trees, rising up and up. "What is all this noise about? You embarrass yourself, Edmund, shouting and racing about like an ill-mannered street urchin!"

"I am going to be king of Sicily!" Edmund repeated, facing up to his older brother with a fierce look in his eyes.

"Well, one day, I will be King of England!" returned Edward.

"But that will be many long years yet!" piped Edmund cheekily. "While I will be king soon and hence mightier than you!"

"Well, you're not King yet, and as I am your elder and our father's heir, there is nothing to stop me from twisting your arm until you admit to being a horrid, uppity brat who embarrasses our family."

Edward reached out and grabbed Edmund's arm, yanking it behind the smaller boy's back as hard as he could. Edmund struggled in his grip and began to howl. Everyone in the palace stopped and stared while the frantic nurses wrung their hands, wanting to take control of their charge but fearful of interrupting Edward's chastisement of his brother.

"I have had enough…from both of you!" I snapped. "Edward, you are old enough to walk away from such foolishness. Edmund, you are to go to your chambers with your nurses and I will send the chaplain to you, and you are to get down on your knees and pray for forgiveness for your presumptuous and arrogant behaviour!"

Glowering, both boys leapt apart. Edmund began striding away, his anger and humiliation shrouding him like a cloud.

"Bye bye, little King!" Edward called mockingly after him.

I rolled my eyes. I prayed there would not be rivalry between my sons forever…as there was between Henry and Richard.

Predictably, Richard *did* object when he heard that Henry wished for Edmund to take the crown of Sicily. A special emissary of the pope has arrived from Rome and an investment ceremony scheduled to be held in Westminster Abbey. All the nobles of the land were expected to attend, including the Earl of Cornwall.

Glum and glowering, Richard stood with Sanchia, his brow knitted in a black frown while my sister was pale as snow and casting him nervous glances as if she feared he might suddenly strike out in wrath at those nearest him.

Down the great nave, to the thunder of the organ, traipsed young Edmund, wearing the native costume of Sicily, which the King had imported for the occasion.

"A fop! They dress the boy as a fop! And he does not even have a crown as yet!" Richard's broken, spiteful whisper echoed through the vast caverns of the abbey church.

Several nobles turned around to stare, several choked back unseemly laughter; I noticed Sanchia nudge her husband with her elbow, obviously warning him to silence. She looked as if she might faint or be ill.

Henry was walking down the aisle, his robes trailing on the newly laid Cosmati tiles, seemingly unaware of the hostility and disbelief amongst many of the attending lords, not just Richard of Cornwall. Reaching the altar at the Confessor's chapel, he went on his knees alongside Edmund, a small figure almost like an oversized doll in his outlandish, parti-coloured Sicilian wear.

Unsmiling, the pope's representative took a great ring, carved and emblazoned with an insignia, and ceremoniously slipped it on Edmund's small white finger. A ring declaring his new position as ruler of Sicily…after Manfred was deposed, or paid off, of course, and his Mamluks sent packing back to their hell-hot countries.

"In the name of St Edward, the Confessor," cried my husband, staring up towards the Rood, with its magnificent screen. Vermilion and gold flashed down at him; the ruby and sapphire of new glass set in the pointed windows cast showers of colour over the floor, over the kneeling King and the child who was the would-be Sicilian monarch. "I will send a mighty army in the name of my son, Prince Edmund, to defeat the usurper Manfred. May God smile eternally upon Edmund, King of Sicily!"

"He is not King yet!" I heard Richard's harsh rasp again; a murmured, frightened retort from Sanchia. "And Henry will not get one mark from me to support this folly!"

In the days that followed Edmund's investiture, Richard continued to make his displeasure known. He told Henry to his face that he disagreed with a military campaign for such a fractious, far-flung kingdom, and then, his rage rising and boiling over into cruelty, he turned on Sanchia and berated her before the court. "And as for you, Madame…What is wrong with your acquisitive family? You all push for this boy's prominence before mine, although I am a man grown and more deserving. Bah, the lot of you are all the same, springing from modest blood but seeking crowns and positions at the expense of your betters! Why is this foolishness tolerated?"

Henry reacted with anger at his harsh words; for although they were directed at Sanchia, they clearly were also aimed at me…and at Henry. "Go from me, Richard!" he stormed. "Go to your lands in Cornwall or wherever else you might wish, as long as it is far from me. I will do without your cursed money, which you love beyond all else! Ah, the grief of it…that my own flesh and blood attack me!"

"I attack only my brother the King's unwise decisions, not his royal person," said Richard icily, and he swept from the hall, leaving a humiliated Sanchia behind. He did not glance back at her, nor did he send for her when his entourage marched from London that eve.

I took Sanchia into my apartments, where she burst into tears. "Forgive me, Eleanor," she said, "and please, speak with the King and beg his forgiveness for what has occurred. Do not let him come to blows with Richard!"

"Why is your husband so thorny in his moods?" I handed her a kerchief to wipe away her tears. "Why does he speak ill of our family? Our family that is now also his!"

"He burns with the desire for a crown. It eats at him like a cancer. And…" she bowed her head, "he has grown tired of me. He loves me not."

"How could he not love you, Sanchia? He was mad for you when he first saw you at our parents' castle and would have no other. He beamed with pride to hear the troubadours sing that you were of beauty beyond compare. His eyes were locked on you at your wedding feast; it was as if any other woman was invisible."

"That is long ago," she sighed. "He has grown tired of me now."

"But you are still beautiful. And you have given him a fine, healthy son."

"Whom he ignores, Eleanor. He has no care for his second son, just the first, Henry, who is twenty years old and can ride and drink and wench with him."

"It is a pity you have no daughter to be at *your* side." Little Edmund lived in the royal nurseries with his cousins, according to the old custom. It must have been quite lonely for my sister without him. "Pray to God that you might have another child."

"It is unlikely I shall have any more children, Eleanor," said Sanchia mournfully. "Richard seldom comes to my bed. He prefers the company of mistresses…and harlots. He even has a child with one, Joan de Valletort. He thinks I don't know, but I am not stupid—I do."

I hung my head, unable to meet my sister's tormented gaze. It was no secret that Richard had been equally inconstant with his former wife, the long-deceased Isabella Marshal. He had moved heaven and earth to wed her, despite disapproval over the difference in their ages…then within a few short years, he lost interest in her, replacing her with easy women. As she lay dying, he virtually abandoned her and went about his own business.

"Have you any joys, sister?" I patted Sanchia's cold hand. For the first time, I noticed how thin she was, her beautiful features like whittled alabaster.

"Oh yes," she said, and though her smile was wry, her face lit from within. "My abbey at Hailes. Do you remember it, Eleanor?"

I nodded. The King and I had attended a grand celebration at its opening, accompanied by thirteen bishops.

"Richard founded it in gratitude for surviving an ill-fated sea crossing," Sanchia continued. "It was one of the most joyous days of my life when I first walked in the choir and the ambulatory and stepped inside the chapter house. The memory brings me much joy even now. I only wish Richard would find solace in such simple pleasures, and less in sinful pastimes and gaining money."

"I will pray for him and for you, sister," I said softly, although, in truth, I knew that Richard of Cornwall would never change his ways. He was, perhaps, more like his father John than Henry was—John had been a rapacious womaniser and stolen the very rings off his baron's fingers. How lucky I was to have married the King I did, for all that some disloyal men called him 'weak.' One sister had married a saint and the other an inconstant, fickle prince. Beatrice's marriage secrets, I knew not, for we seldom communicated.

I honestly did not think God would listen to my pleas for poor, neglected Sanchia…but pray I did, for I had promised to do so.

And a miracle happened.

To everyone's surprise, not least of all mine, Richard was offered a crown in Europe. This time, he did not waver, did not hesitate while counting his coins. With a little bit of bribery, and some help from the sisters of Provence, who approved his claim on Sanchia's behalf, he won the election for the title.

Richard had been elected as a ruler in Germany, and with his kingdom came a dramatic and impressive title.

Richard of Cornwall would be King of the Romans, and my sister Sanchia would be his Queen.

I was glad for Sanchia and hoped Richard's new, much-wanted crown would keep him occupied and away from the affairs of England.

I had my own worries to attend to.

I feared greatly for the health and well-being of my own daughter, Margaret, sent as a child to be the Queen of Scotland. In the intervening few years, the letters between us had dwindled to nothing, my missives going unanswered. Even Margaret's governess, Matilda de Cantilupe, seldom responded to queries about the Queen of Scotland's health, and then only with flat, useless words that meant nothing and unlocked no secrets. *//The Queen is hale and sends her greetings//*

For some reason, the silence from Meggie filled my heart with dread. I did not wish to lose my daughter. Already I was terrified for my youngest, Katharine. At birth, she had by far been the fairest of my children, but as she grew, her nurses noticed something unusual about her.

She could not hear us. We clapped our hands in her face, Edmund blew a horn by her ear…she did not respond.

She also could not speak, made only mewling sounds. She was a fair as spring flowers, with curling gold hair and eyes like sapphires, but my little daughter was both deaf and dumb. She would never amount to anything; we did not even think of a marriage for her…but, Christ Jesu, we loved her nonetheless. Almost desperately so.

But it was Margaret's situation that tormented me now. What if the Scots were treating her ill, hoping she might die so they could break the terms of the marriage treaty? What…what if she were already dead? Not even my best spies reported ever seeing the young Scottish royals together in public. Whatever was happening to my daughter, it was hidden behind the grim, grey walls of Edinburgh Castle.

"Henry, I must see Margaret…" I approached the king with true desperation, after many sleepless nights where I tossed and turned, plagued by evil dreams. "Such silence is not normal between mothers and daughters, even when they dwell far apart. I do not trust the Scots to keep our daughter well. Let us insist on a meeting. Write to John Baliol and Robert de Ros, who keep the royal couple during their minority."

Henry gestured to me to sit. I did so, and he gazed at me in silence for a long while, stroking his beard while taking in my uncharacteristically dishevelled and worn appearance. "Be at peace, Eleanor. I am sure your fears are only heightened because of Katharine's illness. But I will write to the Scots and propose we meet with Margaret and her husband Alexander at York."

York was miles away, a long, hard journey up the Great North Road. But it would be better than nothing. I had to see Meggie, no matter what.

As the messengers to Scotland rode away from Windsor, I watched them go, with trepidation. *You are being foolish*, I told myself. *Good news will come. Margaret will write and tell me how silly I am being. Yes, good news will come….*

It did not.

Within a few weeks, the dusty couriers returned, presenting a rolled parchment to the King. He read it through and I saw the colour drain from his face; his lips were compressed into hard lines.

"What is it, my lord?" I asked, breathless, my heart thumping against my ribs. "I can tell by the look on your face that something is amiss! Tell me of my daughter!"

"Come with me!" Henry leapt from his high seat and escorted me into his private closet, dismissing his squires and servants as we entered. "We cannot discuss this before all."

"Henry, you frighten me." Tears pricked my eyes. "Something is wrong, isn't it? What news did the messengers bring?"

"The Scots have refused to meet in York. They say it is impossible for the Queen to travel so far…even to meet with her parents. No reason was given." Henry's teeth were gritted with rage and frustration.

My hands fluttered to my face. "I knew within my heart of hearts that the Scots were playing us false! The Scottish lords hold my daughter and likely hope she will perish in their cold castle, so that they may start their hostilities towards England once more while keeping all she brought to the marriage!" I then rounded on my husband, strident in my desperation, maddened beyond reason with fear for my missing daughter. "This is unacceptable, Henry! My child…unable to visit or communicate with her royal parents! What are you going to do about it?"

"What can I do?" Henry cried, holding out his empty hands. "They refuse to bring her to England. She is married, Eleanor…she belongs to Alexander, not us!"

"She is treated as a prisoner, that much is obvious!" My voice rose dangerously. "We should go north with an army! At once!"

Henry slammed his hand on his desk. "Don't be stupid, woman! You would see the borders of England burn? Like it or not, the wellbeing of the country comes before that of Margaret. It pains me too, Eleanor, but so it must be. There is no reason to believe she has been harmed, after all. "

Tears ran freely now, diamonds on my cheeks. Would Henry be moved by tears? I was not a woman who normally wept to get what I wanted. "There must be something that can be done. At the very least, my mind would be eased if an emissary from England could see her. They could then report back as to her treatment and let us know if she seems content."

"It may be possible but we must be careful, we must not offend." Henry chewed his lip thoughtfully. "The physician, Reginald of Bath…Do you know him?"

"Yes. What of him?"

"I could send him to Edinburgh. He is renowned throughout the country for his great learning, and I doubt they would refuse him entry to the castle. Upon arrival, he could then request an audience with

118

Margaret; there would be no good reason to deny him his request. If they will not send Margaret to us, we will send our people to Margaret. Once Reginald has seen her, he can then report back on her condition…"

I would have rather sent the army…but I knew that Henry's ploy was the best that could be hoped for. "Send Reginald of Bath, then. Send him as soon as possible. I must know that my daughter is well or I will go mad!"

Reginald went and Reginald returned.

Embalmed and wrapped in cere cloth, lying in a coffin.

On his way home after leaving the Scottish court, the good doctor had halted at an inn on the borders of Scotland. He had eaten, drank, gone to bed. That night, a terrible deadly flux came upon him, and he died before dawn's light.

"I am sure it was poison, your Grace," one of his attendants said. The man was weeping; Reginald of Bath had been much loved. "He was hale when we departed Edinburgh, though eager to reach your Grace. Too eager; he made the mistake of stating his name and business at the inn where we stopped for the night. I am sure they slipped poison into his meat…but proof? We have none."

"And my daughter, what did he say of my daughter?" I asked. "What did he find out when he was in Edinburgh? Do not hold back, I beg you. I must know, even if my heart is shattered!"

The man's face was grim. "The doctor was appalled by the treatment of Queen Margaret, your Grace. Her guardians allowed him to meet her, but with bad graces, and the Scots lords stood around them like gaolers and listened in on every word they spoke. Reginald said the Queen was thin and sickly, depressed in mood and full of melancholy. She managed to communicate that she kept apart from her husband, King Alexander, while Baliol and de Ros did as they pleased. She had no proper ladies-in-waiting; her only real companion was the woman de Cantilupe, who was so cowed by the likes of Baliol, that she was unduly harsh towards her charge."

"Gentle Jesu, have mercy on my daughter," I whispered. "And on the soul of loyal Reginald of Bath. No doubt he was poisoned because of what he knew."

"That is also my belief, your Grace," said the man. "I am convinced Master Reginald did not die a natural death. The Scots were desperate to keep his tidings from reaching your Highness's ears."

"I am sure they were...those hard-hearted knaves." The motherly tears that had afflicted me for days suddenly dried in my eyes. Anger replaced sorrow.

I had confirmation that my daughter, a princess of England, was being mistreated by her husband's so-called advisors. I would impress upon Henry that he *must* act, lest he seem a useless king and uncaring father. If he refused...well... I had a large contingent of Savoyard and Provencal relatives, many with large households full of stout young men. I would march on Scotland alone if I had to! Any animal protects its young—why would I not do the same for my child?

Full of righteous wrath, I stormed to Henry's quarters, as warlike as his grandmother, that other Eleanor who caused her husband so much strife. "Henry! You have heard the news. Reginald of Bath is dead, treacherously slain at the hands of Scots poisoners. Margaret is ill-kept and pines alone in the cold castle of Edinburgh. She is even shut away from her own wedded husband—they are both prisoners while De Ros and Baliol dine like pigs at the trough. We must ride forth with an army, even if it breaks the peace. I fear for the safety of both children!"

Henry groaned; he would not look me in the eye. "Wife, be seated, calm yourself...I will have wine brought. We must be calm and sensible about this situation. Look, I have held talks with my brother Richard and with the Lord Treasurer. There is, I fear, not enough money to mount an invasion. To say nothing of the fact, the Barons would never agree to it."

"You will leave our daughter in distress?" My voice shrieked like a mad woman's, all decorum forgotten. I fought the urge to throw something.

"No, no, of course not, but I am sure this problem can be solved diplomatically, without need for bloodshed...or angering the barons. I will send the Earl of Gloucester to Scotland, along with an armed retinue. On my behalf, Gloucester will insist that the regency be ended and Alexander and Margaret take their rightful place as rulers of Scotland."

"And if they refuse?"

Henry slumped in his chair, looking miserable and rather aged. "Then war it will be, baron's opposition or no. I will just have to raise taxes...again....to pay for it."

Fortunately, it did not come to war. Upon Gloucester's arrival, the Scottish lords capitulated; he was a man that brooked no insolence and the soldiers he took with him were highly skilled in the arts of war. Baliol and De Ros lost their power, and the young royal couple emerged from their virtual imprisonment to the cheers and acclamation of the people of the city.

Hastily, they removed from Edinburgh's gloomy, windswept halls to a more cheerful palace in the lowlands. There they announced that they would soon begin a royal progress, during which they would visit Roxburgh and the castle of Wark.

Wark was near the border of England and Scotland, standing slightly on the English side.

"I will go to my daughter at Wark," I said to the King with great determination. "I know the miles from here to there are great, but I beg you, do not try to stop me."

"I would not dare do so, wife," Henry replied, a wry smile tilting the corner of his mouth, "because I will ride with you. I want to see Margaret too, and make sure she is now well."

I kissed him fervently, which made him laugh. "You are a good father and a good husband."

"A soft one, I think sometimes. But when could I ever deny you, Eleanor? We will set off as soon as possible to meet the royal party from Scotland!"

So we rode north, the wind in our faces, blowing cold from those desolate regions.

I did not care that my cheeks were burned by the wind. All I could think of was my daughter Meggie, gone from my side for what seemed an eternity.

Wark castle was a desolate place, frowning from the grassy summit of a man-made mound that stood like a fat boil above a bend in the river Tweed. Many times in its history, the Scots had attacked and burned the stronghold to the ground. Its bleak battlements rose like fangs against the sky, shrouded in low, fluttering clouds. The day was so dark, the light so tenuous, I wondered if the sun ever shone with proper strength here.

Riding beneath the heavy portcullis, where the stiff wind made little shrieks as it rushed around the barbs, my heart began to flutter. Would Margaret be glad to see me? I hardly knew what to expect after all this time. Perhaps she would be angered that we had left her so long to reside in misery in Edinburgh.

Reverently I was escorted by the white-haired castellan through the dank and winding passages of the castle, lit by torches that sent up showers of black ash to stain the walls. The air smelt fuggy and damp; I wrinkled my nose in dismay—pomanders should have been strung up for the royal visit, but there was no helping it now. Nor could anything now be done about the dirty floor, with its mud-clumped rush mats that should have been cleared out by the servants months ago.

At length, I was led into the presence of my daughter and her husband, the King of Scotland. They sat stiffly on a pair of wobbly-looking chairs under a rather threadbare canopy, in what was a dismal great hall, with stern, bare walls and only a few vast iron candelabras to shed light. Alexander had grown into a thin, wary-eyed young man with a shock of curled reddish-brown hair, while Margaret...ah, Margaret, I hardly recognised her! She had grown tall, outstripping me in height, but the roses had been washed from her cheeks by the bitter Scottish rains, and her expression was both serious and haunted. She looked like a pale doll, wrapped in cloth-of-silver and marten fur.

After pleasantries had been expressed, the young Queen beckoned me to attend to her in private. Henry and Alexander began a discourse about the peace treaties between England and Scotland as we fled away.

Margaret took me to her chambers. They were cold but faced the east so they had more daylight than many of the others. "It's not much of a place..." I said, glancing around at the unadorned room. Even the bed was plain, the only thing of worth its rich green and gold draperies with the Scottish lion roaring upon them.

"Yes," said Margaret, "but not as cold as Edinburgh. The wind screamed almost every night upon that dark hill, and the castle was so huge, it was like a maze. I never saw Alexander. Matilda de Cantilupe was my one companion, and she was beneath the thumb of de Ros and Baliol; she did nothing but chide and criticise. I felt so alone..." A little sob caught in her throat. "I thought you had forgotten me, lady mother."

"I would never forget you, Margaret," I said, with maternal fierceness. "I would have come to your aid even if it meant war. Your father was the problem; he would not cast caution to the wind. But it is of no matter now—we are here, and you and your husband are free from the cruel and unnatural regency."

Margaret nodded, heaving a great sigh. She was so drawn, great dark circles under her eyes. She almost resembled a little old woman, not a young girl. I thought how happy and radiant I had been when I wed Henry and felt deep sorrow for her. However, having seen the boy-king Alexander, he seemed a serious and intelligent lad and eager to speak in peaceful terms to his father-in-law. Without the interference of the Scottish lords, perhaps the marriage could be made good after such an unhappy start.

"How is Edward?" asked Margaret, a wan little smile crossing her features. She was closest in age to Edward and had great affection for him. "I have heard he is married now. To the daughter of Alfonso of Spain."

"Yes, another Eleanor. Maybe one day you shall meet her; you are not dissimilar in age, and she seems a kind, biddable girl. Edward is enamoured of her, and she is the same with him."

"Well, he is so handsome, is he not? Even if he is my brother! So tall and with his golden hair."

"You might find him changed. Even taller now...and the golden hair...Well, as he has grown from youth to man, so too his hair darkened. It is nigh on black, almost as dark as mine."

"I do long to see him, and Beatrice and Edmund too...and the new baby, Katharine. How strange to think I have a new sister that I have not ever seen."

I bowed my head, thinking of silent little Katharine, bound forever in her quiet world. What would become of her? She could not marry, and she did not seem suitable for a nun's life either, although the sisters might take her in out of charity.

"You look so sad, mother...What is it?" Margaret threw off any queenly pretence and came to me, putting her arms around my waist, while her ladies in waiting moved discreetly to the opposite side of the chamber.

"It is nothing. And I am not sad, Margaret. I am gladder to see my eldest daughter than you will ever know."

Wark castle had belonged to Robert de Ros, who, along with his ally John Balliol, had made my daughter's life miserable.

Now it was his no longer.

The King had taken it.

Red-faced, shaking with rage and fear but trying to contain himself, de Ros knelt before Henry's throne at the end of the great hall.

"Your behaviour…was just not good enough, de Ros," snapped Henry, prodding at the kneeling lord with the sharp toe of his boot. "What have you to say for yourself?"

"I did my best, your Grace," said de Ros defiantly. He was a short, pig-faced man with a thick bowl of chestnut hair.

"Did you? Did you truly? When my daughter, the Queen of Scotland, was kept isolated, and her husband the King barred from her side? When we were told we could not see her, and when our physician was murdered?"

De Ros made a choking noise. "The couple were too young to be together, let alone rule. Baliol and I were to govern in their innocent years. You know that, your Grace."

"I know that you and bloody Baliol thought you would have an extended period of ruling their kingdom for them! Enjoying wines off their tables and food from their kitchens, while they languished as near prisoners, eating the dregs and wearing old garments!" Henry bawled. He looked nigh crazed with anger, reminding me once more of his foul-tempered father… a side I seldom saw, God be praised.

"Your Grace, you misjudge me!"

"No! You misjudge me! You thought I'd seek the Scottish peace above my own daughter's happiness. You thought, far away in the north, you could do as you pleased and live like a king along with Baliol! Well, you will pay the price for your folly, de Ros. Your lands…they will revert to the crown, including this castle. I want you and yours gone by the morrow. Oh…and I think a monetary fine is in order as punishment for your misdeeds. 100,000 marks sounds fitting."

"100,000 marks!" Robert de Ros fairly screamed. Shocked, he tried to lurch up from his knees; two guards prodded him down with the butts of their spears.

"Yes, you heard me, de Ros. You're not deaf, are you? Just stupid."

Defeated, Robert de Ros stormed from the hall. I could hear women weeping in the corridors, and saw the startled, frightened faces of his servants. Little sympathy was within me, however; not after seeing my languid daughter, aged by her experiences, directionless without careful nurturing, sitting next to her equally pallid and maltreated husband.

"It is a just punishment, is it not?" Henry looked pleased with himself once de Ros had departed from Wark.

I nodded. "Taking a man's lands will always make him very sorry. And what of Baliol, his colleague?"

"I deemed him to be the lesser evil of the two, the follower hanging on to the hem of de Ros's cloak. I am inclined to give him a pardon...but only when he shows me the colour of his money." Henry rubbed his hands, gave me a grin that made him look wolfish in the flickering torchlight. "Think of it, Eleanor. All this new money in the treasury. We shall get that crown for Edmund yet!"

Chapter Seven

Katharine was dead. Oh Jesu, help me, my little last daughter was no more.

Over the past year, Katharine's health had declined even more. No physician could say what was the cause, only that her troubles went far beyond her deafness and lack of speech.

She had lain in her bed, unable to move, hardly able to swallow food. The look of sorrow and pain in her eyes had torn into my very soul. She implored me silently for help…and I, Queen or not, could do nothing.

The King too had been distraught. It did not matter that our daughter would never be wed or have a true vocation. We loved her as God had made her and wanted her to live.

In a panic, Henry had ordered a silver statue of Katharine crafted by the most skilled silversmith in London and set it on the shrine of St Edward the Confessor in Westminster. With her nurses Agnes and Avisa tending to all her bodily needs, Katharine was taken by litter from Windsor to the Swallowfield house of her governess, Emma de Spenser, where there were other children her own age that the doctors thought might cheer her. She seemed to rally for a while as a stream of learned doctors went in and out of Emma's home, and once or twice, I saw her smile or make the small, twittering sound that was her laughter. The King ordered a wild goat captured in the Great Park and brought to Swallowfield for her amusement; she watched it from a pallet, made weak clapping motions with her small, bloodless hands as it bucked and gambolled in the gardens, chased by the able-bodied children.

The brief respite in her health was not to last. Soon she lost the ability to eat, and would only take fluids from a horn inserted in her mouth. Emma panicked, wrote in haste saying that Katharine must be returned to Windsor at once, that she could not deal with the decline in her charge's condition. And so Katharine was moved, lying as still and silent as if she were already dead, her nurses snuffling tearfully beside her litter

She lingered a few days, curled like an unopened flower on the linen sheets of her bed, fair-smelling roses sprinkled about her to sweeten the air she breathed. Then, on the third day in May, just after that wild raucous night when the commons leap the fires in the woodlands and young maids wear garlands in their hair, that time when all the world comes to life, field and furrow, man and woman, our Katharine breathed her last. The passing bell tolled over Windsor, and all knelt, crossed themselves and prayed for her soul.

Katharine was taken from me, embalmed and wrapped in layers of cere cloth. The King ordered her buried in his beloved Westminster Abbey, while a silvered effigy showing her in the guise of her namesake St Katherine was to be fashioned and placed above her tiny grave.

I could not bear it.

Never had I felt such pain; it was if swords stabbed into my heart day and night. "You must eat, your Grace." Willelma tried to comfort me, to push a tray of sweetmeats in my direction. "You have grown so thin."

"I care not if I live or die, Willelma," I told the old lady-in-waiting "I know these are wicked words, and an affront to God, but it is how I feel in my heart of hearts. For me, it is as if the sun has fallen from the heavens and I sit in eternal night."

"But what of your other children, your Grace? They need you."

"They are all growing up; some are married already as you know. They have no need of me. Katharine had need of me, yet in the end I could do nothing to save her."

"It is God's will," said Willelma softly, "you must remember that, my Lady. God wished for beautiful Katharine to dwell amongst the angels. She was an angel, sent to earth for but a brief time."

"Sometimes…" my tears began to fall, as they did daily since Katharine died, "sometimes I hate God."

Willelma was stunned into silence by my blasphemy. She crossed herself once…then again. "I will get the doctor for you, your Grace. I fear you are ill…very ill."

"I am not ill…but do as you wish, Willelma!" I snapped at her, and put my aching, tortured head into my hands. My rings caught the long, unbrushed strands of my dark hair, ripping them out; I cared nothing for the pain. I must have looked a madwoman, my eyes swollen and red, my hair a wild snarl.

But it turned out Willelma was right. I *was* ill.

Soon a fever raged within me, a fever that assailed both mind and body. Drenched in sweat, screaming against demons that haunted me, clawing for my soul, I was carried to my bed. I railed against God and begged for the peace of death as the physicians tried to minister to me and bring the fever down. My ladies gathered around, weeping, brave

Margaret, wiping my brow with rosewater and Willelma and Christiana saying noisy prayers as rosary beads clacked through their shaking fingers.

Through the haze of illness, I heard a voice speaking, gabbling in the gloom like geese. "It is bad news...bad news indeed." A man's voice, solemn at the grave.

"The Queen must not be disturbed by any more troubles!" Willelma's voice was sharp as a whip, protective. "Do you not see how it is with her?"

"She must be told."

I struggled to rise amidst the froth of pillows, dank with the sweat that flowed like water from my pores. Something wrong...my children...what of my other children?

"There is surely nothing she need be told that is so pressing it must be brought to her sick bed!" Out of a blurred eye, I saw Sybil approach the messenger, her jaw set and determined, as if she would push him back out the room, no matter how urgent his business. "Come back when the doctors say she is recovering!"

The man swallowed. "Lady Giffard, it is the King..."

"What about the King?" Sybil's brows lifted, but her voice held the hint of a fearful quiver.

"His Grace is ill with the same malady as the Queen and has taken to his bed. He barely knows himself and moans in agony. Before he fell senseless, he said he had the Lady Katharine much on his mind. The physicians fear for his life, lady, and the Queen must be told."

"The Queen must rest!" snapped Sybil. "You will kill her with this news! Begone, man. Begone!"

I lay in misery, listening in a daze to this exchange, my hair falling in soaked ropes around me, unable to respond to the conversation between Sybil and the messenger. Henry was ill! Henry, the King of England, was dying of heartsickness over the death of our little daughter.

And I knew this evil could not be allowed to happen. Edward was too young to rule a country as yet. He was not ready.

With an effort, I suddenly sat up, pushing myself upright on my elbows. Groaning with the pain of my wasted, aching muscles, I swung my frail legs over the side of the bed. Willelma and Roburga both uttered little shrieks and tried to swathe me in the bedclothes. "You must not move, Lady. Let me get you some water!" cried Willelma.

"I have lain in bed too long," I gasped. "I have heard everything. I must go to the King, who needs me more than at any other time! My ladies, dress me and make me presentable. Messenger…" I gestured with shaking hand to the open-mouthed man standing near the door. "Let a message be carried to my husband's chamber that I shall join him there anon."

The man rushed away, and shakily I stood before my women, struggling against the waves of dizziness that rushed over me. "Quickly, quickly," I ordered them. "I must go to the King's side as soon as possible."

They threw my linens and over-tunic on me, hastily covered my hair. I did not bother with girdles or jewels—I needed to see my husband.

Weakly I stumbled down the hall, Roberga and Christiana supporting me, striving to keep me on my feet. The floor seemed to sway beneath my soles, the tiles whirling into a haze…yet strangely, as I approached the king's apartments, I began to feel a strange new strength flooding my limbs. The mist of illness and despair was lifting from my brain; the fire that burned my skin and ravished my body was extinguished. Katharine had gone to the Heavenly Father and would never return but I still had a purpose, a duty. I would not shirk my appointed task…as a wife, as a Queen.

Thrusting past the guards at the King's chamber door, I pushed my way through a heaving crowd of doctors and attendants with bowls and towels and medicines. "Out of my way, all of you! Let me see my husband!"

They tried to draw me away, their hands flapping at me uselessly, not daring to touch my royal person. "Your Grace, you need rest. The situation is in hand!"

I glanced over to where one doctor held a sharp-bladed knife. Below the implement, his apprentice held a large copper bowl. They were about to bleed Henry, to cut his vein and let perceived bad humours out with the flow of blood.

I did not believe in blood-letting, not for the evil that had gripped him, which was born of melancholy. And melancholy could pass without mortification of the flesh…

"Get out!" I cried at the doctor. "Stay at your peril!" The apprentice, terrified to see his Queen bearing down on him like a mad woman, dropped the bowl with a loud clang.

The physics all fled, their robes flurrying like a trail of fallen leaves as they hastened from the room.

I knelt by Henry's side. His face was waxy, yellow-grey, his brow furrows awash with sweat. He mumbled to himself, a jumble of mostly incomprehensible words. "Katharine…" I heard him groan. "I am a King and have the power of life and death over most men…but I could not will you to live."

Reaching to touch his shoulder, I called out his name. He did not speak. Slowly I began to sing, a song of the Blessed Virgin sung to the Christ Child, but with words that mirrored our bitter loss:

"Always recall in thine heart these three things:
whence thou came, what thou art,
and what shalt become of thee.
Lulley, lullay, my little child,
lullay, lullow;
with sorrow thou wendest into the world,
with sorrow thou shalt go."

Henry's eyelids flickered. "Why do you torment me, woman?"

"Because I would not see the King of England fade away like our dearest daughter. It is not his time."

"How dare you tell me what my time is?"

"I dare because I am your loving wife. I have lain abed too long…and so have you." I took his hands, hot, dry. "Rise, your people await you. Katharine awaits you too…in heaven. But your time of meeting is not yet. Rise, because she, so innocent and sweet, would not see her father perish on her behalf."

Henry groaned, but he kept his hands entwined with mine. "What day is it, Eleanor?" he asked. "How long have I been ill?"

"It is the end of May," I said softly. "You have been bedridden since not long after Katharine died. I have equally suffered but now I wake anew. Our duties call, to God and men."

A tear trickled down his yellowed, sunken cheek. "You are right…you are almost always right. I must find strength…somehow. I have four other children. I have you. I have England."

"Robe the King!" I ordered the hovering squires, who were gazing at me as if I were some sort of miracle worker.

The King staggered to his feet, beard tangled, hair matted from the pillow and from sweat, but with a new light slowly dawning in his grief-dimmed eyes.

My husband had returned to himself, as I had likewise returned from sickness and despair to the realms of living men.

Chapter Eight

The Pope was threatening to excommunicate Henry! I could scarcely believe the menacing letters he had received from the Holy Father. It was a true nightmare, as if the shade of Henry's father John, who had been excommunicated and brought England under Interdict, had arisen to haunt us.

The problem was Sicily.

Edmund's prospective crown.

We had not been able to raise enough funds to mount an invasion. Richard refused to aid us, the barons turned up their spiteful noses. The fines Henry acquired from Baliol and de Ros had ended up lining other pockets. Henry's financial obligations to Pope Alexander had not been met, and the Pope was an angry man indeed, for all his heavenly worthiness.

I had hoped Uncle Thomas might help finance Edmund's claim if Richard would not but troubles had beset my poor uncle when travelling in Switzerland. The perfidious Swiss had seized him on a flimsy charge and cast him into a dungeon. While I managed to ransom him, with financial and diplomatic help from my mother and sisters, by the time he reached the safety of England, he was suffering badly from his long incarceration. His limbs were wasted, his ankles raw from chains. I could not ask a man for money when he was so ill he was being carried around in a litter…even for Edmund's sake. And Thomas certainly would not be leading an army into battle; not then, not ever again by the look of him.

I also felt uneasy and guilty. Edward and I had fallen out. Over the Lusignans, of all people.

I had decided to aid in the expulsion from England of Henry's half-brothers, the Lusignans, the other children of Isabella of Angouleme. I hated them all; none were the least like Henry in temperament and he favoured them in a ridiculous fashion, granting them the best castles in the country, where they lived like petty kings.

While similar accusations were thrown at me over my preference for Savoyard and Provencal kin, at least *my* relatives were learned and cultured. In my estimation, the Lusignans were no more than piggish thugs. William de Valence, for example, was a poacher who had raided the lands of the Bishop of Ely. After his illicit hunting was done, he then broke into the manor house and drank the Bishop's wine, leaving the wine-casks open and flowing on the floor in an additional act of careless nastiness.

In his youthful naivety, however, Edward loved these foolish louts, almost admiring their insolence and, when he got the chance, joining their dissolute ways.

In high dudgeon, wanting the bad influence on my son to cease, I had gone to Simon de Montfort, to see if the English barons could assist me in removing these detestable leeches. Disloyal? Call me what you will. I truly thought it was best for my husband and son to be away from those wilful, useless kinsmen. And de Montfort was the only man forceful and powerful enough to take them on.

I must admit, however, it was with heavily beating heart that I waited for de Montfort in secret, hiding in one of my special knot gardens at Winchester. I had dismissed my women; they lingered on the verges of the garden for propriety's sake, though well out of earshot.

In the rose bower Earl Simon came to me, brooding as he ever did, his dark face full of that savage fire that had both affrighted and entranced me when I was a little younger. His eyes, ever wolfish, pierced me like swords. His jaw was granite, clean-shaven but dark with stubble…he had ridden many days. He still wore his mail and a dusky blue cloak, covered in grime of the road. "You wished to see me, your Grace?" his voice was as rough as his appearance, still holding hints of his French accent.

"How is Nell?" I said, trying for niceties, because, I had to admit, he unnerved me, and such trivialities could often give rise to deeper conversations. "I have not seen her at court often and I miss her. I have not even seen her youngest daughter, Eleanor since she was born."

Simon cut through any courtliness, any games I might have sought to play that would get him on my side. "I am sure you have not summoned me here to talk about my wife and youngest child." He used no formalities in speaking to his Queen…and no niceties either.

Anger at his arrogance gripped me, and chastisement burned on my tongue but I decided, with much difficulty, to hold my peace. One must fight fire with fire. The Lusignans bore the same sort of arrogance as Simon. The Earl of Leicester could be my fire to burn that cancer from the land

"No." I tilted my head and narrowed my eyes in a way I hoped would look haughty. "You are correct, my lord. Let us dispense with formalities, shall we? It's the Lusignans that concern me. They are running amok in England, and my son is infected by their barbarous ways."

His cruel mouth quirked upwards, amused. "You tell me nothing new there, your Grace. Does the King wish for something to be done about these feckless relatives of his? Does he see their true colours at last?"

"No, sadly he does not!" I said sharply. "That is the problem. He loves the oafs dearly, as does the Lord Edward."

Simon's brows lifted under his thick brown fringe. He was smirking now; I wished to slap his arrogant face. "So...you wish to go against your husband, the King? A dangerous game, my lady, I should say."

"I would never 'go against' Henry. I love my husband dearly." My cheeks began to burn. Why did this man always unnerve me so? "I merely seek to remove those would use him because he is blind to their faults."

"And I would guess there are some nice Provencal uncles and cousins who might better benefit from the Lusignan kindred's lands?"

A shocked breath hissed through my clenched teeth. "You speak far too freely of matters that are of no concern to you, de Montfort!"

He laughed; it was rich and rolling, thunder on a hot August night. "I always speak my mind, lady, for good or for ill. But...I still am at a loss here. What do you want me to do about the King's problem relatives?"

"You have great influence among the barons, perhaps the greatest influence of all. There is to be a parliament held in Oxford. See to it that the great of England vote that these interlopers be cast forth like the feckless devils they are!"

"Feckless devils, indeed!" De Montfort laughed again, his mouth pursing. He mocked me, I knew it, and I could do nothing to stop him. "I would not like to get on the wrong side of you, my Lady."

"Enough!" I said, attempting to assert my authority. How this man unnerved me!

De Montfort bowed; he was standing so close I could smell the dust on his garb, the faint scent of sweat and horses. "I will do my best, Madame," he said, and his eyes were locked with mine, unflinching, mesmerising as a serpent's unwavering stare. Was that how the Serpent in the Garden stared at Eve? "I just pray the result will be to your liking." He gave a deep chuckle as if at a private joke.

And then he was gone, leaving me leaning against the castle wall, surrounded by the tender May time flowers, breathing heavily as if I had just run a race. A race indeed. But had I won or lost?

Simon de Montfort did as he promised. Most of the barons despised the Lusignans as much as I did. In Oxford, during the sitting of parliament, they voted almost unanimously to seize the Lusignans' lands and castles. When Guy, one of the King's half-brothers sprang up to protest, Simon faced him down with a threat, "Yield your castles or you will all lose your heads!"

The Lusignans fled for the nearest port, even Bishop Aymer...

But what a hollow victory for me. De Montfort had more on his mind than expelling the Lusignans. Once they were dealt with, he proceeded to establish a new council filled with his own cronies. An Act called the Oxford Provisions was passed and Henry, Edward, Uncle Peter and me were all compelled to swear that we would abide by this Act (Richard was abroad in Germany and escaped, while his son pleaded that he was too young to swear). The Provisions stated that Henry must bring any matter of import to the council before it could be acted upon; essentially, it made the King a figurehead and nothing more. Once again, the spectre of Henry's father John rose before us all, defeated as a ruler, inept, bound by the terms of the Great Charter forced on him by his barons.

The strictures on King John had brought war...What would the Provisions of Oxford bring?

As de Montfort departed the hall of Oxford castle, he passed in front of my seat, smug, swaggering, wearing garments as rich as any king's. Our eyes met briefly; I broke eye contact first, calling upon my ladies in waiting to attend me. Simon smirked. I detested him in that moment. And feared him more than any man living. And to think at one time I had begun to warm towards him. Now he chilled my blood.

Earl Simon was hardly foremost in my mind, however. Edward was a greater problem. He was furious at the loss of his Lusignan uncles and shouted at me for wanting them out of the country. But it was more complex than a tantrum over losing his ill-mannered kin. He also had a close friendship de Montfort's two sons, his cousins through their mother Nell, and they held much influence over him. Whilst he was angered that he had been forced to swear to uphold the Provisions of Oxford, he noisily exclaimed that he agreed with many of the barons' concerns. This was tantamount to speaking against his father's rule—a dangerous, inflammatory situation.

I decided to smooth things over, to make certain Edward's friends were not of equally baneful influence to the exiled Lusignan lords. My son was a prince; he could not be permitted to fall under de Montfort's unwholesome spell and maybe be urged by unscrupulous men to rise against his father.

Urgently, I called him before me at Windsor.

He procrastinated…but then sent a message. He would come.

Edward arrived, scowling, still wearing the stained clothes from his morning's hawking foray in the Great Park, possibly to show that he disregarded my opinions, that he found his entertainments more important than my concerns. "Is it an emergency, mother?" he snapped in clipped tones. "I was…busy. I see no reason to come here, otherwise."

"I deem it an emergency," I retorted. "I must warn you about de Montfort. Take great care, my son, lest his strong beliefs bring about war and ruination in this kingdom…a kingdom that will be yours one day, provided no ill befalls."

His eyes widened, then narrowed; cold blue ice in his bronzed face. "I am twenty years old, Madame," he said stiffly. "I have my own household. I can—and will—choose my own friends."

I wanted to tell him that twenty summers he might be, but at this moment, his behaviour was that of an impudent boy of thirteen…but I restrained myself. Such chiding would only rile him further. "Your duty is to your father before all," I said in a quiet voice.

"When have I ever been undutiful?" he flared, his fists clenching at his sides. "It is you, Madame, who have been undutiful to your husband. Promoting your own relatives at the expense of his. Hating his family when they outshine your own. The whole country is abuzz with your behaviour…how Eleanor the Queen hands grants out to her foreign relatives and no others."

I gasped.

"Yes!" Edward cried, thrusting a long, impertinent finger in my direction. "Hear me, mother. They also talk about this ridiculous bid for the throne of Sicily for Edmund! Oh, how they talk…calling it folly. Sheer folly. And they are right!"

"Do not speak so of Edmund, your own brother! How can you resent him a crown?"

"I do not, lady! But he should not have one if this crown is to bankrupt England and cause friction with the Pope! Do you want interdict passed upon us again, as in my grandfather's day? When the dead could not be buried, and lay stinking in crowded churchyards? When no baptisms could take place or any sacraments be given, even to the dying who begged for them? Would you see such horror again? Be sensible! Edmund will never rule Sicily; why can you not admit it? It makes me cringe when father calls him 'King of Sicily'; you can see the courtiers smirk, for they know it is a hollow, meaningless title!"

I longed to argue with him...but my tongue would not move; deep in my heart, I knew he was right.

"Mother, with this recent parliament, I fear you have reaped the whirlwind," he said, his tone bitter, "I am not talking about just the Lusignans." He gave me a curt bow, and then stalked away, back to his bright young men and their hunting and hawking, leaving me staring at his retreating, sword-straight back with sinking heart.

After he had departed, I hurried to Henry's chamber; my husband was sitting on a brocade-covered stool by the narrow window, leaning forward as if a great exhaustion had enveloped him. He looked suddenly very old; the light picked out silver flecks in his beard and hair. Shadows hovered like nightmares under his unhappy eyes. His drooping lid hung lower than ever with weariness and strain.

"Henry," I said sharply. "We must go."

"Go?" He raised his head and gazed blearily at me.

"Yes, go!"

"Where?"

"From England!"

He looked horrified. "What are you suggesting? We cannot abandon the people. There was famine in the country but last year, and this year a promising harvest was wrecked by floods! Plague had struck in the city!"

"We are not abandoning anything, husband...but I deem we must lie low until recent troubles abate. We will go to the court of my sister, Marguerite. She will help us, and so will Louis, now that he is your friend. It will not be shameful to seek solace there—you have that Peace Treaty that is due to be signed between you. Knowing of the treaty, men will laud you and not whisper that we have made a coward's retreat when the country is in need."

Henry's face brightened and he stood. "Yes, yes, perhaps you are right, Eleanor. Edward can be in charge when we are away. Things will settle with the barons and with the Pope. One thing though…" He licked his lips, looking sheepish.

"What is troubling you?" I said impatiently. My mind was racing with all I must do if we were to sojourn abroad.

"As usual, we have no coin. The treasury coffers are close to bare—the worst I have ever seen them. The barons won't allow us to take the remainder with us, due to their accursed Provisions."

I sighed. "No matter, no matter. I will take all my jewels. They will tide us over if need be."

Within the month, we were sailing across the Channel towards France. My heart gladdened as the tall white bastions of England's shore sank into a haze of mist and spray and disappeared from view.

Chapter Nine

It was wonderful to see Marguerite again. With my sister as my companion, I could forget my woes in England and think on other things. We compared gowns and fashions, and I sighed over all the wonders of the Parisian dresses. We also worked on a match for my dear daughter, Beatrice. We decided a suitable husband would be John, Duke of Brittany and set the date of the wedding for January. Henry wrote to the King of Navarre, anxiously reminding him to turn over lands he owed to the Duke. We had to make sure our daughter was well provided for.

"A January wedding might be cold," I frowned, though my mind was filled with delightful thoughts of colourful brocade and silk, and miniver and marten and fox fur hoods and ruffs. I glanced outside the window of my sister's palace; it was snowing now, small flakes twirling down from a steel-blue heaven.

"Maybe," Marguerite said cheerfully, "but think of the joy a wedding will bring to our hearts in these dull months of winter! The promise of new alliances and new life!"

I embraced her. "Joy. Yes, we all need more joy in all our lives right now. We will smile again soon, and the world will be put to rights."

I do not know if some devil, some mischievous minion of Satan, heard my hopeful words that day and laughed at Marguerite and me, before casting a cloud of darkness in our direction. Misfortune soon fell, like a sharpened sword falling upon the vanquished on a battlefield.

Christmas had passed and Henry and I were dwelling at the Abbey of St Denis, preparing for Beatrice's wedding, when a messenger arrived from my sister's court. The man's face was skull-white, drawn; he wore mourning clothes with the lilies of France pecked out on the breast in white seed pearl, like bones upon a black shroud.

My heart flipped-flopped in my chest as he walked down the abbey cloister towards us, the heels of his tall boots making a sharp, unnerving rat-tat-tat upon the flagstones. He was the bearer of bad news—I knew it instinctively. Was it Marguerite? My mother? The French King?

"Your Graces." The messenger sank down on one knee on the tiled floor of St Denis's abbey. "There is ill news from the Palace."

"Tell us," commanded Henry. "Do not dither, man. If a blow must come, let it be delivered swift and sharp."

"It is Prince Louis, the Crown Prince. Shortly after the Christmas festivities, he fell ill with a fever. Yesterday, he went from this evil earth into God's light."

"Christ have mercy on the poor young prince's soul!" I cried in sudden anguish. "And may Blessed Mary send sweet balm to my sister in her grief."

I began to weep, as the messenger was dismissed, leaving me alone with Henry in the cloister. Monks peered anxiously from nooks and alcoves in the distance. I had only met Marguerite's eldest son a few times, so knew him but little, yet I knew what a loss it must be to his parents. He had only been fifteen at his death and he was heir to the throne, schooled from birth to be king. Marguerite had another son, Philip, who would fill his shoes, but young Louis had been his mother's bright star, born after ten years of barrenness. It seemed so cruel.

"We must postpone Beatrice's wedding for at least another week," I told Henry. "It would be inappropriate when the heir of France has died."

Henry nodded. "Yes, we must don the colours of mourning and join in the grief of our kin of France."

The prince's funeral cortege wound through the winter-bitten streets of Paris out into the bleak countryside around the abbey of Royaumont, where the unfortunate royal youth would be interred. Marguerite and I rode solemnly in a chariot draped in mourning blue; Henry had offered to help carry the prince's coffin on at least part of the journey. With trepidation, I watched him slipping and sliding in the mud and melting snow. Above, the sky was a livid bruise, the hue of a dead man's face. I clutched Marguerite's ice-cold hand and thought of my own lost daughter, little Katharine, lying forever asleep beneath her silver effigy in Westminster.

"Eleanor…" I heard Marguerite's voice, weak and heavy with her sorrow.

"Yes, my sister?" I clutched her fingers even tighter.

"I know it is not good between you and Edward right now. That he behaves foolishly and irks you and the King, even frightens you with his wayward behaviour. Well...I bid you, try to reconcile with him. No, I do not bid you...I *beg* you. I have lost a son to the cold hand of death...Do not lose your son because of stubbornness or pride."

I thought on her words; solemnly I let my gaze travel to Henry's hunched shoulders, bowed beneath their heavy load. Snow was falling again, alighting in his hair, turning it hoary.

Edward was *our* star, our hope. Marguerite was right. We must not lose him through stubbornness, either his or ours. All we had ever dreamed of depended on him. And England, which he would rule one day, depended on the right choices too.

The Treaty of Paris was signed. Henry had to do homage to Louis, kneeling before his throne and placing his hands between those of the French king—a humiliation of sorts—but there was no helping it if we were to have peace...and French assistance.

The treaty completed, my husband and I began gathering up a force with which to take England, paying for it with the jewels I had brought overseas with me. Marguerite procured a loan, and Louis made sure all our hired soldiers were paid. Fierce mercenaries as interested in blood as money joined our cause; uncomfortable men to be around, but unavoidable...and useful.

In the spring we sailed, a flotilla of loaned ships spread out upon the slate-hued waves of the Channel. As the Kentish mainland appeared in view, I strained my eyes to see if any enemy army thronged the white headlands, waiting for us. There was no one.

Unchallenged, we entered Dover harbour, with our loyal subjects cheering from the quayside. No de Montfort...but no Edward either.

Heartened, we marched on toward London, sending messages to Richard of Cornwall and Uncle Boniface as we hastened down the road. *We pray you see to the Lord Edward. Convince him to come to us and rejoin his family. The prince must not be set apart from his father and mother....*

We reached London. The river curled before us; the Tower loomed, a skull-like head in the mist. The bells were ringing, heralding our arrival. Richard of Cornwall had ridden in from his distant estates; he came before us with a grim smile playing upon his features. "It has worked, my brother," he said to the King. "Good news at last. Edward is on his way to London, and he will repent of his former deeds and swear loyalty to you."

An emergency session of parliament was scheduled, high in the stern bastions of the White Tower, where gulls shrieked as they wheeled in off the Thames. Having newly reached the capital, Edward entered the council chamber still wearing his mud-stained travelling cloak and went dramatically on his knees before his father's high seat.

"Edward, my son, what have you to say to us?" Henry asked sternly. "Rise, and speak to all those within his room."

Edward got to his feet, standing head and shoulders above those men clustered near him. "I ask your forgiveness, my lord father…my King."

There was still a certain sulkiness in his tone and in his face, but his words were the ones we longed to hear.

"I never meant to bring grief to my august parents, and I shall endeavour never to do so again. A man cannot serve two masters, as the Bible tells us. I have chosen whom I must serve. The rightful King of England. The Queen, his wife. My esteemed father and mother."

Edward was divested of his dripping mantle, and still with stony visage took his place amidst the King's counsellors, and eventually attention drifted away from him—focusing instead on Simon de Montfort, who was accounted one of their number, perhaps the greatest and most influential of them all. It seemed to me that in the months we had been away Simon had blown up like a great puff adder, dark and deadly. An air of danger had always clung to him, but now his ferocity and disdain was openly displayed.

This man, of noble but not royal blood, whose life had consisted of audacious feats, considered himself as important as a King. Indeed, maybe he saw himself as a candidate for kingship, winning an unrightful crown by deceit and by threat of armed force.

The King was focused on him too, his countenance dark with displeasure. "I see de Montfort is with us. I am surprised he has dared show his face here today, upon our triumphant return to our kingdom."

Simon bristled with ill-contained rage from his seat amidst the barons. "I am on the council; it is my right to be here."

Henry leapt out of his seat, making a strangled noise. "Right? I doubt your right! You are untrue and disloyal to the crown! You treated me with great discourtesy when you laid out those abominable Oxford Provisions and forced me to agree to them!"

A sneer curled Simon's upper lip; he was like a beast, cornered and immensely dangerous. "You treat your *people* with great discourtesy, your Grace. You and the Queen. You spend the country's money on your relatives, and on obtaining a worthless foreign crown for your younger son. England is nearly bankrupt, my lord…because of your wastefulness. Your rule is corrupt, as was your father's before you!"

A gasp rippled through the throng. Edward's lips tightened to lines but he stared at his toes and did not rise to defend his father.

Henry's face suffused with blood; his eyes started from his sockets. De Montfort muttered an oath beneath his breath and started to move towards the council chamber door, but two halberdiers intercepted him, crossing their weapons before his face. Motionless, he stood staring at the honed blades as they glinted dully, threateningly, a few inches from his nose. "Let me pass." His voice was a growl.

Richard of Cornwall left his bench and stalked to the King's side, laying a hand on his shoulder. "Brother, be at peace. Let de Montfort go," he urged.

"Why should I? He forgets his place!"

"It is not the time for warlike action, we must try for reconciliation." Richard glanced nervously at the barons, many of them de Montfort's supporters. They shuffled uncomfortably, eyeing each other, eyeing the King. Some looked shocked, others disapproving, others eager for affray. "We will talk of this later, your Grace. Later."

"May I go?" De Montfort's hard voice sounded again, taut with impatience.

"Yes, go, go, Goddamn you!" Henry shouted, flapping a hand at the halberdiers who parted instantly to allow de Montfort passage. He strode into the corridors of the Tower, wearing his arrogance and fury like a cape.

Henry looked wrathful but also relieved as his rival's footsteps faded into the distance.

Richard gazed down at his brother. "We will talk, in private. Her Grace the Queen too."

We met in the Tower Gardens as dusk fell over London and the sky turned a twilit purple. A thin, fingernail-paring moon ascended the sky, slashing at the turrets projecting from the massive walls. The leaves on the pear trees Henry had recently ordered to be planted around the Garden Tower fluttered in the wind, while the smell of mint and lavender drifted from the herb beds. Far in the distance, the beasts in the King's menagerie were roaring for their dinner, the lion, the camel, the buffaloes, and the bear gifted us by the King of Norway, their cries strangely surreal in the gloaming, echoing and bouncing off the pockmarked stone that contained them.

The King shuffled over to Richard, holding up the hem of his long over-gown as if he feared he would trip on it; two brothers but so different, my husband short and compact, Richard taller and sparer. Both men were growing old, the lines of care and worry increasing almost daily on their faces. Two Kings, two sets of problems. Richard's German kingdom was increasingly violent and unfriendly towards their new ruler; he and Sanchia had near enough fled from the depredations of their bloodthirsty subjects on their recent visit. Further plans to become emperor, a position dangled before him by the conniving pope, had dissolved like smoke from a quenched fire. And to add to the misery, Sanchia was ill, lying bedridden in Berkhamsted castle, traumatised by the terrifying circumstances of their travels abroad...and, I feared, by her husband's lack of care.

"Well, Richard, what advise can you give me that my other counsellors cannot give me?" Henry asked bluntly.

"Good sense, I hope," said the Earl of Cornwall. "I know you long to bring Simon de Montfort down..."

"With justification!"

"Indeed...but it is my belief that the more you rail against him in public, the more it hardens his heart and those of his loyal followers. So my counsel is this...do nothing. Keep quiet."

"What kind of advice is that?" sneered Henry. "Do nothing!"

"Simon is an arrogant and covetous man. However, men flock to him, for he is charismatic and appears strong and just. But after a while, they will see him for what he is...and then he will fall. Let him hang himself, brother. It will happen, I swear it."

"You are suggesting I let this man rule my kingdom and hope for the best?" Henry shook his head with ferocity. "You are mad, Richard! Even if Simon were eventually destroyed by his own ambition, someone else in his treacherous fold would step up to fill his shoes. No...men have often accused me of inaction, but they will no more. I will go to the Pope about my troubles, and I will raise an army."

"Henry, think carefully about this," Richard warned.

"My mind is made up. If you will not support me, let it be at your peril." Henry gathered his robes about him and strode from the garden. The night swallowed him.

I remained with Richard in the descending night. Moths were flittering about our heads making false crowns; they ducked and swayed around the flambeaux burning throughout the mighty bailey. Taking a deep breath, I faced my brother-in-law. "Where will your loyalties lie, Richard?"

"With the King of course," he retorted, shocked. "How low you must think me, Eleanor, to believe otherwise!"

"How is she, Richard?" I breathed, my voice barely about a whisper

"Who?"

"Precisely," I said with bitterness.

Turning from the Earl, I pursued the King back into the Tower. Only shadows followed me.

We prepared for conflict. Henry and I made the Tower of London our permanent retreat, setting uncounted guards upon the entrances and walls. No barons, save those known to be unquestioningly loyal to Henry, were permitted into the city at all, and all citizens over the age of twelve were required to attend special sessions where they swore fealty to their sovereign. In secret, we conferred with those known to be faithful to us, and sent John Mansel the younger to the Pope, in order to extricate documents from him that could free us from the oaths adhering us to the Oxford Provisions.

"I am going to have to do something you won't like, Eleanor," Henry said to me one evening, as we stood on the Tower battlements, unaccompanied save for four archers and the gulls soaring in off the Thames to squabble over old bones and bits of detritus on the Tower roof.

Nervously my fingers knotted together. "And what might that be, husband?" Henry was not as shrewd as many men, and I ofttimes feared his decisions, which were seldom as well thought out as my own. But his will, naturally, must take precedence over mine...

"My brothers...Aymer, William, Guy..."

I pursed my lips. The accursed Lusignans again! "Yes, what about them?"

"I am going to ask them to return to England. I know you have no love for them, Eleanor, but they will support me unquestioningly and bring large armies with them."

Folding my arms, I let out a deep, troubled sigh. The wind felt fresh off the river, making me shiver atop that great height. "I understand why you feel you need them, but I cannot agree to this happily unless..."

"Unless what, wife?" A muscle jumped in Henry's cheek. I could tell by his voice, he was not pleased that I was trying to impose conditions on his decision. But on this matter, I would, must, remain firm...

"Unless they apologise to me for their behaviour in the past, and swear they will not stand in my way or interfere with my business. They need to show me the respect due to me as Queen!"

Henry began to laugh. "Is that all, wife? I think that can be arranged. They won't like it...they are proud men...but to get their feet under an English table once more, I believe they will do whatever I ask."

"They *must* do it. And there is something else, Henry. Edward."

Henry rolled his eyes. "I know you don't like the influence of my kinsmen on our son, but he is a man grown and married. He will choose his own friends. Just be glad he seems to have been weaned off Simon and his cronies."

"It is not that so much. It is his absence! He plays too much these days instead of learning statecraft! Where is he now? France! Not on a pilgrimage or mission of diplomacy, but gallivanting around in a tournament. He must return home at once, and cease his foolish enjoyments in French jousts. I know he wishes to show his prowess to his hordes of admirers, but now is not the time. He is needed in England...the country wants to see a strong prince." *Especially now that the King is getting older and weaker,* I thought, but dared not say.

"You are right." Henry leaned on a crenel, staring into the gloomy sky. "I will see he travels home immediately, in the company of my brothers." Henry made sure I knew the brothers would definitely be coming, whether I liked it or not... though at least the apology they must make was confirmed.

I turned to face the dusk; there were storm clouds on the horizon, their tiered edges limned by fiery light, casting a surreal glamour over London's teeming streets. The wind suddenly dropped to nothing; a strange silence descended—it was as if the great city held its breath in expectation.

A shudder rippled down my spine. Things would be put to rights when Edward returned and Henry's forces were swelled...wouldn't they?

Joy filled London; the bells boomed from church tower and priory. News had reached us that Edward and the Lusignan brothers had returned to England, bringing with them a new ally, the war-like Count St Pol, who commanded a huge force of mercenaries. Outnumbered, realising that his days of liberty might well be numbered, Simon de Montfort surrendered up his control of the government and fled pell-mell for France.

Mansel had returned from Rome; before crowds of watching men, he held up a parchment bearing the Pope's seal so that all might see and witness. The Oxford provisions had been repealed; a papal bull absolved Henry and me of our oaths to follow its strictures. We were free of its oppression at last.

No longer fearful for our freedom, perhaps our very lives, we abandoned the confines of the Tower to meet our eldest son in Winchester. How wonderful it was to ride the roads in a new spring, seeing blossoms deck the trees and the gentle sunlight playing upon the many streams that crisscrossed the land. It was as if a new day had finally dawned, one where we could be at peace, and rule as kings and queens were meant to, without interference from power-hungry lords.

Once we reached Winchester, the great hall was prepared for our guests—the great hall where once King Arthur might have sat in counsel, his company of valorous knights seated around him at the Round Table. The flagstones were polished, mats and imported carpets laid down, candelabrum brought in, sweet pomanders hung from the beams.

In person, I rode out to greet Edward and his companions as they arrived at the town gates. After embracing the prince before all watchers, I made great show out of being reconciled to the Lusignan brothers, who hung their heads and muttered apologies for their former treatment of their Queen. I was benevolent, forgiving; I smiled sweetly (with just the slightest hint of sarcasm) and gave them gold and silver. St Pol was also gifted with rings and jewels to show our gratitude for supporting our cause.

That night, after a huge feast, we met with Edward and walked with him in my herb garden. He gazed at us solemnly, hands clasped behind his back. "It is good that de Montfort is gone," he said at length. "Although at one time I almost fell under his spell, I now truly see that I was in error. He wanted power for himself; he would have undermined me, if not worse, the moment we clashed over policy. I swear I will never stray so far from the family fold again. Father…" he turned to Henry, a huge figure in his shimmering blue silk tunic, a lordling as imposing as those Arthurian knights who dwelt at Winchester long ago, "you need never fear my loyalty again. The past is done. Never shall I support those who do not have the Plantagenet interests at heart."

I smiled; with Edward back at our side, the dark times were surely over, even if poor Edmund was no longer in line for a crown. We would find our younger son something else to amuse him, I was sure.

A letter had come, borne by a messenger wearing a badge of the Scottish Lion. A letter from my daughter, Margaret! I read it with burgeoning excitement. She would be journeying to England with her husband, King Alexander.

In Windsor, I waited impatiently for the royal arrivals, stalking around my apartments in excited distress while my ladies tried to find pursuits and fancies to distract me. Gowns, veils, and jewels were laid out; I would consider them, reject them, and then toss them to Willelma or Margaret Biset, asking to see others. I could not rest, could not keep from an almost girlish excitement at the homecoming of my eldest daughter.

At last, an outrider arrived, informing the King that the royal party from Scotland was processing through Windsor town. With Henry at my side, I rode out to meet the cavalcade, both of us wearing our crowns. I had chosen a red damask gown covered in gilt quatrefoils and a deep blue cloak lined in white fur.

When I saw Margaret, my eyes brimmed with maternal tears. She had matured so much, from the frightened child who wed a foreign prince in York and the unhappy girl that I had met at Wark Castle, to a beautiful and confident woman. Slender and upright like her brother Edward, the hair confined by her headdress was a dark golden brown, glowing in the watery sunlight. Gazing ahead, her eyes were clear and calm…and thankfully, happy.

We greeted each other with all the formalities that were expected, but when we were at last alone in my apartments, it was another story. "Oh Meggie, you look so well now; there are roses blooming in your cheeks!" Margaret had removed her austere headdress and her hair hung down in long waves, nearly to her waist. "Indeed, you are blooming all over; you have put on much weight since last we met. Those dour Scots must be feeding you adequately at last."

Margaret glanced at me with a secret little smile. "Ah, I bloom indeed, mother, but not just because there is more food upon the royal table!"

I let out a gasp. Margaret ran to me and pressed her finger to my lips. "I must bid you be silent on this matter, mother. The Scots do not know, even Alexander does not know! They would have never let me travel so far if they had realised I carry Scotland's heir beneath my girdle!"

"Meggie, Meggie, I do not know whether to be angry or overjoyed! You *have* taken a great risk journeying so far...but I cannot deny I am glad to see you. Would it not be wonderful if you could stay in England until the babe arrives? I am sure the child would be more likely to thrive in English climes than in the cold winds of Scotland."

"I agree with you," said Margaret. "This is a warmer and more welcoming place for a baby to be born. I would love to bear my child with you and father near at hand but of course, the Scots will want the child born on Scottish soil. If they find out I am *enceinte*, they will demand Alexander and I return to Scotland at once."

I glanced at my daughter, gaze raking her from top to toe. "When I was carrying you and Edward, I scarcely looked pregnant until I was gone six months. I hid everything beneath my skirts. You seem of similar build to me, though taller; maybe it will be the same for you." I took her hands, squeezed them. "We can play a game, if you wish, Meggie. A game devised between us to keep you in England until the heir to Scotland is born."

Margaret laughed, embraced me as if she were still an excitable little girl. "I would gladly play this tricksy game...but Alexander will find out about my condition before long. He will want to...ah...visit my chambers, and after a few more months, it will not be possible for him to do so. I have already been...*sinful* in holding the truth from him."

"That *is* a problem," I said thoughtfully, "though perhaps if we are clever, a minor one. When he finally discovers the truth, we can tell him that you are too fragile to travel such a distance. He will surely not want to risk the life of his prospective heir, even if all the lords of Scotland demand that you return home!"

"I pray your ploy will work, mother." Margaret let her hand drift to her still-flat belly. She gazed out the window into the gardens of Windsor, with the misted trees standing like rows of sentinels in the Great Park. "I want to stay here, at Windsor with you."

And so we set out to deceive King Alexander, in the nicest possible way. I admired the young Scottish king very much, even to the point of viewing him as another of my sons. He could be witty and amusing and was deeply solicitous and respectful of Meggie. Being a man, he was somewhat simple regarding women's matters and seemed blind to any changes in his wife. When we finally could not hide her condition any further, Margaret finally called him aside, sat him down, and told him with demure sweetness that soon Scotland would, God willing, have a new prince or princess.

Alexander's face whitened and then turned blood-red, matching the fiery tones in his curls. He sputtered in amazement as if it were a wonder he had done this thing. "This…this is wonderful news!" he cried. "I must write to my government and tell them. Then we must hurry home so that you can give birth in Scotland."

Margaret passed a hand over her forehead, looking like a languid maiden on the verge of a faint. "My lord, I shake with fear at the thought of such a perilous ride. My first babe…and I am expected to ride hundreds of miles over rough terrain? So dangerous…."

Alexander bit his lip in consternation. "You are correct, wife, it *would* be dangerous. A litter will be found for you, with comfortable cushions."

Margaret shook her head sadly, wrung her white hands. "The road would still be bumpy and long, my lord. I would worry the whole journey, fearing inclement weather and possible attacks of brigands. We all know the forests of the north are full of fearsome outlaws. Such worry…they say worry is not good for the health of an unborn child."

Alexander frowned. "I have heard that too…I think. No harm must be allowed to come to my heir, no matter what my great council wants. My will supersedes theirs. I deem it best, Margaret, if you stay here at Windsor to birth the child, with your parents' permission, naturally."

"Yes." I had been hovering in the back of the chamber, ready to intervene if necessary. "I believe she should stay at Windsor, too. A journey would be too much for her, especially as it is her first child— look at her, my lord, see how fearful she is to go travelling? She must stay. I swear that she will have the best physicians and midwives in the land."

"But I still must tell the Scottish court," said Alexander uneasily.

"Of course you must," I smiled. "They have a right to know such glad news!"

"But…" he shifted uncomfortably, "they will insist upon Margaret's return to Scotland to birth the babe!"

"Let them insist!" I waved my hand airily. "Who is the King?"

"Yes, Alexander," Margaret chimed in. "Who is the King?"

"I am," he said, his voice flat.

"Then they must obey you," I said, with a curt nod.

The Scots roared and complained when they heard the news about Margaret's pregnancy. As expected, they wanted her to return to Edinburgh immediately. Letters came, vaguely threatening in tone, demanding that the royal party head for home at once.

The constant stream of missives annoyed even Alexander. "How dare they imply that we are somehow held prisoners in Windsor!" he cried, as he hurled yet another unread parchment upon the fire. "I shall not budge one inch, not until Margaret is delivered of the child and all is accounted well for both of them. The lords can go hang for all I care!"

And so Margaret and Alexander remained at Windsor, and no matter how much the lords of Scotland grumbled and threatened, they would not be moved. Henry and I made sure the young couple felt most welcome, presenting them with jewels, plate, and fine cloth, and importing the best foods for Margaret's health.

She continued to blossom, the child growing large within her…but at the same time, far away in Berkhamsted castle, my sister Sanchia waned in strength, the illness that has assailed her since her flight from Germany taking firm hold.

In October, when skies stretched grey and geese flew in flocks to warmer climes, their unearthly voices honking over the misted landscape, Richard deigned to visit her, bringing their quiet little son Edmund with him. Richard looked down at Sanchia, who was so weak she could not rise. He seemed to have lost his tongue.

Swiftly he departed the chamber without uttering a single comforting word, let alone a loving gesture, leaving a frightened Edmund kneeling alone at his mother's bedside. It was fearfully similar to what he did with his first wife, Isabella Marshal.

By November, Sanchia's condition had worsened. The doctors did not know what ailed her, but she withered like a flower torn from the root. Some thought she had a growth at her very core. Richard was informed that she was not expected to survive. He took the news in silence; silence had been his shield from the moment he set foot in Berkhamsted. The next day he galloped from the castle to 'attend to urgent business' elsewhere. The business had included parcelling off Sanchia's land…even before she had breathed her last.

She did not last long after his departure. With young Edmund clutching her hand, she departed this transient life on November 9. In an elaborate funeral hearse decked with images of saints, she was carried to her beloved church at Hailes where she lay, for a brief time, before the high altar, with the monks of the abbey chanting prayers day and night. Boniface and Uncle Peter were there to say farewell. Richard was nowhere to be seen.

I dared not attend myself; the encroaching winter had brought new unrest to the south and Henry thought it prudent we go once more to our secure place in the Tower. There, in the chapel of St John, I had a Requiem Mass said for Sanchia, followed later by another in Westminster Abbey.

It was all I could do. Sanchia, my beautiful younger sister, was beyond my help and in God's hands.

Men say that as one leaves the earth, another comes to take their place. It is true, of course, and has been so since the days of Adam and Eve, Cain and Abel. On a cold, clear February day, my daughter Meggie gave birth to a healthy girl child. It was not the much-hoped-for male heir to the throne of Scotland, but the child was 'bonny' as the Scots account it, and healthy, and proved Margaret's fertility. The baby was named Margaret, after her mother, and in private Alexander called her Maisie, the Scottish pet name for Margaret, which seemed different and unique to me.

"I so wish we could stay longer," Margaret said, as she kissed my cheeks in farewell, before climbing into her litter in preparation for the long journey back to Scotland, "but the lords will not tolerate our absence any longer. Pray we have a safe journey home, mother."

"I will pray for you and for Alexander, who has become like a son to me. And of course for the health and wellbeing of little Margaret…Maisie." I glanced over at the child's nurses, gazing long at the downy head, with its tuft of reddish hair. When would I see my granddaughter again?

Then I stood back, and I watched, steeling my face to queenly sternness, as my daughter's cavalcade left to the accompaniment of blaring clarions. The Lion of Scotland streamed out gold, pawing the sky, and then they were gone.

My heart felt heavy. Too many farewells, too many partings.

Another year passed. Henry still fretted about de Montfort, who was holed up in Paris. Although the King and Queen of France knew of our troubles with him, yet he had their ear—even Marguerite's. Simon was nothing if not persuasive.

"I cannot rest knowing that he is still out there, spewing his poison," Henry said to me. "I cannot sleep at night. I fear he will sour my newfound friendship with King Louis, and then all the French will turn against me. After all, Simon is French himself, is he not?"

"Yes, he is French born...but my sister Marguerite is not. She is Provencal. She will not fall to his persuasive tongue so easily."

"So you say, Eleanor, so you say," murmured Henry, obviously ill at ease.

"You want to go to Paris, don't you, husband?"

"I think I have no other choice. Fear not, I will leave you well guarded."

"You will not, Henry. If you go, I am coming with you; it is my duty to do so and there is no reason why I should not do so. I am neither pregnant nor unwell; I will travel with my husband."

And so we packed our possessions, our crowns and robes and jewelled collars and studded girdles, and set off for France with a large party of nobles that included a jovial Uncle Peter and our son Edmund, who was chaffing at the bit for some excitement, having lost his chance at Sicily's crown. Dates were set up for discussions between Henry and de Montfort.

Upon reaching Paris, Louis presented us with one of his own castles for our personal use during our stay. Hastily, we filled it with our finery and our homegrown servants. Mother, invited from Provence as a mediator, lodged with us, bringing her own household...and many new fashions in dress that I pored over eagerly with Marguerite. England was a bit of a backwater when it came to ladies' gowns, I had to admit.

We all wished for a successful meeting between the King and the Earl of Leicester, but it became clear that our hopes were in vain from the moment we entered Louis' council chambers. Henry and Simon were at each other's throats from the start, hurling accusations at each other in a most unseemly manner.

"You would usurp my right!" Henry accused, pointing at de Montfort as if he were a dog.

"You show yourself to be a tyrant!" Simon retorted, his face suffused with blood. "The people have no love of you!"

Even mother's grace and entreating words of wisdom could not calm the two men as they circled each other like angry dogs, then slunk away to their benches, snarling, neither having gained an advantage over the other. Louis sat impassively on his throne, like a carven image of a saint, saying naught, favouring neither combatant.

This hopeless bickering went on all summer, as tempers frayed and the temperature rose around us. It had become so hot we had to throw all shutters wide in order to breathe easily, and that meant we exposed ourselves to the deadly humours creeping in off the nearby river, which had shrivelled to a rancid brown trickle in the heat.

Before long, pestilence struck the court. One after the other, men and women fell ill, gripped by pains that churned their innards and turned their bowels to blood. I tried to sequester myself away from the others and ordered my women wave fresh pomanders in the air, and it appeared to work; unlike many unfortunates, I did not sicken.

But others did, and others died. The old and the very young went first; the castle reeked of vomit, ordure and death. The local cemetery was brimming, the gravediggers busy at their trade, hacking at the parched earth as heat shimmers lifted up like angry ghosts.

Storms arrived at night, blasting the sky with lightning but still the heat did not abate. Food tasted vile, tainted by rot; I was sure it only added to our illnesses. I spat it out onto my plate and drank wine only; not wine mixed with water as was usual for women, but full strength as for a man. I walked in the castle gardens, noting the dry, cracked ground, the dead vines creeping on the old stone walls. It was like a castle of death in some Arthurian tale…the Wasteland of the Fisher King.

Fanning myself, with my ladies assisting in the effort, I sat within an arbour, where there was some shade and a few dying flowers to sweeten the rank air. "My Lady…" Margaret Biset rose from the stone bench where she was sitting as she fanned me. "The Lord Edmund comes from the keep."

"Does he?" I gazed out between the dangling withered fronds, the twisted grey vines that hung over the arbour's frame. Sure enough, I could see my younger son staggering towards us. Even at a distance, I noticed the whiteness of his face, the sweat that streamed down his brow and soaked his hair.

"Mother, help me!" he cried out as he drew near, and he fell to his knees on the hard flagstones.

"Edmund, what is it?" I cried, although I guessed already.

He clutched his gut, gasping in pain. "The flux, the bloody flux!"

I put my hand upon his brow. It burned like fire; my palm came away dripping. "Jesu, help us," I whispered. "Margaret, Christiana, help me."

We managed to pull Edmund into the shade and into an upright position. He began to gag and I held his head while he was sick. His hair was so saturated with sweat, it was as if he had been caught in the rain. "Roburga!" I called out to another of my younger ladies-in-waiting. "Go into the castle and call for help. Get the physician and some stout men to carry Edmund to his chamber. I cannot lift him."

Roburga dropped a quick curtsey and fled, hoisting up her skirts to the knee, uncaring that any man might see her bare legs. There were few to look anyway; most were hung over chamber pots, being ill, or lying in darkened corners, some near to death. If any of our foes sought to attack us, this would have been the time.

Porters came. We dragged a half-fainting Edmund back into the keep, and I ordered his chambers be changed to ones with better ventilation. Although the physicians were there, I tended him as I would a sick babe, as he drifted in and out of consciousness. I wished old Willelma was there to help me; Edmund liked her and her knowledge of treatments was nigh as good as that of a doctor...but she had retired from my service in the past year due to her age. How I missed her now!

"Your Grace, it is not fitting you do work of a nurse!" one doctor said to me, voice full of disapproval as I handed a pot full of stomach bile to a servant and ordered them to hurl it down the privy...quickly. "You must leave this room, I beg you! You are risking your own health."

"He is my son" I spat back, almost ready to grab the piss-pot back from the servant and dump the contents on the doctor's head. "I birthed him in blood and pain. He is part of me and I will not leave him. Leave me be, or I'll have you removed."

By the next morning, Edmund's fever had broken. The bloody flux had diminished and the stomach pains had gone. Edmund was still pale and his skin felt clammy, but he was able to sip a bit of wine and hold it down. "I feel as weak as a babe," he muttered, leaning back on his pillows. "Or an old greybeard in his dotage."

"You are lucky to be alive," I said to him, laving his brow with rose water. "Another ten have died overnight."

"God rest their souls."

I looked at him, his drawn cheeks, the greyish tint to his mouth. He was too unwell to remain here; if another bout of the flux took him, that would be the end. I wanted him to go back to England to recuperate. The sea journey might be hard in his weakened state, but I thought it a risk worth taking.

"I am going to send you home, Edmund," I told him. "Back to Windsor."

He began to laugh haltingly, and I thought to cry a little, though he fought to hide this perceived weakness from me. "Home….I must admit I thought I would never see it again."

"I will go to your father and inform him at once," I told him. "You will be on your way home very soon, I promise you."

Leaving Edmund in the care of the physicians, I began picking my way down the corridor to Henry's apartments. The air reeked of dung and bile; the acrid scent clung to every stone, a death-shroud. I strove not to gag and walked on with head held high even though my senses spun like a Catherine Wheel.

As I reached the door to the royal chambers, a doctor in his long black gown suddenly stopped me. His arm stretched out before me, barring my way in. He did not dare touch me, as it was forbidden to lay hands on a Queen, but he was close to doing so. "Your Grace!" he said a hoarse, parched voice. "You must not pass."

"Do not tell me what I must or must not do. I am the Queen of England, and my husband the King is beyond."

The man swallowed nervously; I watched a bead of sweat track down his wide, furrowed brow, shining like a slug's oily trail. "Your Grace, you do not understand. The King has been afflicted with this flux. In the course of mere hours, he has gone from being well to being bedridden."

"I must go to him!" I cried in alarm. Henry was no longer young; most of those who had died in this pestilence were either the elderly or the infants.

"Your Grace, I beg you do not risk yourself." The raven-black arm before me did not falter. "You have been unaffected by this pestilence so far, and by God's grace, you will stay that way. I would counsel that you retreat to England until this vile sickness has gone."

"I am sending my son Edmund home to recover," I said, "but I will never leave the King. Never. I will nurse him myself if I have to, just as I did with Edmund! Now let me pass, or by Christ, I will call the guards!"

The physician's arm dropped like a heavy stone and I flew past into the chamber. Henry lay abed, sprawled on his back, his eyes glazed and his body drenched with sweat. "Henry!" I called to him, leaning over his inert form. It seemed that he could not hear me but wandered in some other realm, caught between life and death.

Well, if there was a war on for Henry's life, Death would have to deal with Eleanor, Queen of England. I did not like to lose *anything*.

This was a deadly battle…but one I was determined I would win.

Edmund was sent back to England, despite pleading to stay when he learned that his father was desperately ill. I forbade him to remain, and he was carried from the castle on a litter and borne away towards the nearest port.

Henry continued to burn with fever and suffer the devastating flux, although his wits had returned to him. "The pain in my belly, Eleanor!" he cried, writhing beneath the sodden sheets. "I bid you go from me, for your own safety and because I do not want you to see me so unmanned."

"The doctor told me I should not be with you," I said. "I defied him, and I defy you too, even if you are King of England. I will not leave my husband when he is ill!"

"Ah, Eleanor, I fear I am dying," he gasped, as a paroxysm of pain shuddered through him. "Call a scribe to me, so that I may make out my will. I promise I shall endow you well, as you have been such a loyal wife to me through thick and thin."

I wanted to rail at him, scream that he must not convince himself he was dying, but decided that perhaps to humour him would be better. If he thought his affairs were in order, he might rest more, which would then aid his recovery.

"I will call a scribe so that your mind will be put at rest," I told him. "But you will not die, Henry. I will not allow you to! Do you hear me? I, Eleanor, forbid you to die!"

Slowly Henry began to recover. With feeble and hesitant steps, he left his sickbed and attempted to walk around the chamber. He could only take a few steps at a time before collapsing onto the shoulders of the squires that supported him, but it was enough for now. He would live. My dearest husband would live.

However, news reached me that filled me with anger and unease. I dared not tell Henry for fear of the shock driving him back to an invalid state.

Simon de Montfort had contacted the Holy Father in Rome and sent bribe money. He wanted the Oxford Provisions reinstated, along with our oaths to follow them. While Henry was still in bed recovering, Simon made a dash for England, where he drew the barons together and flung before their startled eyes a document stating the Pope had ruled the Provisions and oaths must stand.

The barons had leapt to their feet, clamouring for Simon as though he were a king. No one knew if the scroll he hurled down before them was a forgery or not, and no one seemed to care. With most of the barons firmly in his camp, de Montfort, smug and assured, returned to Paris.

But I suspected, with sinking heart, that it would not be for long. He had set the Wheel of Fate in motion.

Henry and I began the laborious journey home. The King was still weak, and had to stop many times along the way to rest; once he halted at Reims to visit a shrine where he could offer thanksgiving for his recovery. When we finally reached England, sailing over a frigid December sea, Henry was still so incapacitated by his recent illness that we stayed in Canterbury rather than risk the ride to London on the snow-bound roads.

As we travelled, more evil news reached us but this time, not regarding Simon de Montfort. Wales had risen in a new rebellion, led by Prince Llywellyn, and many of Edward's castles there were compromised. Edward was abroad in Gascony, participating in the tourneys he loved so much despite his earlier avowals to spend more time in his future kingdom.

With a shaking hand, Henry wrote a stern letter, bidding our son to remember his recent promises and return home: *This insolence should bring great concern to your heart. It is no time for a boy's wanton slothfulness. That Llywellyn breaks the truce he swore to brings great shame to you…"*

Prompted into action by his father's doleful letter, Edward rushed home with a band of mercenaries in tow. By force, he wrested back some of his pillaged castles, but a dam had been breached that was long ready to break, and even my valiant warrior son could not hold back the dreadful tide.

Simon de Montfort's presence continued to cast a spreading dark shadow over our lives. His hostile and increasingly violent young sons were at his side, and, to everyone's horror, Richard's son, Henry of Almain, betrayed his own family to ride in the company of this interloper. Richard was stunned and depressed by this treacherous defection; he loved the boy too much, had coddled him and allowed him to spend too much time with influential men who had only their own interests at heart.

Simon and his followers gathered in the city of Oxford, making a city of learning bristle with spears and swords, and insisted that the Provisions of Oxford must be reinstated immediately and the oaths renewed. Any who refused to adhere to the regulations would be exiled, their lands stripped from them. The hardest hit were my relatives, a deliberate move by de Montfort. The castles of Savoyards were attacked and looted, and they were thrown from their houses into the streets. A bishop was dragged from before the altar of Hereford cathedral and hurled into a Gloucester dungeon. Carts of plunder trundled down the streets and the cries for mercy from both men and women were ignored. "To the ports with you or perish!" they were told by Simon and his cohorts.

With the King, Edward, and Richard, I retreated to the Tower of London and together we prepared for a potential siege. De Montfort was coming for us, with baronial support. Archers marched on the tower walls, keeping guard, and ships protected the Watergate. Soldiers marched in the streets, making sure there were no disturbances, and the bridges were blocked and barricaded, with only the locals allowed to cross.

Messages arrived in London from de Montfort's approaching host: *Support the Provisions of Oxford or resist at your peril!* Swiftly the Londoners, those turncoat cowards, began to join with de Montfort's rebels. Rioting took place, and our soldiers were pushed back to safety within the Tower walls.

High in Bishop Gundulf's keep, Henry and I conferred. Richard was with us, advocating that we try to reconcile with our great enemy— doubtless, he feared for the safety of his misguided son. I counselled war—I was furious, and Edward, of my temperament more than his father's, backed me up. Torn, wavering, Henry sat on his chair, his head buried in his hands, worn-out with the strain of all that had befallen in recent months.

"We must fight them, father!" Edward whirled on his heel in sudden agitation and slammed his fist down on the nearest table, causing the goblet set there to tumble, spilling wine like blood. "Do you wish to be a laughing stock, a puppet king? That's what de Montfort and his rabble will do to you if..." his visage darkened, "even worse does not befall you. Well might de Montfort take one step further and dethrone a king."

"He would not dare..." murmured Henry.

"Would he not?" Edward's brows rose. "I am not so sure of it."

"What should we do?" I asked. "All of us, shut in here like prisoners. We need to break free, and we need money too, to pay for soldiers to aid our cause."

Edward looked thoughtful, and suddenly a crooked grin spread over his face. "I have an idea. Gather round, all of you. It is a long shot, and not without risk but I think I must try."

We gathered around the table, as candles burned low and our shadows stretched long upon the flagstones.

Edward stole out the Tower, disguised in unmarked dress, with a party of sell-swords close around him. In the twilight hours, he hastened to the Temple, where the Templars guarded the wealth of London's elite. He told the Master he had arrived to retrieve some of my jewels for an appearance I would soon make, and although the man eyed him suspiciously, he was admitted to the inner chambers. Once inside the main hall, however, he and his companions drew their swords and produced hammers, smashing into the locked boxes that contained the coin of noblemen and merchants.

Purses bulging with money (*I am only borrowing it*! he told me he had shouted over his shoulder as he left), he galloped like a madman for Windsor, seeking to head off Simon de Montfort's army. While his brother hastened to the castle, Edmund marched for Dover to control the port and bring in men and supplies from France. Some of our most stalwart supporters, such as John Mansel and my Uncle Boniface, hated with a passion by de Montfort, began to move towards Dover also, eager to take sail for their own protection. In their train they carried all their possessions, as well as a gaggle of noblewomen from Provence and Savoy who feared what their fate would be should the rebels defeat the King.

Getting wind of this ploy, Simon de Montfort sent Richard's erring son Henry to attack the party on the road to the coast. However, I had placed my own spies in the trees and bushes along the route, and they gave Edmund word of Henry of Almain's approach. My son sent out a huge contingent of soldiers from Dover, and, to his mortification, Henry was captured by his cousin and bundled onto a ship bound for France, where upon arrival he was imprisoned in the nearest castle.

Henry and I were jubilant, with our sons holding two of England's main castles, but Richard was, quite naturally, distraught when he heard that his Henry languished in a foetid dungeon somewhere near Paris.

He looked twenty years older as he sought out Henry and sank to his knees, wringing his hands in distress. "I beg you, brother—have mercy," he said, voice cracking. "Henry is young and foolish; by now he will surely have learned from his errors! Jesu, how will he survive in a dungeon? Henry, for the sake of the blood we share, forgive him his errors! Release him and sit down to the bargaining table with de Montfort and let us try to make an end to this unrest!"

"I am sorry…" I interrupted before Henry could open his mouth to answer the so-called King of the Romans. I had seen the look of uncertainty, of pity on my husband's visage. Sometimes he was not as hard as he needed to be. I was firm in his place. "It cannot happen. Not yet, at any rate. There will be no more attempts to reconcile with traitors."

Sadly, the King overrode my words within days. He could not bear Richard's pleading or the thought of his nephew imprisoned. He grew fretful and did not eat or sleep, pacing around his throne. Eventually, without conferring with me, he went to Richard and promised young Henry's immediate release. He also promised he would speak to Earl Simon, and as a token of good faith advise Edmund to hand over Dover castle to de Montfort's waiting men.

I went mad with anger; never had I been so furious with the King. "What is wrong with you, Henry? Have you gone mad?" I shouted, uncaring that I sounded like some riverside fishwife. "We held

Dover—the port! Edward is still in charge at Windsor. There was no reason to capitulate! None!"

"I am afraid, Eleanor." At one time Henry would have been angry at my outburst. Now, in the wake of his recent illness, he seemed timid and meek, crouched down before me like an old greybeard. "London is hostile; our enemies are encircling the Tower, cutting us off...."

"And what of it, husband?" I flashed. "This is the Tower of London. The mightiest fortress in the land! We have adequate supplies—we could hold out here for a year or more should our foes besiege us!"

Henry hung his head, wiping at his brow with a shaking hand. "I can bear this conflict no more, Eleanor. This horrible stalemate. I will speak truth to you. Not only have I released Henry of Almain and relieved Edmund of his duties in Dover...I have agreed to abide by the Provisions of Oxford once again. I know you will not be pleased, but I truly believe it is the only sensible thing to do. I...I do not want to end up as my sire did."

"You *are* mad!" I flushed hot and then cold. "You are handing your own kingdom away. Our son Edward's birthright. Ah, I cannot bear this folly...."

I stormed to the nearest window, stared out. Below me, the castle bailey was heaving with soldiers; further afield, past the jut of the huge walls, the citizens of London looked like a milling hive of ants. The hot July air shimmered, and stink rose from the sluggish, sunken Thames. July, hateful month, ruled by the pestilence-bearing lion and the scorching dog-star!

I felt like a captive animal myself...and that is when I reached an important decision. I could not stay here with Henry. I had to leave. Now. This very moment.

"I am going," I said abruptly, whirling away from the window embrasure.

"Going? Going where?" Henry looked alarmed now. He clutched at my hanging sleeve; I snatched my arm away as if I could not bear for him to touch me. At that moment, I could not.

"Away from here. To Edward in Windsor. To someone who will fight for his own country and not be cowed like a timid sheep!"

Henry's eyes flared with anger. "How dare you insult me, wife! You have gone too far yet again! I am the King!"

"Are you?" I said, with insolence. "I wonder."

Henry sputtered with rage, banged his curled fist against the wall. A tapestry fell, curling to the floor; he cursed and clutched his wounded hand, knuckles bleeding. "If you leave now, Eleanor, do not expect the gates to be opened again for you if you do not like what lies beyond."

"If that is your will, so be it," I said. "I will be on my way."

"God curse you, Eleanor!" he screamed at me, more impassioned than I had seen him in years, and although the thought of any curse made a little ripple of fear dance up my spine, I was not going to be dissuaded from my path.

I left the King's chamber and called for my ladies-in-waiting to bring me my travelling clothes. I was going to my brave son in Windsor. To tell him to hold against de Montfort no matter what his father said or did.

At twilight, I went down to the Watergate. The last vestiges of faded sunlight glimmered on the sucking, slopping waters of the Thames and the air was full of the squawks of milling seagulls. Carefully, my gown lifted by the two women I'd chosen to attend me, my younger damsels Roberga and Christiana, I alighted onto a small and, I hoped, innocuous barge.

Pulling away under the portcullis in the mouth of the gate, the craft slipped out into the turgid flow of the great river, the rancorous lifeblood of London.

At first, the journey was uneventful. The sun died behind the spires on the skyline and the heavens turned violet, speckled with stars like rows of glittering eyes. Fires appeared on the riverbanks, where men had gathered; London, men said, never slept.

Ahead, the dark bulk of London Bridge reared through the deepening gloom. At its terminals, the severed heads of traitors and miscreants reared on pikes, silhouetted horribly against the darkling sky. Gulls were still wheeling about them, pecking off strips of flesh. Beyond the heads, the shops that lined the bridge's long span were shuttered for the night, locked against thieves and rogues, but I could see torches flickering at their feet. Dozens of people were wandering about on the bridge, passing hither and thither fitfully. Their voices were a dull roar, mingling with the churning of the river.

The barge sailed onwards, gliding toward the bridge's central arch. Growing increasingly uneasy, I sat in silence, staring upwards. Too many people above... Had word got out that I had fled the Tower? Had someone turned their coat and betrayed me to the Londoners, who were never my friends and ever eager for my downfall?

A sudden shout from above confirmed my worst fears. "There she is, the foreign harridan! Show her what we think of her!"

The torches bobbed and dipped as the hordes on London Bridge swarmed to the railings. They heaved and clambered on the stonework, roaring menacingly. A missile flew, striking the water before the barge. Another followed it, this time landing on the barge itself. Horse dung sprayed all over us, and Roberga and Christiana squirmed and shrieked.

The barge sailed closer to the arch, the master determined to pick up speed and get us out of the bridge's ominous shadow. Stones and ordure rained down, rotten fruit tumbled through the air. A dead cat flew by, struck the barge, bounced off and went spinning away on the swell.

The onslaught grew stronger, more frenetic; the falling objects became larger and deadlier. A thrown chamber pot struck one of the crew upon the shoulder; he fell with a scream, his arm shattered by the impact.

We were so close to our assailants now, I could see their hostile, fire-lit faces, distorted by hatred, the countenances of monsters. And I could hear the words they shouted, "Get the ladders! Get her as she comes through on the other side. We'll make the bitch pay for her crimes against us!"

The barge's master heard the threatening words too; sweat ran down his pallid face. "Highness, I dare not go forward!" he said to me with urgency. "They will drop down upon us from the other side of the bridge and we will be lost. I cannot risk it. We must go back or perish."

I knew he spoke truth. Above us, the railing was black with the twined bodies of angry men. Stones were still falling, rocking the barge. I wondered how long before arrows might sail down to strike us.

"Yes, yes, you are right," I said. "We must return to the Tower at once."

Relieved, the captain hollered at his men to reverse and row as fast and hard as they might. The crowds on the bridge, seeing that their prey was making to escape, began to scream and surge forward, many of them almost falling into the river in their eagerness for vengeance. Torches were flung, tails of fire burning the sky, before they were extinguished in the muddy water.

Suddenly a small boat appeared, rowed swiftly through the gathering gloom. I started with fear, thinking my enemies had come upon me but then recognised the fur-lined red gown, hat and chain of office of the Mayor of London. He stared up at the seething mob on

London Bridge and raised his hand on high. "Halt!" he cried in a booming voice. "Cease this outrageous folly! I demand it!"

The crowd paused, surprised to see the Mayor below, and at that instant, a contingent of the Mayor's soldiers rushed onto the bridge with naked swords in hand. Fighting began as rioters sparred with the Mayor's guards.

The Mayor climbed from his small craft onto the barge, surrounded by armed soldiers. "I am Sir Thomas FitzThomas, your Grace. I will take you under my protection," he told me. "Anyone who comes near you must come through me first. Rest assured, all who have participated in this foul act will be punished, severely punished."

The barge began to glide back towards the grey ghost of the Tower, FitzThomas standing before me, hiding me from the view of any miscreant who might be watching from the riverbank.

Before long, we saw the portcullis of the Watergate. It was down, the murky waters making slapping sounds as they sucked at the rusting metal.

"Open the way!" the barge master shouted up angrily at the unlit tower windows. "We return with the Queen!"

No answer came from within the turrets that flanked the gate, though there were pale lights burning within. Someone was on guard; there always was.

The captain held out his hands in helpless fury.

My own anger kindled to life. Standing up, I shouted with all my strength, "Guard! Ignore me at your peril. It is, I, Eleanor, by Grace of God Queen of England. Open at once to me. Our party has been sore abused this night and we seek safety!"

A helmeted head appeared over the parapet. "Your Grace, forgive me, but I am under strict orders not to open the gate. To anyone."

"Are you mad, fellow? I am the Queen!"

The guard's voice was trembling. "His Grace sent word that no one was to be allowed inside the Tower after dark. Even Her Grace the Queen."

I stood trembling, in shock. My ladies-in-waiting began renewed weeping and the bargemen looked stunned.

Sir Thomas, bless him for his compassion and cool head, took control of the situation. He held out a hand to me. "Your Grace, do not despair. I promised to see you to safety. I mean to hold true to that. We will moor the barge on the riverside and I will personally take you to the Bishop of London's home."

Silently I nodded my assent and the barge rocked off to a small dock further down the river, where we disembarked. Shocked into silence by my husband's callousness, I let myself be guided by Mayor FitzThomas to Fulham Palace, where the old ailing Bishop lay on his deathbed. As the Palace gates clanged behind me, I wondered if I would ever come out safe and sound, caught here with a dying man and with hostile foes in the streets around me.

Not a week had passed before Simon de Montfort arrived in London, to hysterical cheering and celebrations from his followers. England was his.

We had lost.

Henry sent a company of armed guards for me; they straggled into the gates under a bombardment of abuse from the hostile Londoners. In silence, I took up my meagre chest of clothes and went with them. "Where am I being taken?" I asked the captain of the guards dully as we marched away from the Bishop's abode. My husband's device gleamed on his surcoat, but Jesu knows I would not have been surprised if Henry was sending me to imprisonment or other punishment after our bitter quarrel.

"Westminster, your Grace," the man replied, but he would not meet my eyes.

Surprised, I raised my brows. "Indeed? With Simon de Montfort at the helm of government in England?"

The man cleared his throat. "I have heard the Earl is permitting you and his Grace the King to reside there."

A cold sensation ran down my spine. We would be as good as prisoners, even if not confined in some sour dungeon! Sure enough, when my party reached the Palace I saw, instead of our men, the soldiers of de Montfort ringing the building. Hundreds upon hundreds of them, mailed and heavily armed. Together the King and I were permitted to take up residence in Westminster Palace, under watchful scrutiny.

As I entered the hall, the first sight I saw was Simon's banner, blazoned *Per pale indented argent and gules.* Bile scored my throat. "Your Grace..." Henry's steward swept up to me, looking haggard and worn.

"Get away from me, man," I said bitterly. "If you mean to take me to the King, I do not wish to see him! Take me to my quarters."

Still angry at being barred from the Tower while in peril for my life, I would not speak to my husband, had no desire to see his face.

However, finally, the coldness in my heart thawed, and I went to him, dressed simply, my anger suddenly turning to sorrow. Henry looked as miserable as I, and in a fit of remorse, I ran to him and wept bitterly upon his gold-clad knee. "Henry, Henry...I cannot bear how it has gone wrong between us!"

I felt his hand touch my hair. "I cannot bear it either, Eleanor."

I rubbed my damp eyes. "How could you have treated me so, barred my entrance to the Tower? I might have been killed."

"I did not know there were rioters and ruffians waiting or I never would have refused your entrance. But wife, it was your stubbornness that caused that dreadful situation. I told you not to go. Do not defy me in such a manner again. It never ends well."

"I will not," I promised—and I meant it. Never did I wish to undergo the terrible feelings I had experienced that night when I left the Tower. I was sure Henry had tired of me and would shrug as the ravening mob took its revenge. Thanks be to God on high, I was wrong, so wrong.

That night the King and Queen shared the same bedchamber.

Several days later, Simon de Montfort summoned the barons to a great council. One of his chief supporters was given the Great Seal and the authority to use it in Henry's name without conferring with the King first. Worst of all, the seal was used almost immediately to summon Henry's forces to attack Windsor, where Edward still held control.

"It is monstrous, Eleanor!" Henry cried, almost purple in the face with rage. "Using the Seal thus, it makes it look as if I make war against my own son! What will become of us? What will become of Edward?"

Seeing how the cards had fallen, Edward was furious but wise enough to know that resistance would only bring needless bloodshed. He could not win against such overwhelming odds, having only a small party of mercenaries with him. With heavy heart, he surrendered the castle and sent his army back overseas.

I refused to be beaten. I sent secret missives to Marguerite, and Louis contacted Henry on the sly. The King of France soon found a way to ease our woes and get us all out of England. When we agreed to the Treaty of Paris, this made Gascony a fiefdom of France. As Henry held Gascony, Louis could summon him to court at any time. And so he did, commanding us to come to Boulogne in September.

Simon had no option but to let us go. He was angry but he had no choice. However, instead of trying to stop us, he decided to accompany us on the journey. He had been friendly with Louis and Marguerite in the past, and such was the man's overweening confidence, I dare say he thought he could easily turn them against us.

He was in for an unpleasant surprise.

When he entered King Louis's great hall, the enraged Queen of France confronted him. Glaring, I stood beside her along with my mother, Beatrice, who began to berate him for all he had done. "You have shamed your King and shamed yourself!" she admonished. "You think men look up to you? No, most now see you only as a would-be usurper!"

"Madame, it is not so!" De Montfort was flustered, not expecting to be attacked verbally by a woman, especially an older one like my indomitable mother. "I wish only for the King and Queen and their son the Prince to uphold the Provisions of Oxford, which they swore to!"

"Which the Pope nullified, did he not?" My mother's eyes narrowed.

"No, Madame…"

"Oh, Simon…" Marguerite butted in; she was on first name terms with him from past days of greater amity. "We all know that you lied about that. The Pope agreed with Henry about the Oxford Provisions."

Simon's visage was like a brooding thunderhead. "What I do is all for the people of England! They see the land given away to foreigners…"

"Like you, Simon? Were you not born in France?" said mother lightly.

Simon ignored her, blustered on, "And not only were lands and castles handed to foreigners and marriages forced on the English nobility, the treasury was spent unwisely on fripperies and frivolous behaviour…such as acquiring worthless foreign crowns!" He stared venomously at me, his dark brows drawn together, attempting to intimidate with his feral stare.

My supporter, John Mansel, spoke up in great anger, pointing an accusatory finger at de Montfort. "You hypocrite. You confiscated my property, and what did you do with it, Simon, eh? Give it to the church, to the poor? No, you bestowed it on your monstrous brood of sons!"

Simon's lips moved; for once, he was speechless and unable to defend himself. He *had* given Mansel's lands to his sons; he could not deny it.

"I will not speak of this any longer," he huffed, nostrils flaring like those of an angry bull. "I am tired of being chided by angry women and greedy churchmen."

Hands clenched, he stalked from the chamber, leaving us all staring at his back.

I would have laughed had the situation not still been so dire.

The Provencal women and the church were steadfast against Simon, but King Louis retained some sympathies for his old friend. He insisted that Henry return to England for the October sitting of parliament, as de Montfort ordered that he do. This was ill news for us. We had little time to drum up forces to take on Earl Simon or to convince the French King of the justness of our cause.

Marguerite and I sat down in private to discuss what I should do next. "Louis still believes in the wisdom of much Simon has to say," she told me. "I am sorry, Eleanor. But perhaps we can contrive a way between us. Maybe you and Edmund could remain in France, while Henry and Edward fare to England. I am sure de Montfort would be pleased if you were not with the King since he, and so many of the English, seem to think you have an evil influence."

"Evil influence!" I snorted. "They just know that I am not biddable and easily cowed, and will not let them sway the King into folly."

"So you will stay? We can write to my brother in law Alphonse and see if he has any ships he can lend us. There must be others willing to help too. Mother will assist with her diplomatic shrewdness; she has obtained many contacts over the years."

Grimly I nodded. "I will stay in Paris. And I will raise an army. I think there is no other way, Marguerite. Earl Simon has caused gross offence to my family and to me personally. I want him defeated utterly. I dare say...I want him dead."

Henry returned to England. I had convinced Edward to work on his father, encouraging him to face down de Montfort and reject his unacceptable terms. At the October parliament, when chaos descended in the council chamber and Simon thundered that the Oxford provisions must be observed, no matter what, Henry and Edward leapt up in wrath and pushed their way out into the night and freedom.

Like a pair of furies, they rode madly for Windsor, with supporters joining them along the road. Edward had recently mollified some of the Welsh barons, and, thankfully, Richard's son, Henry of Almain, decided to abandon de Montfort's cause and join again with the King and Prince of Wales. His defection was as sweet as angelic music to my ears. It would be a hard blow to the Earl, and whispers said he was shocked and grieved to the very core—apparently, when young Henry had promised he would never bear arms against Simon, despite his renewed support for the crown, Simon had bitterly told him, "I cared not for your arms, but for the loyalty I thought you bore me. Go, and take your arms with you. I fear neither them nor you."

I laughed to hear the news, while sipping celebratory wine with Marguerite and mother, and tried to imagine Simon's face as Henry of Almain walked away, his enemy…and now our friend. The confident and arrogant Earl would, I hoped, be shaken to the core by the young lord's defection.

Something must have touched him for the first time…fear? Uncertainty? As summer stretched into winter, de Montfort suddenly contacted King Louis asking him to arbitrate between him and my husband one more time. He swore on the Rood he would abide by whatever Louis decided.

"I will speak to my husband, the King of France." Margaret came to visit me in the solar. It was a sullen, dark day, the torches barely casting light about the room, their flickering flames sending sooty smudges up the painted walls. "I cannot promise he will listen to me, and he once called himself Simon's friend, but he may."

"Do your best, my dearest sister," I laid down the tapestry I had been working on. "I know you will."

By January, King Louis had made his decision. Henry had come to France to witness the ruling, and we rode to Amiens with trepidation to learn the hand fate had dealt us. Simon had remained in England, God be praised—his high-tempered stallion had thrown him and he had broken his leg, making him unfit to travel.

"God is good, God is kind," Edmund sniggered upon hearing the news of de Montfort's injury. "We won't have to put up with the presence of that pompous traitor!"

Nervously we gathered in front of Louis' throne. Servants brought a parchment roll to the King, and he unrolled it and read aloud, his voice carrying down the hall:

"...by our ordinance we invalidate the Provisions of Oxford, and that which has arisen because of them. It is apparent that the Pope already declared them null and void, and we agree that Henry, King of England, and all others who agreed to take the oath to observe the Provisions, should be entirely free from observing them."

As he spoke the words, I could have danced for joy, but restrained myself as a Queen should. We had won, snatching our rightful positions back! Simon de Montfort had lost utterly; his cause was in ruins.

Later, I heard a wicked tongued chronicler claim that it was I who led Louis astray and made him find against Simon; he called me 'a serpent-like-fraud." Nonsense, of course; I had no special influence over King Louis.

I was not the serpent. That had been Simon, pretending to fight for the common man whilst pilfering John Mansel's lands, Simon who lied about the Pope nullifying the provisions, when his Holiness had done no such thing. Louis had seen the truth and made a fair ruling in order to bring peace.

But it was not to be.

God help us.

The French King's peace brought us war.

Simon was in shock...and then his men erupted in fury. "We will not accept the judgment of a foreigner!" they roared.

Armed soldiers marched through the towns of England and the Cinque Ports fortified themselves against the return of their rightful King. London barricaded itself against Henry's arrival and the citizens, including the justiciar Hugh le Depenser, sacked Richard's manor at Isleworth. Wales burned by the hand of Llewellyn. The young men who followed Simon also began to show their true colours. De Montfort could not hold them back. Looting and burning began. Fields were laid waste and cattle carried off. Churches were torched and pillaged, even though de Montfort had vowed to execute any man found plundering a sacred place. Even peasants were not left unharmed; their hovels raided even to the straw of their miserable beds.

Despite his growing age and lack of martial prowess, Henry was unusually stalwart in the face of such unrest. Edward was firmly at his right hand, a solid shield whose determination and fervour was infectious. In February, they sailed, despite Dover being shut to them, leaving Uncle Peter and me under instructions to muster any forces we could. Henry had also given me permission to sell the crown jewels, if necessary, in order to hire mercenaries and ships.

At first, I kept my mind occupied by writing to our potential supporters, cajoling and bartering. I emptied my thoughts of what might be taking place in England. But once the forces were gathered and armies began to move, I was left in a frustrating position—I was far across the sea, and could only wait for news, good or ill.

The first tidings that came filled my heart with gladness. Henry and Edward had ridden from their headquarters at Oxford to the town of Northampton. Simon de Montfort's son was within and the gates barred against the King, but the Abbot of the Prior of St Andrews, never entirely loyal to the Earl, breached the town walls and allowed the King's army to travel over the priory's lands.

The castle was not far away, standing like a stone giant beside the river Nene. The garrison rose to its defence, but the hotheaded Simon de Montfort the younger lost it for his father's supporters. Filled with battle fury, he had the portcullis raised and launched an assault—his charge was so wild that he lost his footing and fell headlong into the stinking town ditch! He was taken captive and his men, seeing the hopelessness of the situation, all surrendered. While they were put in chains, Henry's men sacked the town.

"It will surely only be a matter of time," I said to Uncle Peter. "When men see how easily Northampton fell, they will turn from Simon back to the King. They will know we will not be beaten."

Uncle Peter patted my hand; he looked weary, old. "I pray so, dear...but this trial is not over yet. Pray, Eleanor; it is the best thing we can do."

May. Blossom scent hung in the air, fresh in the morning. I walked in the Parisian garden, informally attired, just enjoying the tranquillity of the place, just as I had enjoyed my gardens at Winchester, Windsor and Clarendon. On such a sunny morn, it was easy to forget the troubles in the world outside.

Suddenly I heard noises; voices raised. It was too early in the morning. Tension rose in my belly in a great wave. Could it be news from England? It had to be!

Feet were clattering in the corridors that led to the garden door. Framed by the light of the burgeoning sun, I stood, a statue, as Uncle Peter approached me with an unknown man dressed in the King's livery. The stranger's hair was like thatching, his face scratched and bruised. His clothing bore tears and bloodstains.

"Your Grace." He fell on his knees before me.

I glanced at Peter, suspicious, alarmed. "He is a messenger. I know of him. He goes by Roger of Abingdon. He is trustworthy."

"What has happened?" I asked, knowing instinctively the answer would not be the one I desired to hear. Bitter bile burned the back of my throat and for a moment, my head spun.

"A battle had taken place at the town of Lewes, in Sussex," said the messenger, Roger. "Nigh on three thousand men lay dead upon the field."

"And my husband and son?" Blood drained from my face; my hands were shaking.

"Alive...but they are taken. Simon De Montfort now holds England as if he were its king."

I fainted dead away.

After I had recovered from the shock of the evil news, I had the messenger brought into the hall and, remembering courtesy, saw that he was fed and given drink, and had water to lave his hands and face.

Remarkably composed despite the situation, I sat down in a seat of estate and gestured to the man. "Now that you have supped, you must tell me all about this battle. Tell it to me as a storyteller might so that I can envision what befell my lord the King. Have you that skill, Roger of Abingdon?"

"I...I do not know, your Grace," Roger stammered, "but I swear I will try my best." Taking a deep breath, he began to tell the tale—at first haltingly and then with greater strength as his confidence started to grow.

"After the King's victory at Northampton, Simon de Montfort made to draw his Highness away from the middle shires. Jews were murdered in London—men, women, babes in arms. Simon attacked Rochester, burning the wooden bridge by the use of fire-ships. The castle held against the invaders so instead they stormed the cathedral, those sacrilegious beasts, stabling their horses in the cloisters. De Montfort could or would not halt them. The King marched to Rochester's aid and Simon moved on. His Grace pursued, faring from Tonbridge to Battle and Herstmonceaux. Here, he caught up with the forces of Simon de Montfort.

"The battle began shortly after dawn. Earl Simon crept through the forest around the town of Lewes with a rabble of men, some of whom he had pressed into service in London. He was mightily fearful of the greater numbers following the King and needed more recruits—he even took on young boys who had never fought before. He charmed them with talk of high deeds; assuming the nobility of a king or duke, he knighted them on Offham Hill where he had camped for the night."

"And Henry's men? Where were they at this time?"

Roger of Abingdon bowed his shaggy head. "Alas, Highness, the King's men had grown overconfident after their victory in Northampton. They had lazed in their own encampment all evening, drinking until their heads were pounding and their limbs heavy. It was the Feast of St Pancras and the monks of the nearby abbey, deeply disturbed by their raucous behaviour, cast curses on them."

I groaned, angry at the folly of men.

"Lord Edward acted decisively though, your Grace," Roger told me eagerly, seeing my dismay at hearing of the dissolute actions of the army. "He rose from his battle couch, donned his armour at once, and rode out with banner flying to meet the front lines of de Montfort's host. Earl Simon had ordered his unruly London rabble to go in first; they stormed over the hill like a bunch of scarecrows, clad in useless, outmoded armour and bearing rusted weapons! De Montfort had given them tabards with crosses on the breast like crusaders, but they were more like foolish children at play, being both undisciplined and untrained!"

"What happened then?" I could not believe such a pitiful-sounding force could have overcome Edward.

Roger gave a harsh laugh. "They saw the horses waiting to charge…they saw the banner of the Prince of Wales…they saw the Lord Edward on his courser, taller than all other men, with his great sword naked in his hand and flashing in the red dawn light. They ran for their lives!"

For a moment, I laughed too, imagining the terror that my tall, proud, war-like son must have struck into them by his appearance alone. Then I remembered…he had lost. "What went wrong? It must have been something terrible. Tell me."

Roger stared at the toes of his boots; so worn his big toe was poking through the aged leather on one. I would see he was supplied with new boots for his good service. "The Lord Edward went after the Londoners. He should have let them go, let the rats flee back to their holes. But he wanted to destroy them, to grind their bones into the dust. He cried aloud to any who listened that he would destroy them for the threats they made towards you at London Bridge. He galloped after the Londoners, intent on their deaths, and his men ended up spread out for miles across Sussex."

Feeling suddenly weak and giddy, I placed my head in my hands. Edward had abandoned the field, leaving his father and Richard of Cornwall to lead the battle. They were both growing old, and Richard seemed to have lost his taste for warfare after going on his last crusade. Worse, Edward had gone on this rampage because he thought he was avenging *me*. I did not care about my treatment by the accursed Londoners; God would punish them! No matter what was in the past, Edward should have stayed near his father during the battle…

"At first, when he stumbled over de Montfort's baggage train, we thought the Lord Edward's charge might have been a good thing after all. Earl Simon, still limping from his broken leg, was rumoured to be riding in a chariot with the baggage. Edward doubtless hoped to meet him there and capture him…but he was gone. Three fat London burghers were bound in the cart instead of the Earl; they were prisoners, who had apparently been caught by Simon's allies whispering about selling secrets. None knows if that tale was true or not. The burghers did not have any chance to speak. In his rage at de Montfort's absence, Lord Edward slew them, along with most of the men in the train."

I brushed aside the account of my son's violence. He was a warrior. Even as a young boy, he sometimes showed excess cruelty. "What of the King? How did he fare? And his brother, Earl Richard?"

"His Highness fought like a lion, Lady, against the might of the young Earl of Gloucester, Gilbert de Clare. Two horses were slain beneath him, yet he was not deterred. The King of the Romans, however…" he hesitated, flushed.

"Yes, what is it? What of Richard of Cornwall?"

"He lost his nerve entirely in the face of de Montfort's advance. He abandoned his men to their fates and was later found hiding in a nearby windmill!"

"For shame…" I hid my face again. To think, Richard had once been idealised in my youthful mind! No warrior was he…he was a fraud.

"When they caught him, de Montfort's men called him 'the wicked miller' and abused him with many taunts," Roger continued. "In the meantime, the King's division was pushed back into Lewes and fighting took place in the town's streets. Blood swirled in the gutters and fiery arrows shot by Simon de Montfort's archers set the roofs of the houses aflame. Eventually, the King was driven back into the gateway of the abbey…and there the enemy took him. His bodyguard fought well, keeping him from harm and defending his body with the might of their arms…Sir Phillip Bassett took twenty wounds to protect his lord."

I cast down my eyes, sorrowing. "Poor Phillip. I know him well. Always loyal. If he should survive, he will be well rewarded."

"Richard of Cornwall was marched down the street by his captors, all white from the flour in the mill. Men continued to jeer at him, laughing at his appearance and at his title 'King of the Romans'. He was dragged into the priory to be imprisoned along with the King."

"And how did they take Edward, my indomitable son?" I was nearly weeping now, trying to hold my emotions in check.

"When he could not find Simon in the baggage train, Lord Edward eventually rode back to the battlefield. I believe he expected to see victory, for the King's forces far outnumbered de Montfort's. Instead, he saw ruin and death, the town burning and his father's army scattered. He attacked his foes like a madman, trying to hew his way into the priory where his father was held, but then de Montfort's men overwhelmed him, dragged him from his steed, and bound his limbs with chains. He was made a prisoner alongside Henry."

"At least he is unharmed," I choked, tears sliding down my cheeks. "By Christ, there will be a terrible vengeance for all that has befallen at Lewes."

Then I steeled myself, wiped the tears from my face. "Thank you for your tidings, messenger. You are dismissed. I now have much to do. I will prepare to fight…to free my husband and son."

The crown jewels were first to go. They brought in a thousand pounds. Mercenaries were promptly hired from all across Europe. Marguerite and Louis stood behind me as I appealed to the Pope to bear upon de Montfort to release Henry and Edward. A papal legate was sent to confer with Earl Simon; with his arrival, came the very real threat of Simon's excommunication.

I chaffed at the bit like a wild horse, tired of waiting, of talking, of useless, endless negotiations. I wanted only to invade. I was even willing to put aside my differences with Henry's half-brothers, the Lusignans, who had escaped the aftermath of the terrible battle. They were, if nothing else, doughty warriors.

Stalwartly, I contacted Uncle Gaston de Bearn, that fickle, martial man who loved war more than women or wealth, and with sweet words and promises convinced him to join my cause. Edward's knights in Gascony were ordered to remember the service owing to their lord and gather in the Low Countries, ready to disembark for England when called for. Mother travelled to Savoy and rallied troops there, while Uncle Peter financed their pay.

"They will fight for you, Eleanor," he told me. "Your army will be huge, unstoppable. And you will lead them. You will be like a Queen from an ancient legend, riding before the troops on a white horse, inspiring them to victory."

I hoped it would be true. I was desperate and my desperation had given me the stomach to ride forth, in armour like a man, if the need was there.

But it never happened.

The papal legate sternly counselled me against war; he wanted a peaceful resolution and I was afraid to fall from his favour by opposing his will.

But the main opposition was not from the Pope, it came from...Henry. Yes, my imprisoned husband Henry, King of England. He wrote to Louis, frantically begging him to stop my efforts as quickly as he might. He was convinced that should I proceed with an invasion, his life, and that of Edward, might be in peril.

I had to think hard on his words; there was a chance he might be right. Simon could not be trusted; he could well react with violence if pushed. But how could I leave Henry and Edward imprisoned?

Even though I am a woman, I have always acted decisively. If my mind were made up to follow a certain course, I would never waver in my aims. Here, I had to stall, my mind in turmoil, the choices before me great and dangerous. For the first time in my life, I was wavering in my plans, uncertain as to what would be the correct move.

If I won, de Montfort and his allies might execute the royal hostages before my forces could reach them and free them.

If I lost, de Montfort probably would kill them anyway, to teach me a lesson, and I might join them in death...or worse.

I hesitated, waiting for a sign...from where I knew not. God? It seemed he had abandoned my family. I watched the skies by day, by night, seeking if not heavenly assurance, some sort of omen. The skies were ordinary, still.

Months drifted by, long, lingering, painful to bear. I knew my chance was drifting by too, but I could not bring myself to give the orders for the invasion of England to commence. In Canterbury, the King and Edward had been forced to swear loyalty to the Government. When Henry protested at some of the terms, Earl Simon had openly snarled at him that he would do as he was bidden if he wished to hold onto his crown. De Montfort was threatening to depose him, perhaps even to murder him. Henry hastily acquiesced, and Edward did the same grudgingly.

Unable to make any headway in all this madness, confounded by Simon's stubbornness, the papal legate excommunicated the Earl then hastily returned to Rome to report his actions to the Pope. I was left with even less guidance than before.

My army started to drift away. Winter was hurling in and the tides were turning. Soon it would be dangerous to sail, but my problems were worse than a perilous journey...I no longer had money to pay the mercenaries.

They abandoned me and returned to their homes, first just one or two at a time, then a vast flood. I was left alone in France, for the first time ever without any plans at all.

I could only listen to the rumours and tales the spies brought. De Montfort had used Henry's Great Seal to bring in his beloved Oxford Provisions once more and expand them. Foreigners were barred from holding office and chased from their lands; such hypocrisy coming as they did from a Frenchman! The King was apparently treated well enough—fed, clothed and bathed—as the Earl towed him around the country, never out of his keen gaze. This vile display was meant to show the people that the King was unharmed, but to any of intellect, it was clear it was to show his impotence, that his true powers were stripped from him. Henry was dangled before the populace like a puppet, impotent, toothless. *Sing, Henry, Smile, Henry. Pass a new law, Henry...*

From my sources, I learned that Edward, along with Richard of Cornwall and Henry of Almain, had been imprisoned in Richard's former castle of Wallingford in Oxfordshire. Poor young Edmund, my sister Sanchia's boy, was trapped there with them. They had their material needs met but were not allowed to wander outside the fortress, even in the bailey; the windows were barred and the gates permanently shut.

Edward was in the keeping of one of Simons's son, Henry de Montfort, an ardent youth who took his assignment of guarding the prisoner rather too seriously. He made himself deeply annoying to Edward, with whom he had once been close, following him whenever he walked down the hall, watching him as he ate his meals, checking on him as he slept, even trundling behind him when he used the castle privy. Edward was fuming over the indignity of it and half-wanted to strangle him, cousin though Henry de Montfort was through my one-time friend Nell. However, he dared not raise a hand or even a protest lest he risk his own or his father's life.

The messenger—Roger again—who told me the tales of my son's incarceration tapped his nose slyly, however. "I would not worry too much, your Grace. Not everyone is happy with de Montfort's enforced rule, or with seeing the young prince, God bless him, in captivity. There are rumours that supporters of the crown are going to try to break Lord Edward out of Wallingford."

"Really?" I could have kissed the man...save that he was sweaty from the road and smelled none too sweet. "Where are they gathered? Who are they? I must get a message to them."

"I daren't tell you, Highness, I am sworn not to say anything...to anyone," Roger said ruefully. "But I can tell you this; at the moment, they gather in Bristol. I can take a message if you wish, your Grace. I know who to look up."

"Yes, yes, please do; you will have my eternal gratitude." I summoned a scribe, but took quill and parchment myself, sending the man away so that none would know my words. Hastily, I penned a note to the would-be rescuers of my son, commending them for their fidelity and bravery and telling them what I knew of the state of Wallingford castle. The walls of inferior thickness and there were surprisingly few guards, considering the important prisoners held within; perhaps de Montfort thought his newly placed bars and gates would keep his prisoners secure. Or perhaps in his overbearing arrogance, he merely imagined that no one in England would dare try to break his highborn prisoner out.

I watched as Roger departed, my message concealed within his jerkin, and hoped for a miracle. As he vanished on his horse into the distance, a cloud fell across the sun. Shivering, I turned away.

Bad news came again. Roger of Abingdon was back in France, leaner and more wayworn than ever. "I am so sorry, your Grace," he said, hanging his head. "I bear evil tidings once more. The rescue attempt failed."

"Tell me." My voice was a crow's croak through strained throat muscles.

"Edward's followers rode from Bristol in the dead of night, under a dark moon. They slept by day, travelled the roads after dark. At length, they reached Wallingford castle, and as you described, Sovereign Lady, found it poorly manned and with weak walls. After the moon had set and all lay in complete darkness, they made their attack, valiantly ripping down part of the curtain wall and storming the inner bailey. Men fell before their onslaught, and it looked as though they might be victorious and free the prince but then…" He shook his head, knotted his grimy hands in sorrow. "Then the Lord Edward's gaolers hauled the prince to the top of the keep, dragging him to the edge of the parapet with a dagger held to his throat. They shouted down to the rescuers that they would fasten him to a mangonel and catapult him over the walls if the attackers came any closer."

I groaned in misery. What a terrible threat! "What happened to my son the Prince after that? Can you tell me, good Roger?"

Roger nodded. "De Montfort moved him, first to Kenilworth and then Hereford. Farther away from centres of rebellion."

I sat still, my hand pressed to my cheek. "Well, at least I was justified in not bringing a huge army to England. My fears would have proved true; they would have murdered him."

"Aye, your Grace, I deem you right. They are desperate men. And may become yet more desperate."

"What do you mean?"

Roger glanced up suddenly, with a gap-toothed grin. "Not all my tidings are dire. There is a fracture in de Montfort's party. Not all are happy with his rule, And then there is…Gilbert de Clare."

"Gloucester? What about him? Is he not de Montfort's man? Didn't he take Henry of Almain and Earl Richard prisoner at Lewes?"

"He did, your Grace but they have since had a falling out. Earl Simon has not abided by the old rules of warfare. All of Earl Richard's lands should, if custom were followed, go to de Clare. Earl Simon took them for himself. Same with the captives; they should have been placed in Gilbert's charge and their ransoms paid to him. But, no, Simon has hold of them and any monies paid will fill *his* coffers. It caused a great row, and de Clare had now fled to join the Welsh lords of the March. De Clare is a powerful man, and influential; this is a great blow for Simon de Montfort. He had learned that not everyone loves what he has done…especially when their own interests are ignored."

It was time for me to do something. A full-scale invasion was impossible and dangerous but something smaller scale was not impossible. Taking horse, I headed to Gascony where I raised a force of men in Edward's name. William of Valence brought men too; for the first time, I could have greeted that Lusignan with joy. Louis gave safe passage to all the soldiers and they sailed—not for England but for Wales. Once there, they met with Gilbert de Clare, who was now openly protesting against de Montfort's rule, and with all the Welsh lords who remained loyal to Edward.

Things were moving, but I, still trapped on foreign shores, could only wait. I grew thin with worry, could not settle to womanly arts, which seemed pitiful and meaningless, a waste of my time.

I thought only of battle, and of revenge.

Edward had escaped his captors.

At last, God had smiled on us after long troubles. The tidings poured over the Channel, reaching eager ears all over France, Provence and Savoy.

Edward had been imprisoned in Hereford, Henry de Montfort still sniffing behind him like some peevish guard dog, watching his every move. A band of other young de Montfort supporters was also billeted at the castle; one man amongst them was Thomas de Clare, the younger brother of Gloucester. A persuasive secret message had arrived for him from Gilbert and on an impulse, he decided to turn his coat and join his brother's cause.

Decision made, Thomas bravely carried a message to Edward, telling him that my men and de Valence's had arrived in Wales and that his own brother had defected from Earl Simon's cause. Along with this message, he also brought a letter from Maud Mortimer of Wigmore. An ardent support of the King, Lady Maud suggested a ruse in which Edward might gain his freedom.

Edward decided to attempt Maud's plan, which was simple and yet dangerous should it fail. His gaolers were impatient young men, temperamental and fed up with lounging about a remote castle with little to do. "Come, lads," he said to them, turning on the charm as he could do at will, "the day is fine and here we sit like withered greybeards! Let us go out of this reeking old castle, and do something amusing. If we do not see to our fitness, soon we will be fat and unable to fight!"

"What do you propose?" Henry de Montfort asked, a hint of suspicion in his voice.

"A race, a race on horses...up to the nearest line of trees, nothing more. Don't worry, Cousin Henry, I know you are not stupid, I am not going to ask you to close your eyes while I run and hide in a game of Hoodman's Blind!"

The other youths had roared with laughter.

"I do not know about this plan. My father might not approve." Henry was still uncertain.

" 'My father might not approve'!" Edward mocked. "God help us, how old are you, Henry? Ten? Or are you just afraid of me?"

Henry made to retort angrily, but the other young men, bored and restless, began to clamour in favour of Edward's idea. "Come on, Henry! Do not spoil the day! Let us race; we have had enough of moping inside these four stone walls!"

Grudgingly Henry gave in. "But my eyes will be locked on you," he warned Edward.

"First, I must find a decent horse," said Edward. "You won't object to that, will you, Henry? You, of course, can try out various horses too, if you wish. And the others."

"I have a fine horse already," retorted Henry. "My father gave it to me. My men here also have swift, strong steeds; I have seen that they are well supplied."

"Well, it is only me who needs a horse then," said Edward, "since mine was stolen from me at Lewes."

Seeking the stables, Edward began to test the stamina of various horses, galloping back and forth in the bailey, rejecting this one, that one, clambering onto another, checking the hooves, the mouth. The others joined him, galloping alongside him on their own coursers as he made to decide. "Come on, Edward," Henry de Montfort sighed. "Choose. You waste the day."

Edward's eyes swept over the horses. "That one then." He pointed to a sleek bay that danced with nerves and with energy. "I wager that horse will be fastest of them all."

"You did not even try that beast!" snorted Henry. "It looks skittish to me."

"You didn't give me the chance to try it! Nonetheless, I like its look best of all; it is the one I will have."

The youths trotted out over the drawbridge of Hereford and fared into the nearby fields. "The race will go to those trees, no further." Henry de Montfort pointed to the line of oaks on the near horizon. "Do you understand me, Cousin Edward?"

Edward mounted his chosen steed, the slender bay. "I understand you perfectly, Henry...but I fear you do not understand *me*!"

Suddenly he swung out with his fist, knocking his gaoler to the ground with a split lip, and then he clapped his heels to the bay stallion's flanks. He thundered away in the direction of the Welsh borderlands, with Thomas de Clare riding like a fury on his heels, joining him in his bid for freedom.

Shouting and cursing, the rest of the youths galloped after Edward, intent on his capture...but my son had been correct. His steed, unridden that morning while the others tired out their horses careening around the bailey, was by far the fastest.

In the distance, at the river ford, he could see a party of armed men in the Mortimer colours, waiting for his arrival.

He was free! With the Mortimer knights surrounding him and Thomas de Clare, forming a barrier of iron, he went galloping away to safety at Wigmore where the Lady Maud was waiting to greet him.

I went down on my knees and gave thanks to God for his safe release, but soon I was up again, my mind in a renewed state of turmoil. Edward's rescue had unleashed the whirlwind. He would attack de Montfort, I knew that, and give no quarter to his enemies. Either Simon or Edward would perish in the forthcoming fray.

But which would it be? Simon was older, had been a soldier for many years. Edward was winning renown for his prowess on the fields but he was young and could be as impetuous as he was ruthless. A wrong move, as had happened at Lewes, could be fatal.

Once again, I could do nothing but stay in my chambers and pace, eaten up by worry, waiting for tidings from across the rough grey sea.

Chapter Ten

August 4. A canopy raised over me to keep off the heat of the sun, I stood beneath a cloudless sky. A strange tension hung in the air and my stomach was in knots; I knew not why such unrest gripped me.

All of a sudden, a hot wind began to blow, whipping up huge swirls of dust within the gardens of the castle where I was lodged. Maids shrieked and ran, pennants were torn from their moorings, a pavilion went down like a deflated blancmange at the banqueting table. The heads of the nearby roses were torn off and petals showered all over me, crimson, ruby, scarlet, like droplets of new-fallen blood.

"It is an omen," I murmured, and as I glanced at the sky, I saw that the blue was fading away, erased by a storm sweeping in from the west, sudden and ferocious; great dark clouds lifted like towers, black and yellow, crowned by fierce lightnings.

With my ladies-in-waiting surrounding me, Christiana shrieking as her headdress blew off, Willelma's daughter Isabel trying to hold hers on, we raced toward the castle hall just as the storm-rain began to lash and the lightning bolts pounded with deadly fury all around us.

A visitor came, riding in from the coast. It was Henry of Almain, Richard's son. He looked exhausted and stubble darkened his young face, but he smiled wearily as he was brought before me. He knelt, head bowed. "My gracious Queen, my dearest aunt," he said. "I have come to tell you of a great victory. The Lord Edward has defeated Simon de Montfort at the field of Evesham. He has utterly crushed the rebels; there are almost no survivors amongst our foes."

Around me the room spun; dark spots danced before my eyes. I shook my head to clear the uneasy sensation. "Henry!" I embraced him, kissed his cheek. "You have brought tidings long wished for. Tell me what happened. Here, be seated..." I gestured him to a stool and called for a servant to bring wine.

"Thank you, your Grace," he said, sitting down with a bit of effort. "Ah, I am all bruises from the fight!"

"How is my son?" I asked.

"Unharmed, and revelling in victory. I will tell you of it, though some parts may not be fit for a noble lady's ears."

"I think my ears will survive, Henry," I said wryly, with a little laugh.

"Then I will begin, your Grace. At the end of July, Edward had gathered a great force, almost twice that of de Montfort. He marched first to the castle of Kenilworth, where the Earl of Leicester's son, also Simon, was ensconced with his troops and took them unawares. Simon the younger only escaped narrowly, rowing in a boat over the great moat. Having thrown the youthful de Montfort's forces into disarray, Edward then hastened towards Worcester where he deemed the Earl was lurking. His intelligence was correct; the enemy was there.

Near the town of Evesham, de Montfort brought his army in readiness, crossing Bengeworth Bridge…a foolish move, for once over the bridge, his route of escape could easily be blocked behind him. He must surely have thought upon it, for he was no fool, but he decided to proceed nevertheless; he had not received word of his son's predicament at Kenilworth. He attended Mass within the great abbey that stood at Evesham, praying before the relics of four holy men— Egwin, the founder, and Wigstan, Credan and Odulf. Men say the Virgin Mary herself had once appeared at Evesham, to a swineherd called Eof…but on that day Our Lady and Christ himself finally turned their faces from that traitor."

"You loved him once," I said softly. "Even when you left his side, you swore not to raise arms against him."

"I was deceived." Henry of Almain flushed to the roots of his hair. "And as he scorned me and my use of arms, so he had to find out that others did not scorn my valour."

I bowed my head. "Continue, Henry…I did not mean to bring you discomfort. The young often make foolish mistakes."

Henry cleared his throat. "When the Earl left the abbey after hearing Mass, he was met by his barber, a man called Nicholas, who had climbed the abbey tower as a lookout. Nicholas spotted a vast host approaching through the dawn mist, and at first was heartened for he recognised de Montfort's banners but his initial joy quickly turned to terror. As the soldiers drew nearer, he could see some of the banners were torn, some bloodied; they had been taken in conflict. Fearful, he raced down the spire to find his master, crying out, "My lord, my lord…we are undone! By the Rood, we are all dead men, for we are surrounded by our enemies and not by our friends!"

"De Montfort then went to look for himself and it is said he spoke calm but terrible words to the knights gathered around him, "Commend your souls to God, my friends, for they…" he gestured to the marching host, "*they* will have our bodies." He knew, even then, that he was doomed."

"Go on." I leaned forward, almost indecently eager. In my mind's eye, I could see Simon's eyes, so well remembered—those hard, wolfish eyes that both attracted and repelled.

"De Montfort gathered his army and began to march towards Green Hill. He had the King with him…"

My poor husband! I crossed myself.

"…dressed in Simon's own colours to disguise him, and with an oversized helmet placed on his head, so loose and ill-padded he scarce could see. When the Earl reached the hill and the road beyond, he found it blocked by the men of Lord Edward and the Earl of Gloucester. He began a frantic attack, attempting to ram his way through the middle of their forces and escape."

"But he did not succeed."

Henry shook his head. "He was determined, my Lady, that was for certain. The line of Lord Edward's army broke…briefly…in the centre. But then Roger Mortimer arrived from his castle of Wigmore, bringing up more troops from the bridge. The trap had been sprung."

"And then…?" My breath railed between my teeth as I tried to envision the carnage of that distant field in Worcestershire.

"As a huge thunderstorm descended, almost like a token from heaven, Edward's army slaughtered that of the Earl of Leicester. Nigh all of them. Few prisoners were taken, no ransoms were desired. Henry de Montfort was cut down before his father's very eyes. His son Peter was also slain. Hugh de Spenser, John de Beauchamp and many more… All slain, all food for the crows."

"And the King? What of the King?" I almost dreaded asking. I knew Edward was victorious and unharmed, but what of my husband, an old man, weakened from illness, dragged into the fighting on the enemy side?

Henry of Almain bit his lip. "He is safe, your Grace, fear not…but I must tell you, he is wounded and suffering from fright. Simon had hold of him within his inner circle of knights. He cried out constantly, *I am the old King, I am Henry of Winchester! Do not harm me…I am an old man and unable to fight*! Nonetheless, he was hurt in the melee and driven to his knees. Luckily, the helmet Simon had forced him to wear fell away and he was recognised and pulled from the fray. Edward took his father to safety himself, then rejoined the battle."

I gasped a heavy sigh of relief. The King was safe if the worse for wear.

"When Edward returned to the battlefield, the slaughter was terrible. De Montfort's men began to flee. They drowned in the river and were cut down in the garden of the abbey, even in the nave of the abbey church itself. Their blood polluted the steps to the high altar."

I crossed myself again, envisioning that mad final flight of the rebels...and the rage of my warlike son.

"The circle of knights around his Montfort broke. His standard-bearer, Guy de Balliol, was slain. De Montfort's horse was speared and fell beneath him. And that...." Henry of Almain took a deep breath. "That, God be praised, was the end."

"I want to know." My voice came out hard and cruel. "More. All of it."

"Your Grace?" Henry looked dubious; he reddened again.

"You heard me, Henry. All of it."

"Edward's men closed in, like leopards around prey. They chanted at their quarry, tormenting him: *Old traitor, old traitor, it is not possible that you shall live.* Then Roger Mortimer surged forward, tired of the baiting and eager to finish it. He stabbed de Montfort in the neck, and as the Earl fell to the ground, others leapt upon his body, hacking and hewing." Henry licked his lips. "Men vented their anger upon the traitor's dead body. They stripped him and cut off his head and hands. They also..." He stared at the tiled floor, embarrassed, "cut off his...his...ballocks and draped them across the nose of his severed head...I am sorry, Madame, to foul your ears with such horrors but you..."

"Asked for it, Henry. Asked for it. Yes, Henry, I did. And what became of his remains after that?"

"The monks of Evesham took the torso for burial. The hands and feet were sent about the kingdom. The head—and its...its decoration— was sent to Lady Mortimer at Wigmore, in honour of her husband Roger, who struck the fatal blow. It is said she held a banquet that very eve, with de Montfort's head towering above the high table on a spike."

"A hard woman," I said, "but she saved my son."

"Indeed. Much is owed to Lady Maud's courage."

I stood up, turning my back on Henry of Almain and gazing up into the summer's sky. It was of the deepest blue, royal blue, all storms now past. Simon de Montfort was dead, and never more would those wild, yellowish wolfish eyes haunt me again, those brutal eyes that repulsed and yet intrigued at the same time. My husband was King once more, unchallenged. The treacherous barons were slain almost to a man.

I was Queen and no longer needed to linger in exile.

I was going home.

Chapter Eleven

Homecoming was a strange time. Although they did not hiss or boo my passage in the wake of Simon's failure, the people of England yet did not cheer me as part of the victorious party. They looked on, almost blank-faced as if I had become, almost overnight…somehow irrelevant.

It was my son, Edward, imposing and terrible in his polished golden armour, who was cheered, along with his wife, Eleanor of Castile, his dutiful little shadow. She was, I had to grudgingly admit, a fine counsellor, filling her husband's ears with wisdom while keeping her own profile that of a meek, demure wife. She had borne no sons, only several daughters who had died shortly after birth…but there was still time. Plenty of time. I noted that no one spread cruel rumours of barrenness about *that* Eleanor.

I was taken to reunite with my husband in London, and we fell upon each other with many embraces and tears—but how aged he seemed, how frightened and tremulous. His shoulder was wounded and in bandages, and pained him greatly, the sight of which made me weep anew.

"We will live quietly now, Eleanor," he said, holding me as if he feared I might run away. "At Winchester and Clarendon, or even your small castles in the wilds—Ludgershall and Marlborough. Anything of import that needs to be done, let Edward handle it. The people love him as they do not love me, and he has strength of body and mind that I do not."

So we retired to our various homes, and let Edward deal with the last pockets of rebellion burning in England, particularly that of the younger Simon de Montfort, who had holed up behind the broad red walls of Kenilworth. The castle eventually fell to Edward's siege engines but Simon escaped and fled abroad, along with his brother Guy, who was still half crippled from the injuries he received at Evesham.

Henry and I might have faded into the background of political life had it not been for the parliament held in Winchester in September of 1265. Here Edward was given Dover and Edmund was handed Simon de Montfort's earldom. London was fined for its treacherous behaviour and support of the rebels, and London Bridge…Well, Henry awarded it to me, in memory of the infamous day when I was attacked there while on the river.

Between the fine of £1000 and my taking possession of the bridge, it was too much for those still of rebellious nature. Troubles broke out across England. Towns burned and men were murdered in their beds. Like so many times in the past, Henry and I retired to the safety of the Tower, fearful of the potential rise of another man like Earl Simon.

Edward and Edmund fought valiantly, keeping our foes at bay.

As months slipped into years, an uneasy peace descended...

Having an ever-active mind, I kept abreast of all that happened in both England and abroad; I was never the type of woman to be satisfied solely with needlework and such mindless if proper niceties. I noted the activities of my youngest sister Beatrice and her husband Charles, the younger brother of Louis of France—they were busy claiming the throne of Sicily, which I had once earmarked for my son Edmund. When his name had been withdrawn from candidacy, a crown-hungry Charles had snapped at the chance like a starving dog snaps at meat. He had taken an army over the Alps, and Beatrice had ridden with him, defying all danger—they were crowned in Saint Peter's church in Rome.

At last Beatrice, whose jealousy of her sisters had pained our hearts, who with sadness we suspected of harbouring Simon de Montfort's supporters, was at last a queen herself. But a queen without a proper throne or country—Manfred still held Sicily and Charles would have to fight him...to the death.

And so he did, against great odds, with the lives of many Frenchmen given for the cause. Manfred had Saracen bowmen amidst his troops and fearsome German cavalrymen. However, one of Charles' keen-eyed knights noticed a chink in the armour of the enemy—their armpits were exposed when they raised their swords to strike. "To your daggers!" he exhorted the French troops, and they cut down their enemies through the weak spots of their mail.

After long and vicious fighting, Manfred's army broke and scattered. No one knew where Manfred himself had gone; he had vanished during the rout. But two days later a common soldier wandered into a nearby town, leading a mule stumbling beneath a heavy load while calling out in mocking tones, "Who buys Manfred, who buys this usurper?' And when men came running to see what the commotion was about, they saw the body of Manfred slung across the back of the mule.

So Beatrice really was Queen now; she was an equal. I did not care any longer, as long as she left us alone.

She had no time to do anything otherwise. In July of that year, she sickened and died while her husband was besieging a castle. Her corpse was sent home to Provence, to lie beside the tomb of our esteemed father, Raymond Berenger.

I could pray for her; that was all I could do for Beatrice now. Guiltily, I thought prayers would have to do, as I had never loved her much in life, the smallest sister I had known so little, and who had envied all her siblings to the point she would have betrayed us.

Evil also befell Marguerite. Saintly, faith-driven Louis decided to attempt another Crusade. Desperately, vainly, she tried to dissuade him; his ministers tried too. He would not be moved. He ordered his lords to gather to him at fear of his displeasure. Even nobles confined to the sickbed were not excused from attendance at his court in Paris where he discussed his plans for warfare in the east.

Although the older barons, remembering Louis' earlier failed Crusade, baulked at faring to the Holy Land once more, crusading fever began to run rampant amongst the uninitiated young. The Crown prince took the cross; so did Marguerite's other sons Jean Tristan and Peter; so too did her daughter Isabelle.

The unwholesome fighting fever spread, as I feared it might, to my son Edward, who had grown bored as the unrest died down in England. He had no money to fare away on campaign but Louis, glad of his young nephew's fervour, offered to lend him a veritable fortune. Henry and I prayed that the idea of repaying such loan for years on end might turn Edward aside from this path, but he remained enthusiastic and determined.

He came before our high seats, all fire and passion, his eyes alight like brands. Edward loved nothing more than war, though Eleanor his wife came surprisingly close. "It will be a great honour, can you not see that, mother, father? A great honour to convert the wild infidels, to bring the pagans to God or put them to the sword!"

"Please remain in England," I said, speaking calmly for I knew argument would avail me not at all. "Remember that Louis was unsuccessful years ago, and the results devastating. The loss of life to the heat, to illness, to treachery, to the paynim sword…"

"Louis didn't have me at his side then, did he?" Edward interjected with overweening confidence. He tossed his head arrogantly. "Those foreign dogs shall submit or perish."

"What about your wife, your children?" I tried to prick his conscience, make him think about Eleanor of Castile. And of the children they had produced after such a long wait, all still small and in the nursery.

"That is all decided," he said. "The children shall remain here, but Eleanor will travel with me. She is as eager to go as I am."

I stared at my hands. Henry, silent next to me, looked sick at heart but said nothing.

"Will you not at least give me your blessing?" Edward's temper began to rise; he clearly noticed our lack of enthusiasm.

"I would rather you stayed here and assisted with the running of the realm," said Henry at length. "I am old, my son, and weakened by the injuries received at Evesham and Lewes…"

"Both years ago now! You will live, father!" Edward snapped. "I cannot believe you both want me to remain here, frittering away my time in pointless tourneys between dull castles full of dull courtiers, when I could be riding into battle on God's business! How could you not support my just cause?"

"I support you!" My heart sank as my second son, Edmund, stepped up to his brother and clasped his hand in amity. Edmund had always been in his brother's huge, tall shadow; robbed of the crown of Sicily, he was looking to make his own mark in some way.

Edward clapped his sibling on the shoulder, obviously pleased. "Then we shall do it. Our cousin Henry of Almain is eager to come to the Holy Land too. We shall ride out and make the unrighteous quail before us."

Henry and I kept silent. We could not dissuade our hotheaded sons. They were not boys any more, easy to command; they were stern men with wills as hard as the steel they wielded.

With their companies of knights, they rode for the town Northampton, where, along with Henry of Almain, they took the Cross in the church of All Souls. Then they were on their way to Louis' Crusade, leaving England and their families behind him.

Neither of my sons ended up fighting for Louis in the end.

Disaster befell. The French king sailed to African shores and marched towards the ancient city of Carthage, with its primaeval columns jutting out like broken spears from amidst newer fortifications. He camped on the swampy plain outside its sprawling walls, and in the terrible heat of that accursed land, foul humours arose and brought plague and pestilence to his army.

Jean Tristan, born all those years ago on his sire's earlier Crusade, sickened and died almost immediately, while the Crown Prince fell ill but fought through. Lords died, retching into the fetid desert soil, common foot soldiers fell and never rose again. Priests collapsed too, prayers shrivelling on dusty, parched lips; even the attending papal legate died, choking in his own bile as the pestilence took hold.

Louis himself sickened. His bowels and belly heaved. He was weak already and aged; his doctors knew he would not survive. Feeling his demise near, he called for a special bed to be prepared, strewn with grey ash to signify the transience of mortal flesh. His heir Phillip, weak, stumbling and thin as a skeleton from his own sickness, came to kneel at his bedside and be given his blessing and final words about how to be a good King to the people of France.

Then Louis placed his emaciated hands together, raised his eyes to heaven, and cried, *"I will worship in Thy Holy Temple. O Jerusalem! Jerusalem!"* And with that, he expired, his body worn beyond mortal endurance by illness, sorrow, and regret.

Edward and Edmund arrived in Tunisia long after King Louis' death and found Charles of Anjou in control, and turning the situation with Emir Mohammed to his advantage. The French, glad to abandon the campaign of death and destruction, were already pulling out of the country and making for Sicily.

Edward, Edmund and Henry of Almain decided to go with them, for they had few choices…and misfortune chased them like a living entity with Death firmly towed in hand.

First, a storm battered all the crusaders' ships, sinking many even as they reached the shelter of the Sicilian harbour. Isabelle of France's husband, the Navarrese king Theobald, died in port, overcome by illness. Isabelle herself began the arduous journey home almost right away but succumbed to the rigours of the road shortly after. Isabella, the pretty and heavily pregnant young wife of the new French king, Phillip, also died on the journey back to France. In a mountainous region of Calabria, she was flung from the saddle when her mount stumbled on stony ground and her spine snapped in the fall. She gave birth to a dead child upon her own deathbed.

Unwilling to have journeyed so far for nothing, Edward decided to continue the crusade despite the bereaved French returning home. He would go to Acre with Edmund. He released Henry of Almain from his service, however, asking him to seek Gascony and tend it in his absence. And it was there, when Henry paused at Viterbo to pray within a church, that Guy and the younger Simon de Montfort, who had joined forces with Charles of Anjou, fell upon their cousin unawares, intent on terrible revenge.

Before the high altar, while he was on his knees, they stabbed him with long daggers, and his life-blood slid across the tiles, a crimson banner, and fouled all that was holy. Then Guy, the more vicious of the two brothers, grabbed Henry by the hair and dragged his lifeless body from the church, leaving a trail of blood like a beacon to his unforgivable sin, and he threw the body onto the dusty ground and mutilated it horribly in revenge for his father....

The word of Henry's murder came to Richard of Cornwall while he was at court. His face turned the colour of driven snow and he clutched at his heart; I thought he would fall and die before our very eyes.

Wine was brought and the Earl was escorted to a bench. "Oh Christ, no...my son, my son!" he moaned. "How could they kill him with such dishonour? And after young Simon was extricated from Kenilworth, to think I begged for clemency for him! The de Montforts are serpents, murderers, assassins...and defilers of God's House."

Grabbing a nearby vase, he hurled it against the wall; it shattered as his heart had shattered at the news of Henry's murder. Then, his angry outburst done, he began to weep. "What shall I do? My heir is dead! Henry is dead..."

"My lord," I said to him gently, "this is indeed a great tragedy but do not forget, you have another son."

"Eh?" Richard gazed up at me blearily, with reddened eyes. It was as if he had forgotten young Edmund, his son with Sanchia, altogether.

"Edmund," I said softly, thinking of the pious, good-natured young lad, so like my dead sister in looks and temperament.

"Oh, yes...yes, Edmund. The boy..." Richard wiped his eyes on his sleeve. "I must go, make arrangements for Henry's coffin to be brought to England. He will be buried in our church at Hailes, God assoil him."

Inconsolable, Richard staggered unsteadily to his chambers, supported by his squires.

Henry and I could offer no comfort, just hope such a fate did not come to either of our sons, both making their way into the steaming deserts of the Holy Land.

Henry of Almain was buried in Hailes Abbey in a tomb beside that of Sanchia. A fine alabaster effigy was set atop it; the young man in prayer. Before burial, his heart had been removed and sent to Westminster for special interment there.

Richard never recovered from the shock of his eldest son's murder. He fell into melancholy and drank too much, day in and day out. He grew thin and haggard, and his hair whitened. He took another wife, the renowned beauty Beatrice of Falkenburg, which surprised everyone, but his health seemed so poor, I would not be surprised if the union was never properly consummated.

In December, he attempted to celebrate Christmas with a splendid feast. As the revellers dug in and the entertainment began, he suddenly stopped eating at table and stared dazedly ahead, as if he saw ghosts or visions. He could not move or speak and his mouth drooped; it was as if the right side of his face was candle wax, melting.

An apoplectic fit the physics said, brought on by his grief; the ailment the country folk called 'elf-stroke' for its awful, sudden devastation to the body.

He never recovered. Four months later, he passed into the care of God, his final trials over. After his heart was removed and sent to the Oxford Greyfriars, he was buried at Hailes, alongside his beloved son Henry and my poor, gentle sister Sanchia, of so little import in the scheme of things that the people of England even got her name wrong.

The King was unwell too, his maladies worsened by the death of his brother, whom he loved despite all their quarrels. He was like a great oak with its limbs gradually being lopped off. He never recovered wholly from the injuries taken at Evesham and he walked with a marked limp. He had agues and griping of the bowels and strange aches and pains that made him breathless. He was terrified of renewed rebellion and for the welfare of both our sons. He wrote to them, in a spidery, shaking hand, and begged them to return, *"for I am ill, and not like to last much longer, being five and sixty and sore pressed with many griefs."*

After an eternity, a letter came from Edward. Short. Abrupt. *"I must carry on with what I have sworn to do, lord father. God be with you in your trials, and I pray you kneel at the Confessor's shrine and ask him that he may assist with mine."*

Henry cast the terse letter on the fire, bowed over like a willow tree, full of sorrow. "I am an old man, and failing, Eleanor," he said. "And my own sons hate me."

"They do not hate you," I chided.

"I need the doctor to be summoned." Henry pressed his yellow, spotted hand to his belly. "I am unwell, Eleanor...unwell."

Henry did not recover. He lay in his bed, drugged with calming droughts, and stared at the gilded ceiling. He was dying, I knew it.

I tried to keep his condition secret, in fear of uprisings in the kingdom, but servants' tongues flapped all too often, and soon reports reached me of fighting in the streets, of petty lords building illegal castles and stealing others' goods and lands.

As November rolled around, with its harsh, screaming gales and sunless skies, I feared the end for my dear husband was near. We were at Westminster, and outside the Palace the Londoners rioted, burning our effigies in the streets, bursting with wrath because of the strictures we had placed upon them long ago. I dared not show my face nor move to quell the troubles lest I inflame them more. I could not risk another London Bridge.

The priests gathered around the King, ready to give final unction. Barons clustered in the halls, awaiting the passing of their monarch in strained silence. Gilbert de Clare, Earl of Gloucester, was foremost amongst them, and surprisingly kind; upon bended knee, he swore to uphold Henry's last wishes and to help quell the unrest in the realm when he is gone.

Soon it would be time for me to leave the room, to leave my husband of so many years to the mercy of God.

Gently I placed my hand on Henry's clammy brow, gazed into the pallid face and suddenly, as a shaft of light fell through the window casement, it seemed wondrous, as if all his lines and wrinkles were melting away, and he was becoming a young man again.

"Eleanor..." he whispered, his voice a broken rasp over flaking lips. His eyelids flickered...and then he was gone.

Outside, beyond the palace precinct, the rioters screamed and howled like demented animals. I could hear glass shattering and women screeching...and then, drowning the ruckus out, the passing bell began to toll, slowly, sadly, endlessly.

My time as Henry's Queen was over.

He was buried in Westminster, that place he loved so and had rebuilt in such splendour. I did not attend, as crowned heads do not attend the funerals of other crowned heads, but I was told of the funeral in detail. First, he was laid in state, wearing a funeral crown and his coronation robes; men poured in to see, and weep, and wonder. Never had Henry looked so magnificent, so kingly; and his quiescent face bore a peace that it had not borne in life, the wrinkles and cares smoothed out in death. Gilbert de Clare attended him, along with John de Warenne and Humphrey de Bohun; as the King was laid to rest, these great magnates all knelt to swear an oath of fealty to Edward, their new King. Edward, first of that name.

Edward, who was far away, in the blazing heat of Acre, with his brother Edmund at his side.

Grieving, clad in widow's weeds, I went to my castle of Windsor and waited for my sons' return from crusade. I suspected the wait would be long, and I was lonely, although I did have my grandchildren with me at the castle in the royal nursery. After her long delay in conceiving, Eleanor of Castile had produced two living children. There was little Henry, nicknamed Hal, a frail and sickly little boy who was now heir apparent after the loss of another son, John, who died in 1271. I loved him dearly; perhaps he reminded me, sweet and fair and doomed, of my lost daughter Katharine. His sister, pretty clever Eleanor, who we called Leonor, was in residence with him, along with their cousin John, child of my daughter Beatrice of Brittany, who we called by his pet name—Brito.

The children gave me great joy, and my prayers were answered in one respect—the younger of my sons had returned home, sunburned and sorrowing, but hale. I greeted him with great joy and many tears.

"I thought I might not see you again, Edmund," I told him. "So little news came, and after the devastation that overtook the French….I scarcely dared hope you would return unscathed."

"God smiled on us, and hopefully will continue to do so on my brother, the King, who serves Him in Acre still." Edmund, who had been somewhat frivolous and light-minded as a boy, now seemed truly mature, a grown man of gravity and stature. He had gained the epithet 'Crouchback' while on his travels in the east; not for any perceived deformity but because of the Cross he wore upon his back while on crusade.

I glanced at him shrewdly. "Now that you are home, it is time you set up a proper household with Aveline, the wife your father and I chose for you. She is now of an age for the marriage to be consummated. You are a wealthy man since de Montfort and his allies were crushed at Evesham; you hold his earldom of Leicester and the honour of Lancaster."

"And the earldom of Derby," Edmund added, a smirk on his face.

"Yes, how could I forget Derby?" Aye, how could I? The Earl of Derby, Robert de Ferrers, had twice betrayed King Henry and been held prisoner at Windsor for his crimes. Edmund was custodian of his lands during his time in gaol. When de Ferrers was freed, he was granted back his lands, but only as long as he paid an immediate fine of £50,000. He was unable to do so, for no man had such vast wealth to distribute freely and instantly, and his earldom passed to its keeper, Edmund. Men whispered that Edmund had gained this earldom by cruel deception…but I saw de Ferrers as receiving his just desserts, and so did Edmund and the new King.

"I have so many lands and titles now I can almost forgive you for not getting me the crown of Sicily," said Edmund, leaning in the window embrasure and staring out into the gardens where his nephews and niece were playing with their nurses in attendance.

"You wouldn't have wanted it anyway, Edmund," I told him, laying down the needlework I had absently been picking at. "It was a poisoned crown, always fought over. Charles of Anjou holds it now but still there is controversy. He had to fight hard to obtain it from Conradin…the Boy."

"Oh yes, I've heard of the Boy. A sixteen-year-old warrior, wasn't he? But he was defeated; he lost his head, executed as a traitor. I am sure I could have beheaded him as easily as Charles."

"It wasn't easy from what I've been told," I said, "but let us not talk of crowns that can never be. We must talk of Aveline."

Edmund grinned. "What is there to talk of? She is my wife and by now I hope she has grown from the wan little flat-chested creature I wed before you and father in Westminster!"

"Edmund!" I chided him for his rude speech. "You will do your duty by her, no matter her appearance. She is the granddaughter of my friend the Dowager Countess of Devon, and we paid much money for her as she is a very wealthy young heiress."

"I shall, I shall," he said. "You know me, mother, ever dutiful— whether to my parents or to God."

"And fear not, I have heard she has grown very comely indeed."

Edmund grinned again. "Good. I shall look forward to seeing her."

"Well, if that is settled, I will attend to my own needs. I am growing a bit weary of Windsor; perhaps I shall retire for a short time to the royal palace at Guildford. It is quieter there."

Edmund was suddenly serious; he laid his hand on my shoulder. "You look weary, mother, as I have never seen you before. It concerns me. I think you should definitely go to Guildford and recover your strength."

"I will, and I shall take my grandchildren as company."

Guildford Palace was beautiful, set hard against the wall of the castle with its upright keep of golden stone. The great hall had painted glass and the walls were adorned with images of Lazarus rising from the dead. The royal apartments were coloured a deep, forest green and embellished by gold and silver stars; my chamber windows had been enlarged and the window-arches supported by fluted columns of Purbeck marble. There were several chapels and a great cloister, leading to gardens filled with roses, white and red, and sweet-smelling herbs in intricate, interwoven beds that formed vast patterns.

Here I waited for Edward's return from crusade with my grandchildren at my side. Leonor and Brito were bright, lively children, eager and ofttimes headstrong, but Hal, quiet and withdrawn, continued to fail to thrive. While Leonor danced and sang for my entertainment and Brito was engaged in rough and tumble sports with other noble boys and with the dogs from the kennel, poor Hal sat with me in the garden, shivering even when the day was warm, clutching the hand of his loyal nurse, Amicia de Derneford.

I frowned. "Why do you not play with your cousin Brito?" I asked him.

He drew his cloak around him. "The wind is cold, grandmama. And I am tired."

"Did you not sleep last night, Hal?" I looked into his thin face; ivory skin, dark eyes. No colour, like an effigy on a tomb.

"I did, grandmama."

I glanced at Amicia. "He did, your Grace. It was hard to rouse him this morning, but I thought the Lord Henry should take the air with your Highness. I thought it might brighten his cheeks."

I glanced over the short, pruned hedge as a laughing screech came from Beatrice's boy, Brito. I could see him bounding haphazardly through a herb-bed to the dismay of my imported Provencal gardener, with a couple of puppies racing at his heels, yapping and snapping. His tunic was smudged with mud, his cheeks flushed with exertion and good health.

So different from the little pale boy next to me on the marble bench.

"Henry, come to me," I ordered.

Shyly, slowly, Hal released Amicia's hand and walk towards his grandmother. He was small for his age and seemed so wobbly, like a newborn calf trying to find its legs. As he stood before me, I took his little hands...so cold, frail as bird bones. His grip was weak, and as I looked down, I could see, where his loose sleeve had slipped up, a series of dark, ugly bruises.

"What did you do to get these?" I cried, horrified. "Tell me, Hal!"

He shook his head. "They just come, grandmama."

"Amicia? Why is my grandson thus marked? Has his master beaten him at lessons?" I rounded on his nurse, who burst into tears, fearing she might be blamed for her charge's malady.

"No, never! The Lord Henry is a most biddable and polite child. I myself noticed the marks a few weeks back but thought little of them. Children often trip and fall, hurt themselves in play."

"But when does Henry ever play? This cannot be right." My brow creased. "I will send for two noted physicians, Hugh of Evesham and William la Provencal, to attend Henry immediately."

The physicians, sadly, were as perplexed as I was. They considered bleeding him but I did not like the idea in so small a child. They thought that maybe a dispensation could be obtained so that young Hal could eat meat even on Fridays. I thought that might work, help to make him robust.

Yet worry gnawed at my heart and I slept so ill at night I had dark rings beneath my eyes—black as the bruises marring Henry's pale flesh.

When would Edward return from crusade? The child needed his father, and with my husband now gone, I wanted my son's strength behind me, supporting me whatever befell.

Chapter Twelve

King Henry had died upon November 16 1272; almost two years passed before Edward and his wife, Eleanor of Castile, returned to England. But return they did, alive, if a little battered by their long adventures.

Edward showed me a white scar upon his arm and a smaller blemish on his brow. "See these marks, my mother? I was attacked one night by a member of the secret order of the *Hashashin*."

"Who are they?" I asked; the name was unfamiliar, ominous sounding.

"A Saracen order of Assassins," he replied. "Known for their deadly stealth. It is said that if they wish you dead, you might as well dig your own grave."

I shuddered. "Obviously this assassin failed, praise be to God."

Edward nodded. "The would-be killer rushed into my tent one night after silently dispatching my guards. I was drowsing, not yet fully asleep; I caught the flash of a blade in the gloom and sat up as he struck at me. The dagger aimed at my heart struck my arm instead. We grappled and he smote me in the face … but as I fell back, unbalanced, I grasped a nearby stool and clouted him with all my strength. He lost his deadly dagger…and then, once I had pinned him down, his misbegotten life."

"But the wound was poisoned." It was Edward's wife, Eleanor of Castile, who spoke. She was in the solar with him, and with their children, Henry, Leonor and a baby I had only just seen—Alphonso, who had made his appearance when his parents were in Gascony on their way home. There was a new daughter too, Joan, born while her parents were in Syria, but Edward had left her with his maternal grandmother, the Countess of Ponthieu. "I was terrified, I thought Edward would surely die. He writhed on the floor and had terrible visions of demons."

"But you saved me, did you not?" Edward looked at his wife lovingly. To see his devotion pleased me; my stern, martial son could be hard of heart, even towards me, his mother…but he loved his Castilian bride dearly and valued her opinion far more than most husbands did. "You fell upon your knees and sucked the venom from my wounds until the physicians could devise an antidote!"

"A miracle!" I whispered, stunned. "God bless you, your Grace Queen Eleanor." I saw a look pass between the couple and was not quite certain if the story of sucking poison was some kind of ribald private jest...but I would not pursue the subject.

"Now..." Edward swung round and suddenly picked up young Henry, lifting him up before him, "we must prepare for my Coronation. How do you feel about that great day, my young prince?"

Hal just hung there, limp as a rag doll, clearly overawed by this giant of a man with his loud, hard voice and decisive actions. I could see vague disappointment on Edward's face, and felt pity for my sickly little grandson. He was not the kind of son a warrior king might desire.

"Never mind." Edward thrust Hal back towards Eleanor of Castile, who in turn thrust him towards Amicia at the back of the chamber. "No more time for niceties. Preparations must be made!"

The Coronation day came, not without some drama. Edward and Edmund had fallen out; Edmund had insisted that, as steward, he should have the right to carry the great sword Curtana in the procession. Edward has disagreed, wishing to give the honour of carrying the sword to the Earl of Gloucester for his faithful services.

"I followed you on crusade—what greater service do you wish for, brother?" Edmund had snarled, and he retired to his estates to sulk and be comforted by his young wife Aveline, who he appeared to have grown to love dearly.

Edward clearly did not care. "Edmund could always act the child when the mood took him," he said breezily. "His absence will not spoil my day."

And, I must admit, it did not. Crowds were out and in a celebratory mood, and wine sprang from the conduit at Cheapside that any man might stop and drink a toast to the new King and Queen.

In Westminster Abbey, the royal couple knelt, were undressed, anointed, robed again and then crowned. Eager to impress that his reign would be different to that of his forebears, Edward took off his crown mere seconds after it had been placed on his head by Archbishop Kilwardby, and vowed that he would not wear it again until he won back the English lands lost in recent years.

Listening I cringed, my face burning with embarrassment; to me, it felt as though Edward was criticising his father, who lay so near in the Confessor's Tomb.

Then it was on to the banquet, a splendid affair, though I thought, with a lingering sense of sadness, more for the young than for an ageing widow. The nobles of the realm and the King of Scotland rode into Westminster Hall, each followed by a hundred knights on horses. Once they had assembled before Edward, they dismounted their steeds…then set them free.

"Any man here may take these horses for his own!" it was announced. "Just let him catch them!"

Once the excitement of the horse-chase was over, we sat down to feast. I had a position of honour, naturally, but it was far from the glittering table of the king, with its samite canopy and golden flags and huge silver saltcellar shaped like a turreted fortress.

Eating only small portions of swan from the trencher before me, I let my gaze drift down the lines of guests at the high table and the rest of the trestle tables. So many faces missing, gone forever, though I was gladdened to see my daughters Margaret and Beatrice, both now in their thirties, and so radiant that all who gazed upon them remarked at their great beauty. I also cast my eye towards little Henry, the heir apparent, sitting in his newly-made tunic of fine green Ypres silk, with his food lying untouched before him. Looking even more tired and weak than usual.

By midnight, I wish to retire. The child needed to leave too; he was half-sleep, his shoulder shaken every few minutes by a worried-looking Amicia. Approaching the King, I curtseyed—how strange that felt—and asked permission to leave for the palace at Guildford with the young prince.

For a few long moments, Edward stared appraisingly over my shoulder at Hal and then nodded. "Yes, take him, take him from London. I do not think the air here agrees with him."

It is not just the air that ails the child, I thought, but said no more. It was clear to me that Edward had had already given up on this small son he hardly knew and was not bothered if he were present or not. Hal was, at present, his heir…but if he were to perish by some mischance, he had another boy, Alphonso, waiting in the wings to take his place. It seemed heartless, but it was the way of the world, the way of Kings. Children died too easy; it was not good to become too attached, as I had learned with Katharine.

I took Hal from the hall and we rode for Guildford, both of us sharing the same chariot. As the carriage wobbled along the rutted road, I gazed out from behind the rich velvet curtains at the risen moon and drank in the night air. I was glad to be away. For the first time, I felt alien at court; because it was no longer my court but Edward and Eleanor's. They were the future, I was the past....

Little Hal yawned on the seat across from me. "Father looked so tall in his crown...but the crown looked so heavy. Do you think I will find it heavy when I grow older and become king?"

"I hope you will not," I said and stared up at the moon, a white, unfeeling eye. Nightwind kissed tears from my cheeks

"Why are you crying, grandmama?" asked little Hal in concern.

"I am not, it is only the brightness of the moon that makes my eyes water," I lied.

Little Henry's illness worsened in the days that followed the Coronation. As late summer gripped England, bathing it in an unusual heat, he lay abed in his chamber at Guildford, the doctors fussing over him but unable to do more than give him a few moments of temporary relief.

I was frantic as he weakened day by day. I purchased *mensurae*, candles that were measured to Henry's own height, and sent them to various shrines about the country, including one to St Edward's at Westminster and one to the grave of his grandfather. I prayed to God not to take this grandson who had become dear to me.

He did not listen. When the summer burned itself out and the first sullen skies of October descended, and the geese flew in V-shapes across the lowering sky, little Hal passed from this life and into the next.

Edward and Eleanor of Castile did not come to his bedside, even at the last.

I held Hal's hand as its usual coldness became even colder.

The days that followed were blurry and drear. I founded a House of Dominicans in Guildford in Prince Henry's name and bestowed upon them my grandson's heart in an ornate urn. His body was sent to Westminster for burial near his grandfather and my much-mourned daughter Katharine.

His death hurt me the most, but it was not the last. The next year was one of nothing but tragedy and pain for me. Edmund's wife Aveline had become pregnant but died in birthing twins, aged but fourteen. Edmund was mad with grief, almost to the point that I feared for his own life. Then in February, messengers came from Scotland, dressed in mourning garb—my eldest daughter, dear sweet Meggie, had succumbed to a winter fever. A month after that Beatrice was also dead; she had delivered a daughter, Eleanor, and all looked to be well; then, without warning she had collapsed, unable to breathe, and swiftly died.

Guildford, which had seemed a haven of peace, now felt more like a prison. A prison of unhappy memories. After sorting out a pension for Hal's loyal nurse Amicia, I gathered my household and headed to Wiltshire, staying between my dower castles of Ludgershall and Marlborough. Whilst there I tried to interest myself in earthly things, such as the running of my estates; I visited Gloucester where the monks of Lanthony priory allowed me to build a bridge to access their gardens from my castle and toured King's Cliffe, Havering and Gillingham—a journey I did not much enjoy. At Gillingham, a vile greasy smoke rose into the air at evening and assailed my nostrils, turning my stomach and ruining my appetite. It must have been something foul that the locals burnt upon the hearth fire.

I wrote letters regarding the Milton Regis gaol, a market for Pevensey and a meeting at Marlborough. I also evicted a Jew, Jacob Cok, from Andover town, with the blessing of my son the King, who had issued a statue that forbade Jews to practice usury. It did not quite go as I wished, however; for when my steward, Guy of Taunton, evicted the Jew, Cok turned around and sued Guy for robbery! The court case dragged on for ages.

Edmund finally remarried, taking Louis IX's niece, Blanche, as his new bride. I prayed to the Virgin that they would be blessed with healthy children. Soon they were parents to a fine son they named Thomas.

I looked with hope to a better future.

I heard via my network of spies that the King and Queen would be making a journey to Glastonbury, where the monks were planning to rebury the bones of King Arthur in a tomb before the high altar. I had visited Glastonbury briefly with Henry not long after we were wed, and I was consumed with a desire to journey there again, one last time. From youth onwards, I had loved the Arthurian legends—Geoffrey of Monmouth, Marie De France, Chretien de Troyes, the tale of Tristan, the Lancelot Proper. As a young girl, I had dreamed that I was another Guinevere, albeit a loyal one who did not dishonour my marriage vows. I had seen Henry as another Arthur, leader of chivalry, or I had *wanted* to see him that way. We had failed to replicate the valour and nobility of those great ones from the past, but we had tried. We had wished to make England as great as France, to turn it into a country of power and great importance within Christendom. It had not happened in Henry's reign but perhaps Edward would be more successful. Perhaps striving for greatness upon this earth is the best any mortal can do.

I went to Edward, and in all humility asked if I could accompany him and the Queen to Glastonbury. He did not seem pleased; his gaze, heavy with his drooping eyelid, drifted to Queen Eleanor, who sat with demure composure, staring down at her folded hands. "I do not think it will be possible..." he began.

I would not beg, and with a sigh made to turn away and retreat to my apartments. However, the Queen suddenly raised her head and spoke, "It would be a kindness, your Grace. It is little enough for the Dowager Queen to ask."

Edward paused. He listened to Eleanor of Castile more than most men listened to their wives.

"It means making adjustments," frowned Edward. "The monks will not be expecting the Dowager Queen."

"Your Grace...my son..." I turned back to Edward. "I gave you the knowledge of Arthur the King, placed books about his deeds into your hands when you were but a small boy. I went to Glastonbury when your father and I were first wed and I prayed for Arthur's soul then and for all his brave knights—Lancelot, Tristan, Gawain, Percival, Galahad. But I did not see his gravesite or his bones; time did not permit it, the King was on business. Would you not grant an old woman one small pleasure? I will not come as Queen Mother, only as a pilgrim. None would know."

Edward was still scowling but said in a sullen voice, "If it is your wish."

I would go with my son but dressed only as a woman of the court with no adornments and no rich gems to mark my status.

The King came to Glastonbury to great acclaim. Furled in a cloak, I walked behind the Queen, unrecognised. In a great procession, we wended our way through the heart of the town toward the abbey, one of the wealthiest in England since the finding of Arthur and Guinevere's bones. The roof of the great church veered up, shining like gold in the aftermath of early rain. Beyond, rose the hill known as the Tor, a green finger that prodded the sky, its eminence capped by the ruins of St

Michael's church, which fell in a terrible shaking of the earth some three years previously. The common folk said the hill was haunted, that otherworldly palaces resided within, and that Arthur lay there, sleeping...but I did not want to believe that the King slept, caught in some unnatural world of faerie glamour. I imagined that he had died like other men, and had his reward for his valour at the throne of God (I thought not so much of Guinevere's fate, for she had been adulterous...but I hoped forgiveness was hers, and that prayers of those who loved her had saved her sinful soul as one day prayers would save mine.)

The abbey gates reared up before us, opening slowly as if they were the gates to heaven. The abbot, John of Taunton, emerged to greet the party, with the lay brothers gathered close about him, and ushered us into the grounds and then to the doors of the abbey church.

It was one of the largest churches I had ever visited, containing amongst its many chapels, one dedicated to Joseph of Arimathea, who had visited Britain with the young Christ-child and planted the Holy Thorn upon a Glastonbury hillside. Tall windows let light in through panes of coloured glass and the smell of incense and tallow was sweet balm to the senses.

Abbot John was speaking to the King. "In the last century, whilst digging foundations for a new building, a grave was found many feet below the surface of the land. In the pit lay a coffin wrought from a gigantic oak tree, rough and rude but imposing. Upon opening it, the brothers found the bones of a mighty man, surely a warrior of great renown from some elder age of the world. Beside him lay the bones of a slender woman, presumed to be his wife; about her skull lay hanks of hair that still shone as golden as wheat in the field. An air of great majesty and sanctity cluing to these mortal remains, and learned men pronounced that surely they must be the bones of the puissant King Arthur and his wife Guinevere."

"Did not Guinevere die at Amesbury, where she had taken vows to atone for her sins in the last years of her life?" To my surprise, I heard my own voice speaking. I had not meant to speak out of turn but was used to saying what was in my mind without censure.

Edward moved his leonine head to look at me, his expression sour and full of warning. The Queen suppressed a little smile behind her hand, pretended to cough. She was laughing.

Abbot John looked startled at my presumption in speaking aloud; he did not recognise me in my plain clothing and head covering. He spoke to me as he would to a simple soul, some woman attendant of little consequence who had loose lips. "Indeed, that is so, Madame. The nuns of Amesbury, 'tis said, did however contrive for the Queen, as in her final wishes, to be borne to Glastonbury, to lie forever next to her rightful lord."

The abbot pointed to an ossuary box of polished marble, inlaid with gemstones, and seated on a little stool of carved oak, with the upswept hands of gilt angels supporting its heavy base. "Their remains are enclosed there in new reverence, waiting for reburial within the choir."

I fixed my gaze on the stone box. The abbot proceeded to talk with Edward; their voices blurring in and out amidst the hazy candle-smoke and the soft chanting of the monks. My mind flew back through time, recalling the legends I had once adored…and tried to emulate in the glories of my court.

Amesbury…a little Wiltshire town I had frequently visited when on my progresses across England. Not far from Marlborough; midway between there and Sarum. An abbey that now served as the village church, where Eleanor of Brittany's bones lay buried before the altar graced by the relics of Saint Melor, his fate so like that of her own unfortunate brother Arthur. A river and hill and a plain beyond, where the Choir of Ambrosius stood in awful, time-ravaged majesty, its gaunt ruins dappled with light and cloud shadow, its soil rich with the bones of slain men. A community of nuns in a daughter-house of Fontevraud, nestled by the bend in the river and sleeping in the lee of the great wooded hill. a place where Queen Guinevere sought to ease her distressed heart and atone for her sins, where at last she gave up the ghost and the nuns took her body, surrounded by candles like a myriad of will o' the wisps, to fabled Glastonbury with its blood-tinged spring and misty Tor.

Suddenly I longed for quiet, dreaming Amesbury, where swans rode, gleaming white, on the swells of the Avon near the priory's ivy-swathed wall. Longed for solitude, for sanctuary, for a quiet and contemplative ending to my own eventful life.

The Queen that was…

Chapter Thirteen

In the summer of 1286, I sought out the priory of Amesbury, with the intent to stay there for the rest of my days. I was not alone in my haven, for my granddaughter, another Eleanor, the daughter of Beatrice, had taken the veil there, and so had Edward's young daughter Mary. I did not know what kind of nun Mary would make, as she seemed a frivolous and headstrong girl, who like game playing and had no particular piety, but such was her destiny, decreed by her father. She would do her duty to her kin as princesses must.

I had attended Mary's veiling, along with the entirety of the royal family, brothers, sisters, cousins, the King and Queen. Pavilions and golden canopies stretched across the verdant lawns outside the priory, and musicians played as if we were all at a great fair rather than a solemn veiling of a young nun. Goose and swan were served on silver plates, and there were subtleties fashioned into the shape of church towers.

It was a fine Plantagenet party, one of the best in recent years, but it was soon over. The pavilions were dismantled, the entourage passed out upon the road that led to Old Sarum, where Henry's grandmother had once been imprisoned, and thence to Salisbury, where the fine modern cathedral, consecrated a mere thirty years ago, towered over the fine new colleges of De Vaux and St Edmund's. A busy, happy place, where the cathedral clergy taught a burgeoning array of theological students.

I would not see such sights again.

I retired from the world, and the gates of the priory closed, clanging behind me with steely finality. My fine dresses were packed away in chests and the rough grey robes and wimple of a nun brought to me, though, unlike my granddaughters, I was not professed and by special decree, still kept control over some of my dower lands.

And so the years passed, in prayer and solitude. Where once crowds cheered—or hissed—I heard only birdsong, the lowing of cattle in nearby fields, the ringing of bells, the churning of the river, the rush of wind through the trees on the nearby hill.

Once I walked out with Mary and Eleanor and went down to where the river wound around the flank of the hill. Here, the waters broadened out, forming a pool that was mildly warm to the touch; on cold days, we could see wisps of mist rising from it like ghostly hands. A little bathhouse stood nearby, used by those who suffered aches in the bones as I had begun to do; at certain times the waters would rise, covering the floor and the bathers huddled within.

Mary was down by the waterside, amidst waving reeds and long grasses. She was prodding at something on the water's edge with the toe of her shoe. "Grandmother, look at this!"

Bending, she picked a large chunk of rock up from the mud and proffered it.

"Why would grandmama want an old stone, Mary?" said Eleanor contemptuously.

"It's not just an 'old stone'!" insisted Mary. "Look at it! Look at it, grandmama."

I took the stone from Mary, uncaring that cold mud slopped onto my robes. The stone was purple, a deep rich royal purple.

"It's magic," said Mary. "It must be…because Guinevere lived here once!"

"Don't be silly," said Eleanor with the arrogance born of being a few years older than her cousin. "Magic doesn't exist, Mary; and to believe it does is sinful. You should put these notions out of your head now; you are a nun and should fasten your mind only on Our Lord. As for that Guinevere—she was a wicked adulteress, for all she was a great queen. She is probably in hell being roasted by devils even after all these hundreds of years!"

"You're so boring, Eleanor," said Mary. I am sure she would have stuck her tongue out at her cousin but for fear of being reported to the prioress. "What do *you* think, grandmama? Is the stone magic? "

"I do not know." I turned the damp stone over in my hands. Its rich hue…I was reminded so much of my royal robes of long ago. Now Eleanor of Castile wore them; my robes were a uniform grey. "But it certainly is a colour fit for Queens both old and new."

"Plantagenet purple," said Mary defiantly, eyeing Eleanor. "I would wear it still if I hadn't been made a nun."

"Plantagenet purple." I laughed and tossed the violet-hued rock back out into the pool before my two granddaughters, veiled or not, got into an unseemly battle of words or worse. Ripples ran wide; birds soared up out of the brush and vanished into the treetops, shrilling in alarm.

"I saw her," Mary breathed, suddenly catching my sleeve. "Didn't you see her too? Just now. A woman in the trees, with hair like gold. Guinevere's spirit. It has to be."

"Come, Mary, it is time to go." I glanced at Eleanor's pursed lips and dragged my younger grandchild from the water's edge.

A magical day, a strange day that left me wondering. And drawn. For I, in one brief second, thought I too saw a golden-haired woman hovering like a white phantom amidst the slender trees. Beckoning in her robes of purple hue.

News reached me in the priory. Even in remote Amesbury, it often did, and the nuns enjoyed a bit of gossip as much as any, although they pretended to eschew such idle talk. Rumour had it that the late Louis of France was to be canonised by the Pope. The thought somehow pained me. He was saintly, that was for certain, and pious to the point of mania; his failed crusades testified to that, and his wish for Marguerite to live as his sister at one point. But a saint? This man who led most of his kin to death in a miserable field in Tunisia?

Becoming a saint would wipe out all his mistakes, his failings, and raise him above all other earthly men. People would come to pray at his tomb. France's esteem would rise in the world, while England's would languish.

I wanted Henry made a saint too.

I had already spoken of this matter to Edward a few years ago; in fact, we had argued bitterly over it. "Edward," I had said, "your father, for all his faults, was a pious man and great builder for God's glory; he worshipped the Confessor and he built anew Westminster Abbey that men should marvel for a thousand years. Do you not believe it is time to ask the Pope if he may join the ranks of the saints?"

Edward had thrown back his head, roaring with laughter that made me wince with its harshness. "A saint? Father? Surely, you jest, Madame?"

"I do not jest." My tone was crisp. "Once, shortly after your father's death, a knight sought special audience with me. He had been blinded in a cruel jousting accident, but afterwards he had knelt at Henry's tomb and was miraculously cured, his eyesight restored! He swore upon the Holy Rood that his tale was true. He came to tell me what had transpired because he believed the King should be made a saint."

"He came, Madame, because he thought you were weak and would pay him for his sweet and flattering words! Mother, this knight, whoever he was, most assuredly was a charlatan and a thief. I hope you did not pay him overmuch for telling you of his wondrous recovery at my sire's grave."

"He asked for nothing, Edward! I believe he told the truth."

"I thought you were more intelligent than that, mother. Maybe encroaching age had withered your brain."

"Edward, you dishonour me, and your father's memory! How dare you speak so!"

"How dare I?" He glowered at me beneath beetling brow, a look that would make most men quail. It even stopped my heart a little. "Let me tell you how, Madame! Because I am King of England!"

He had turned his back on me then and would speak of the matter no more.

Now, hearing of Louis's forthcoming canonisation, I wanted to write to Edward and beg one last time...but the fire in me was slipping away, dwindling. I had begun to feel old and tired. One night in my chamber I wrote a short missive that began *'Your father deserves to be a saint.'* I never finished it. Reading it over, with a soft curse I tossed it on the embers in the brazier.

Edward would not listen.

The Queen was dead. Little Eleanor of Castile who, despite the sternness of Edward's temperament, he loved beyond all others, whose council he had always valued. When they were returning from Gascony after their crusade, she had contracted the quartan fever, which had robbed her of good health from then on. After the birth of her last child, Edward of Caernarfon, in 1284, she had relied more and more on the ministrations of physics in order to perform her duties. Finally, when travelling from Clipstone Palace to Lincoln with the King, she fell seriously ill near Harby in Nottinghamshire. Carried unconscious to the house of a local man named Richard de Weston, she breathed her last amidst humble folk with simple things around her.

Edward bore her body to Lincoln, where it was embalmed and her entrails buried in the beautiful cathedral on the hill. Then, surrounded by black-clad mourners, he set off for London, arriving in the city in eleven days. Eleanor's heart was sent to Blackfriars, and her remains placed in a tomb at my husband Henry's feet. Grief-stricken, Edward swore that he would erect a cross to Eleanor at every spot her cortege rested upon its doleful journey to Westminster.

My son was a doting husband, no matter what any may say of his other attributes.

Eleanor of Castile's death filled me with great distress in more ways than one. She was a sweet girl, of much charm; her demise saddened me, and I know she was a restraining influence on my headstrong Edward.

But I was distressed for another reason.

Years ago, I had arranged for my own future death. My heart would be removed, placed in a golden casket and buried at the house of the Franciscans in London. The rest of my earthly remains were to be carried to Westminster and interred beside Henry, as befitted his faithful Queen of many years.

The latter was not going to happen now. My privilege had been usurped…on the orders of my own son.

Eleanor of Castile, whom he loved far more than me, lay in my appointed place in Westminster Abbey.

Summertime.

Midsummer's Eve, the day of St John, has come. I am not well. The canker the doctors say gnaws my belly like a worm has flared in the night, giving great pain. Outside the window in my quarters, the morning sky is the colour of a blush; all around in the local villages, Amesbury, Durnford, Woodford, the people have been lighting fires for three days solid—smoke trundles through the air, blending with the mist that coils off the river.

I am weary, earlier I forced myself to go to Nocturn and pray for my family, for the bereaved King, my son. Then, after a brief sleep, I sat down to reading scripture, but my eyesight faded in and out, in and out.

Now, sitting alone, my limbs feel like heavy clay, drawing me down, down, down. Soon, it would be time for Lauds, and the sun would rise. Would I even have the strength to attend?

I glance out the window again. On the high hill above the old pool with its royal purple stones, amidst the waving leafy green boughs, I see a fire burning, a tribute to the rising sun, a beacon heralding the forthcoming day. A pagan symbol that should have filled me with revulsion, yet strangely brought a fierce, desperate excitement.

I pull myself into the window embrasure, holding the edges with trembling hands. Somewhere it seems I can hear chanting and singing in an unknown tongue; it is not the sisters in their austere church. Is it coming across the Plain, brought down the wind, perhaps from the old stones of Ambrosius' Choir, where, it is whispered, men gather on Midsummer's night?

Or is it just a dream, the fancies of a woman who is...dying?

Suddenly I see her.

Out amidst the trees, still furled in night's blue shadows. Her hair is gold like wheat, like ripe corn, and her robes are royal purple.

"Guinevere!" I cry joyfully, as my hands fall from the window ledge and I fall after, the young Eleanor leaving the old and running free, free across the dewdrops, seeking the legends she has always loved, seeking the truth, seeking eternity....

Epilogue. Sometime in the 2000's

John Webb's palatial mansion stands watching over the site of Amesbury Priory, stiff columns and fancy portico, wide, sun-catching windows opening on the day. Behind it, over the ornate grey bridge, the river still coils past the Chinese garden house; it floods in heavy rain, turning the fields below the hill known today as Vespasian's Camp into a lake that shines like a silvered mirror.

The sacred spring, uncovered by recent archaeology, warm even when it is cold, flows dark and mysterious on its primaeval course, giving up its secrets slowly. Stones lie within it, magic stones that turn a rich royal purple when exposed to air.

Magic? In our age of science, it is the algae *Hildenbrandia rivularis,* combined with warm water that causes the vivid colouring to form.

Under the green lawn, carefully trimmed, lie the foundations of monastic buildings. Of a church razed to ground level, a victim of the Reformation and then of 'modern progress.' Not one stone remains above ground, yet the bells of nearby St Mary and St Melor still ring out over the buried treasures below, soothing, counting the hours, as they always did, time out of mind. As they did in *her* day.

A Queen lies there, sleeping, wrapped in a green mantle of grass.

Undisturbed.

Lost.

Waiting, like King Arthur in the stories she loved, for a glorious return.

THE END

Historical Notes

Eleanor of Provence was not the easiest medieval royal to research. The time she lived in is well-covered by historians, but, like many women of the era, her personal life falls between the cracks; we see just a hazy ghost, the shadow of a woman. Her unpopularity in England was also a problem, as the views of the chroniclers were often biased against her; this was mainly because she was 'foreign' and favoured her 'foreign' relatives.

What we do glean from the writings of the time is that she was well read and educated, enjoyed Arthurian legends and romances, and was genuinely beautiful, not just called so as a convention. She remained close to her sister Margaret/Marguerite all her life, and was a loving mother to her children, getting sweets for a sick son, insisting she stay with another while he lay ill in a monastery (horrifying the monks), worrying about a daughter married young and living far away in conditions she couldn't see. She showed similar affection to her grandchildren. On the negative side, she liked to spend and favoured her own family too much; she was also very shrewd maintaining her own properties and knew how to get cash when needed—usually at someone else's expense.

There are only two extant biographies of Eleanor (one of which is also about her three sisters) and even fiction seems to have passed her by—I can think of only two modern novels that cover her life (and they are not exclusively about her, but also the sisters), and one older novel, THE QUEEN FROM PROVENCE, written by that doyen of historical fiction, Jean Plaidy. She gets a mention in novels and non-fiction on both her husband Henry III, her son Edward I, and Simon de Montfort, of course…but nothing much more than that.

Therefore, establishing a clear timeline of Eleanor's life was occasionally quite difficult. Several books disagreed with each other in various places. I have tried to keep to what is known but in several segments of the novel have combined events into a shorter time frame, such as the death of Eleanor's sister Sanchia and the birth of her daughter Margaret's baby.

Although the famous battles of Lewes and Evesham are covered, since I have written the story through Eleanor's eyes, of course she could not 'see it happen' in person. It is covered instead through information gleaned from messengers. I didn't want the story to get away too much and become just another retelling of those battles and their consequences for England; I wanted to show how Eleanor might have felt, with husband and son captive and then, beyond all hope, decisively victorious at Evesham.

Nearly all events covered in the novel are real. It is thought the story of Eleanor sending a poem to Henry's brother, Richard of Cornwall, might be apocryphal but it has become such a part of Eleanor's personal 'folklore', that I decided to include it. The visit to Glastonbury at the end is an invention, although it is true Edward I and his wife did visit on that date. Eleanor of Provence was a great aficionado of Arthurian legends; I think she would have liked to have seen the King's bones reinterred. I also did not make Eleanor actually become a nun at Amesbury; there is no evidence she was ever professed. She kept many of her lands by special decree and may have built her own quarters at the priory.

As for a few other strange little points: the purple stones of Amesbury do in fact exist, lying around the warm spring behind the priory where Eleanor retired; she may well have seen them in the last years of her life. Inigo Jones and his colleague Webb did indeed visit the priory ruins and had a peep into a tomb that contained a skeleton in rich dress...I strongly suspect that they may have stumbled on to Eleanor's now-missing grave that day. (Some have hoped her remains are buried somewhere in the older Abbey church of St Mary and St Melor, since geophysics show there are two grave cuts before the high altar, but contemporary descriptions seem to imply the priory was a more likely than the abbey, which had by then become the parish church. It is possible a stone head in St Melor's is meant to be Eleanor, and one of the mysterious graves could be the tragic Eleanor Fair Maid of Brittany (another story!)

Will Eleanor ever be found? It is always possible. After all, who would have thought Richard III would be located, especially as legend placed him in the local river? We might not have a straight line of mtDNA for Eleanor as we did with Richard, but an isotopic analysis on her teeth should clearly show that her first 12 years were not spent in Britain but in France.

Books to read on Eleanor:
FOUR QUEENS by Nancy Goldstone
ELEANOR OF PROVENCE-A STUDY IN QUEENSHIP by Margaret Howell.

PLACES ASSOCIATED WITH ELEANOR IN WILTSHIRE
Amesbury Abbey, site of the Priory—private. The grounds and river can be seen from the road. There are occasional open days for community events; check local pages. A possible fragment of the priory's perimeter wall may exist near the later gatehouse near Countess roundabout.

The Church of St Mary and St Melor, Amesbury. Church associated with an earlier abbey in the town. Open most days in summer but check times. Possible carving of Eleanor's head near the door. Interesting painted medieval corbels. Also striking carved heads of a King and Prince.

Amesbury History Centre. Church Street, Amesbury. Contains much information on the town's history, including Eleanor, the priory site, the church, and the Mesolithic camp that existed behind the priory.

Marlborough Castle. No stonework remains but the huge mound on which it stood lies in the grounds of Marlborough College. This is not, as was once thought, a Norman motte, but is in fact a huge ceremonial

Neolithic mound, similar to Silbury Hill. Marlborough is often known as Merlin's Town, which would have intrigued Eleanor, who loved the Arthurian legends.

Clarendon Palace. The ruins of this huge Plantagenet palace lie along a forested trackway not far out of Salisbury, headed in the direction of Winchester. There is no carpark, just a track, and then you walk uphill into the woods from there...so you will need a map first. Badly ruined, but very evocative and haunting, with red roof tiles still scattered all over the ground. The stunning coloured floor tiles so loved by Henry are now in the British Museum.

Ludgershall Castle. Earlier castle made into a hunting lodge by Henry III. Eleanor spent a fair bit of time here. Free admission, English Heritage.

OTHER BOOKS BY J.P. REEDMAN

MEDIEVAL BABES SERIES:

MISTRESS OF THE MAZE: The Legend of Fair Rosamund.

THE CAPTIVE PRINCESS-The tragic life of Eleanor, Arthur of Brittany's sister, imprisoned for life for her claim to the English throne.

THE WHITE ROSE RENT—Latherine Plantagenet, illegitimate daughter of Richard III seeks her way in the new Tudor world

THE PRINCESS NUN. Mary, daughter of Edward I, is an nun at Amesbury…but she's a nun who likes to gamble and travel!

RICHARD III

I, RICHARD PLANTAGENET. The life of Richard III, told from his own first-person perspective. Either in one huge volume, or available as parts one and two. In total, over 700 pages and 250,000 words! A Richard neither cardboard saint of Shakespearean monster— loyal brother, ruthless soldier, scoliosis sufferer, husband, father and king.

SACRED KING. Historical fantasy novel about Richard III's return in a Leicester carpark, after a journey through the otherworld.

WHITE ROSES, GOLDEN SUNNES. Collection of stories of Richard III, mostly dealing with his childhood and youth, including exile in Burgundy.

STONEHENGE

STONE LORD and MOON LORD. A retelling of the Arthurian tales with a twist-- in two volumes. Arthur is now a chieftain of the early Bronze Age. A look at the possible origins of some of the Arthurian mythos. First book shows the shaman known as the Merlin choosing the young warrior who will united the tribes; book two has

Mordraed, bastard of Ardhu the Stone Lord, attempting to destroy Stonehenge in a dreadful revenge.

GODS OF STONEHENGE—Non-fiction. Essay on possible deities at Stonehenge, as suggested by mythology and local folklore.

FANTASY

MY NAME IS NOT MIDNIGHT. Dystopian fantasy set in an alternative world 1970's Canada. A young girl flees the slave orphanage where she had been places and goes on a quest to find the Rose of the World…and her own true name.

BETWEEN THE HORNS. Collection of funny, quirky fantasy tales set in an invented central European land between two great rivers. Giant hares, trolls, child gobbling witches, man eating snowmen, a Krampus, flying pumpkins and more.

Printed in Great Britain
by Amazon

68792520R00132